Melvyn Bragg

Melvyn Bragg's first novel, *For Want of a Nail*, was published in 1965 and since then his novels have included *The Hired Man*, for which he won the Time/Life Silver Pen Award, *Without a City Wall*, winner of the John Llewellyn Rhys Prize, *The Soldier's Return*, which won the WHSmith Literary Award, *A Son of War* and *Crossing the Lines*, both longlisted for the Booker Prize, and *Remember Me . . .* He has also written several works of non-fiction including *On Giants' Shoulders*, *The Adventure of English*, *12 Books that Changed the World*, *In Our Time* and *The South Bank Show: Final Cut*. He is President of the National Campaign for the Arts, and in 1998 he was made a life peer. He lives in London and Cumbria.

For Want of a Nail

MELVYN BRAGG

SCEPTRE

First published in Great Britain in 1965 by Martin Secker and Warburg Ltd.

First published by Sceptre in 1988
An imprint of Hodder & Stoughton
An Hachette UK Company

1

A CIP catalogue record for this title is available from the British Library.

ISBN 978 0 340 43101 6

Typeset in Minion by Hewer Text UK Ltd, Edinburgh
Printed and bound by Clays Ltd, St Ives plc

Hodder & Stoughton policy is to use papers that are natural, renewable
and recyclable products and made from wood grown in sustainable forests.
The logging and manufacturing processes are expected to conform to the
environmental regulations of the country of origin.

Hodder & Stoughton Ltd
338 Euston Road
London NW1 3BH

www.hodder.co.uk

To Lise

PART ONE

PART ONE

CHAPTER ONE

Though a score of Indians, Nazis, pythons, Zulus and midget Japanese aircraft had been shattered by Tom's index and middle finger, his grandfather had shot nothing.

Tess howled out her frantic warning. Crack!

A crazy shot, nearly the full length of the field.

'Damn an' blast, an' hell and bugger it!'

Tom could have been sent to court for just one of those words. He rolled them quietly around his closed mouth.

'Bugger it!'

Surely they would go back home now.

'Hey lass!'

The dog snuffed its instinct immediately and galloped towards them, turning a wide circle to trundle up to their legs from behind.

'I never even saw it,' said Tom, untruthfully.

Another cartridge pressed into the broken gun.

'Not a thing.' His grandfather was savage.

'Maybe it's too cold.'

'Not one bloody thing!'

They set off again. At first Tom tried to patter along as lightly as Tess, and then he strained to match the long step of his grandfather. Soon tired, he looked around for something to shoot.

To his left the tarn stretched out, flat, grey and empty. His mother could have gone swimming in it one day and suddenly been chased by an alligator. With a long yodel, Tom plunged in and

3

raced across the water, knife between his teeth. Over and over he rolled, the alligator thrashing the water with its tail, all the other creatures of the lake scurrying down to the bottom edges for safety. He stabbed and stabbed again, losing his knife in the scaly belly, forcing apart the great jaws with his bare hands. Blood spurted on to the surface of the water and spread like oil. He was hurled into the air by some last concentration of the reptile's force, but with that effort the alligator died.

And then his mother would admire him and praise him and tell everybody what he had done, and never shout at him again.

He was very hungry. He could feel his stomach sharpening its claws, impatient to grasp food and tear it into the appropriate portions for each part of his body. They had come out straight after dinner and it was almost dark. At home, the paraffin lamp would have been lit.

They went through a gate. The only sounds apart from their own came from the few black rooks which cawed harshly in the hidden tops of bare trees, and from the echoed yelps and bluster of a hunt which had ghosted around them throughout the afternoon.

The cold had eaten through his wellingtons, through his two pairs of socks, and now its invisible current sparked painfully against his skin. His fingers, swollen big, dug numbly into his mittens.

'They've scared off every damned thing there is.'

Tom nodded. He would like to ride a horse. Jodhpurs, agricultural shows, girls in velvet jackets, silver cups.

'What do they want to make such a noise about? Eh?'

'They should go somewhere else.'

'They should be stopped a'together!'

The empty bag swung down to the top of his wellingtons, scraping against his chapped knees.

They had been out many times before. They had walked through these fields when the sun had scarcely had time to glisten the dew: they had been out in the pitch dark with a torch when all the ignorant rabbits for miles around had rushed to look at the light. They had always shot something.

4

'With their bloody horses and dogs and trumpets!'

They were now directly underneath 'The Saddle'. Tom had never climbed it. From his window it looked like the soft pencil swell of a hillock, with its central dip no more than an innocent curve. Now, beside it, he saw the open jaw of rock which made that slit look like a trap of sharpened flint, ready sprung; and the side of the fell, so soft when dark, now seen to be covered with slithering, shifting screes, balanced, unsupported rocks, wire bushes with thread-brittle roots.

Tess trotted out briskly in front of them. For some time, Tom was again mesmerised by the syncopated rhythm of the dog's quick feet. He was sure that there were moments when all four paws were off the ground. He stared at Tess's uncurious behind and tried to fix the pattern in his mind. His own feet started to misbehave. His left foot shot out quickly with a double kick and then his right swung slowly along to join it. His feet came together and he could not decide which one to push out first. Tess pranced on. His grandfather did not interrupt his step for a moment: knees never straight, arms stiff; only real movement – an occasional pecking shift of the head.

Tom ran to join him.

The hunting sounds were growing louder.

'What can you do?'

Get a machine-gun and ambush them.

'They've spoiled it for us,' said Tom.

'By God! I'd like to see some of them get off their horses for a minute!'

A thin jet of spit shot from the old man's mouth.

'Not one bloody thing!'

Tom accepted his grandfather's misery as his own. Hardly even sketched out by his own experience, he was coloured by whatever was strongest. The cold was now running up and down his back like a packet of sliding ice – but they could not go home until something happened.

The old man muttered away to himself. Tom was too absorbed in his own coldness to listen.

5

His feet pressed down the grass and, without looking, he knew it would bend back to its original position. All the way behind him a track of a million leaves of grass unbending, popping up straight like so many frogs. There was a girl at school who ate frogs. Ate frogs, did not wear knickers, could not read, shaved her head, killed cats. He derived no pleasure from thinking about her. He was too cold.

The sky was a tight grey tarpaulin, ashy with the strain of the last pause before snow. It pressed on top of 'The Saddle'. The whole of 'The Saddle', Tom knew, pressed down on to crystals and fossils and ancient rocks and gases, hidden springs, caves, stalagmites and stalactites, and it moved and cracked and exploded inside itself so that, right at the bottom, there was coal. Thick black coal under his very feet.

Wild yells and long, starved barking. Tess yapped back.

'Shut up!'

His grandfather stopped – face blazing red with cold and fury.

'They've spoiled it! We'll get nowt! We needn't have come! My God! If I could have one of them here for a minute . . .'

He turned and walked on, still cursing and whining to himself, but going on. Afraid for himself if he broke his rule and shot nothing.

'Not even a crow!'

He was about ten yards in front before Tom remembered that he would have to walk after him. He could feel his mind misting to cover the pain of his fingers and toes. He was scared that he might start crying . . .

The fox had crossed the river which ran into the tarn. Crossed it diagonally and under cover of a high bank. The hunt was well behind. He came into the field which Tom and his grandfather had just left. The two small figures under the fell on the other side of the low hedge did not interest him. He could go through that hedge and then he would have three good alternatives. Bush stiff, he darted down the field. Hardly even sweating. Through the hedge. Now. Either a break up and over 'The Saddle', or a run along the fields to more open country, or a dash for the lair. For a fraction of a second he paused.

Crack!

'Come on!'

'It's a fox!'

'Come on!!'

'It's a fox, Granda!'

A tight hand grabbed his shoulder. Almost pulled him off his feet.

'Get in here and keep quiet!'

'But, it'll . . .'

The hand slapped across his mouth.

A warm trickle rolled down the inside of his leg.

'This is criminal!'

'Lunatic!'

'Disgusting!'

'Shot?'

'Good God in heaven!'

'Bass! Cornice! Treble! Chancel! Nave! – away now!' The whip curled out around the dogs. 'Away now! Come away! Come away!'

'What's this?'

'Down wind.'

'Tenor! Alto! Hassock! Come away! Get away from there!'

'Never . . .'

'Best day . . .'

'Water . . .'

'Shot! Some – chap – actually – shot—'

They were very near. By daring all the fates and raising his head just a fraction, Tom could see them clearly.

The noise was terrifying. The dogs, deprived of their food and prey, howled like chained monsters in caves, and their wails bounced off 'The Saddle' to ring around and around the hills. Horses bumped and thudded about, snorting. Fierce words came stabbing through the bedlam like steel darts.

The scene was even more terrifying. It was nearly dusk and, in the half-light, the riders swirled around incessantly, man and horse together making up a sinister mythical figure. The dogs

7

had scattered; some of them were on the side of the fell, others had crowded into the field, one or two were pushing their noses towards Tom and his grandfather: the ground squirmed with their shapes.

The old man sat in his tight huddle without a movement. Whenever Tom looked at him – a blank face absorbed his glance without a response.

Tom palpitated. His grandfather was holding Tess, one hand over her mouth, and the boy caught the terror of the dog's awful heaving and shuddering. They would get him. Kill him.

'Wasted day . . .'

'Bring 'em in . . .'

'Treble! Bass! Tenor! Come away! Tenor! Here, boy!'

Tom almost fainted. A long black nose peered down at them. Galvanised, his grandfather shook his forearm, dumbly miming the foulest recriminations imaginable if the dog did not go away.

'Home . . .'

'Drag them out . . .'

Mouth working idiotically: 'Get away! Move! You bastard!' The tiniest whisper behind the gaping. Tess straining to expel even the last echo of a cry.

'Get on with it!'

The long, driving wail of the horn. The hound in front of Tom began to yelp.

'Bass!'

'Drag them out! Drag them out! Drag them out!' The horn blew.

'This way!'

'Bass!'

The dog – indifferent now to the puzzle of Tess's silence, planted its feet and began to bark.

The pack moved towards them. A black horde from out of the side of the mountain. Always the horn riveting their action, the whip cracking; the ground drumming a tangled, sonorous tattoo under the hooves.

'This way. This way!'

'Bass!'

Bass howled out its secret. Other dogs arrived around it – chests swelling and emptying like bellows. Tom panicked: jumped up!

They were in the middle of it all. He clung to his grandfather – still holding Tess. The heads of the horses threatened to bump into them. The dogs got among their feet. Great capped pillars leaned down from the sky and stared and cursed. The octopus slowly settled its arms around him and sucked him into jelly blackness; filthy green sewage ink squirted all over him, eating through the part of the skin that it touched. It had started to snow.

'Is that Paislow?'

His grandfather stiffened to attention. Tom had forgotten that he was not alone.

'Old Paislow?'

'Damn the man!'

'Paislow?'

'Yes.'

One word. Everything cleared. The enemy were all around them. They must wait for an opening.

'Well?'

The old man shifted his feet and clamped himself to the ground. Tom dare not look up. Snow floated down; soft, white flakes.

'What did you want to shoot it for?'

'Couldn't see.'

'What do you mean – "couldn't see"?'

'Couldn't see.'

'*I* can see all right!'

'Ask him what the hell he thought he was playing at!'

'Quiet!'

'Arthur's enough.'

Tom prickled with sweat. The swamp sucked at his feet. He would be pulled under. Man-eating roots waved and laced around him.

'Just tell me why you did it.'

'I know what I'd do to the old sod!'

His grandfather paused.

'Thowt it was a hare.'

A great frustrated raspberry of incredulous cries spat on them.

'It's nearly dark – thowt it was a hare,' the old man repeated, stubbornly, quietly.

'You're a liar! Do you know that?'

The voices were beginning to distinguish themselves. The interrogator was uncertain. A few men behind him were urging him to insult and action. Some voices were far off.

'Aren't *you* ashamed of yourself?'

Yes. Tom was ashamed. He was anything to get them away. He said nothing.

'Let's go back. You'll get nothing out of him.' A softer voice.

'At least are you sorry for what you've done?'

'Thowt it was a hare.'

'Are you sorry?'

'Come on. Say it.'

Silence.

'Let's get back.'

'He's got to say he's sorry! Well?'

Silence.

The interrogator pulled back his horse and moved away, his face contorted in disgust. Someone leaned down to his grandfather, holding out a short whip.

'See this, Paislow?'

Silence.

'Say you're sorry or you'll taste it!'

Tom's whole body went dry.

'I'll give you three . . . One . . .'

'Tim! Don't be a fool!'

'Two.'

'Come on, Tim!'

'Thowt it was a hare.'

'Tim!'

10

The crop slashed down on to the old man's shoulder.

'Fool!'

The mass began to break up. Dogs were called in. Horses pulled around in small circles. Snow melting immediately on their flanks. Tom and his grandfather stood quite still.

The shapes moved away. Chatter – distant snorts and bitten words. A long shuddering silence.

It was dark. Tom's hand went up to his head. A little layer of snow had formed a thatch.

An elegant, tapered slither of moon floated up from behind 'The Saddle'. The flint jaws gleamed silver. Silver flakes of snow swayed down on to the milky ground. The fell withdrew into its gentle pencil softness. Crabbed hedges changed to pretty, tinsel hedgerows. Feet settled silently on the soft snow.

They began to walk back.

'They've taken it with them.'

A scuffle of marks on the ground – already being covered over.

'Did it hurt?'

'What?'

'Your arm.'

'I wouldn't let *them* hurt *me*.'

'They couldn't,' replied Tom.

The loudest sound was a night whisper.

Both of them knew the path blindfold.

Just a few years ago, Tom had discovered the world by following that path. Before that, there had been the house, the river-neck, the tarn, and the path across the fields that led to a town; his mother went by that path: he followed her for a few yards and then came back to his grandfather in the house. And then his mother had taken him along the fell-path – all the way along it to the main road. The house had disappeared. Tom had been terrified that they would never be able to find it again. He had started to explore for himself, after that. The house had become a lot smaller.

His grandfather was muffled into himself. Tom bent his mind to reconstructions of exactly what he should have said and done to the huntsmen.

'I'm glad they didn't ask *me* owt.'

A grunt. Tom lowered his voice.

'I *knew* it was a fox!'

'Dis te think I didn't?'

'You said . . .'

'I said! I said! I said! Tell them nothing. Tell them not one thing!' He spat out gleefully.

'I *did* them!'

They walked on. Tom would never be able to be as clever as that: he would not be able to keep it in.

It stopped snowing as suddenly as it had started.

At first Tom thought it was the buzzing in his mind that he got in his dreams; then it might be his stomach, or his grandfather's back – full of noises. The movement grew to recognition.

'They're coming back!'

The old man stopped. Again an arm snatched out at the boy for control.

'Still!'

The mushy, even clopping of a horse. One only. At least they could deal with one.

'I came back to see if that fool hurt you.'

Tom edged behind his grandfather. The horse snorted right up to them. Its rider was a straight, black stump, smooth-headed.

'Whoa ist?'

'Me of course!'

'Henry?'

Of course! Tom recognised his uncle's voice and peered out to see him more clearly.

'Hello!'

'Tom? I thought you'd have more sense than let your grandfather do a stupid thing like that! Aren't you supposed to look after him?'

The old man pushed Tom away. Tom could feel the anger spread from him like a scent.

12

'Dis thou mean to tell me that thou was among that lot that tried to kill me?'

'I kept well away from it.'

'Ah bet thou did! Ah bet thou did! Thou'd be flaight te cum a laal bit nearer case sumbody might remember we were related. Ah bet thou kept away!'

'Now then! There was nothing I could do. You asked for it!'

His grandfather snatched out at the bridle. The horse pulled back but the old man held on. Tess stood firm two yards away and barked maliciously at the larger animal.

'Let go!'

'Aave got summat te tell thee!'

'Let the damn thing go!'

'That's reet! Damned thing! Damned lot of you!'

The horse began to stamp. Tom could just see the fudgy shape of his grandfather, hanging on, scuttling from one position to another.

'Paislow! You'll be hurt!'

'I *knew* it was a fox!'

The horse reared. The old man jumped back.

'Look out!'

Man and rider thrust out in front of them.

'An' ah'll shut ivery bloody fox that I lay eyes on!'

Tess chased their sound for a few yards and then turned back. The old man started to walk immediately.

Tom crept right to the bottom of his mind, curled up, and tried to forget everything. His grandfather's muttering – in broader and broader dialect as he became more and more angry – spattered against his ears like hailstones.

'Aw mad! Aw't' family . . . Garn up't' Saddle on a horse . . . crackers . . . oor Annie shud niver ha bothet hessel . . . Crackers! . . .'

They reached the house, paused to make sure that Henry was nowhere around, and went in.

CHAPTER TWO

Even though the door had been closed, Tom went to check that it had been closed properly. In the larder beside the door, the window was open one notch. He pulled it tightly shut.

The last time his father had been really angry with him had been in the summer. His mother had taken him swimming in the tarn and stayed in long after Tom had got out to go and build a house in the wood. When he came back, there were three men with her. She was laughing with them; one of them had rubbed Tom as hot as coal with his towel and carried him back to the end of the tarn on his shoulders. When he had told his father, first his mother had cracked him across the head and then – for the first time in his life – his father had sent him to bed without any supper.

He knew that he would be angry this time.

The lamp threw a fuzzy-edged circle on the low ceiling. The ordinary brown and deeper brown wallpaper was tinted to a velvet cosiness. The fire pushed out more shadows – and the whole room was full of a mystery which would have been inconceivable in daytime.

Edward Graham sat at one end of the long table. The other part was being laid for supper. He was a wispy-looking man even though he was quite tall and broad. Perhaps it was because his blond hair was so lank that it still curved over his face, schoolboy-fashion; and the constant brushing it away made him appear fussy. Perhaps it was because he always looked overwhelmed by his projects – forever surrounded, as now, by plans of every this and that. Perhaps it was because of his meekness – generally – in front of his wife. Whatever it was, he was wispy, and though Tom sensed this to be evidence of inconsequence – to be ignored – he feared any possibility of its change.

But nothing was said. His grandfather sat in the big chair in his stockinged feet – resting them on the fender. He had kept on his cap and his jacket was still buttoned.

Tom slid on to the pouf at the other side of the fire. The silence meant that it was even more serious than he had imagined.

His mother managed the making of the meal with a boisterous violence. When she banged the oven door so loudly that Tom jerked like a scared rabbit – he did not know whether to laugh or flinch. Anne Graham – though she appeared to Tom to be just one step away from the encroaching senility of her father – was about thirty. She had changed little to Tom – and to everyone else – since he had first distinguished her from her voice and hands. She clamped around the kitchen like a wild foal.

'Right!' Edward pushed aside his papers.

'Don't start on him now!'

'I've got to, Anne.' His voice was slender among the thick vowels of the rest of them.

'Oh! You are a fool!'

She stamped out to the kitchenette. Tom thought that she was laughing to herself.

'Now: first, you, Tom.'

That was his grandfather. He was 'little Tom' on such occasions. She must have been crying; she could not have been laughing.

'Henry told me all about it. I'd like to hear your side.'

Why would she be crying? Uncle Henry rode into the kitchen on the horse and kicked her in the face with its hooves. The boy put his hands to his brow: he was sweating.

His grandfather said nothing. Edward was pleased to pontificate. He made a steeple with his fingers.

'I'm . . . Henry's my brother – step-brother – we all know that.'

Grandfather belched violently, bent almost double, and sizzled the flames with a squirt of spit. Tom made a cockerel with his fingers.

'He found Anne this house when I was away; I work at his factory; he's a solicitor.'

'For God's sake, Edward!' From the kitchenette. A pan banged on the stove.

'Why did you shoot a fox?' Edward spoke more quickly.

No reply. Edward looked towards the hidden voice. Tom thought that his mother must be terribly angry to hide.

'He came here.' Edward played on the table with his fingers. 'He told me all about it. I knew all about it! They could have – taken you away. He was right to be mad!'

Silence. Edward crumpled a piece of paper.

'Aren't you going to say anything?'

'Ah'd shut ivery damned thing that they were after. Ah'd shut them if I could.'

'Tom!'

The old man stood up. His right arm jerked up in front of him, and then down again: up and around like a windmill.

'They're . . . nowt . . . but . . . trouble . . . they're . . . nowt . . . but . . . nuisances . . . they're . . .'

'Father!' Anne came hurtling through the doorway. 'Sit down! Father!'

'Tek . . . ivery . . . bloody . . .'

'Sit down! See what you've done there now! Upsetting him!'

'Edward's anger rose to the surface at last.

'He's the one who goes around upsetting everybody. Not me!'

'Anyway, I thowt it was a . . .'

'There.'

'Tell him to stop upsetting Henry!' Edward was yelping.

'Henry would get upset on a main road.'

'Henry is my brother. And – listen – he's my boss! He shouldn't be made to look a fool just because . . .'

'He might have to admit to his relations! Well. We are his relations and he can lump it!' Anne spoke with her back to him.

16

Edward was standing up. He spoke deliberately.

'It could cost me my job. This sort of thing.'

'We can afford that!'

Edward blushed. Tom's arms were locked around his knees. His grandfather had become completely immobile.

'You know his eyesight's bad. You should tell him what he's looking at,' his mother turned on him.

Tom squirmed.

'Next time – tell him!'

Edward sat down: one hand strayed to his papers.

'I was coming to you.'

'Leave the boy alone!'

'He's just as much to blame . . .'

'Blame! You're the only one who's blaming anybody. Nobody would have blamed anybody at all if you hadn't started with your speeches.'

'Anne! Please!'

'Edward! Thank you!' Mimicking his accent.

Silence.

Tom held his breath. It might be over.

The old man spluttered and trundled into movement. He stood up.

'Ah'm off oot!'

'There's no need for that, father.'

'Oot!' The arm straightened out beside him. 'You'll be leavin' me, anyway, when you go.'

'Sshh!'

His daughter glared at him. For a moment, he faltered, and then he stumped across the room to the back door.

Anne giggled.

Tom looked into the fire. The logs spluttered a thousand flames. He could never make out any pictures in them. He gazed full at the roasting colours while his face swelled to a scorching red.

'Plates!'

He went to help.

At supper, his mother helped his grandfather to all the best bits. Edward said little; whatever he did say was ignored.

Outside the door, around the noise, there was the softness and quiet of an even life, a cragged, centuries-still landscape, whose very power and mysteries forced them to fling this tiny cacophony on its unmoved surface.

And then, for no other reason than the shifting of a chair or the curl of a flame, the circle disappeared, the noise vanished, and they merged into the silences which the wind brought up in slow waves from the lakes and hills around them.

Settled alone in the kitchenette with a little heap of brasses to polish beside him, Tom raced towards the dream which at this time both obsessed and comforted him.

His duty was to build an impregnable fortress. For some reason, he always set it in the middle of a plain: hills rimmed the flat land but their skirts rested flat on the ground well away from the centre. It would be built of stone; he had seen what flaming arrows could do to wood. There would be an underground cave in which all the animals could be safely kept – able both to breed and to be accessible for supplies, because, although the corn would be packed and stacked in such a well-camouflaged place and in such abundance that it could last for a year – he had to imagine the siege going on forever. Ammunition was a problem he did not have to deal with until after the first six months. The real and constant difficulty was water . . .

Edward Graham had married Anne Paislow just before the war. His father, a chief cashier, had worried himself to death before Edward had had time to memorise him. His mother had remarried – it had seemed – immediately: to Mr Falcon, a solicitor. Henry had been born very soon after that and the step-brothers had been brought up in such a way as to have had the least possible contact with their father, rumours of whose behaviour crystallised when their mother died a hideous and hysterical death. Edward had been

18

completely unsettled by this and, two years later, he had left the bank to go South; news of his step-father's death had followed him to London only to confirm his decision to stay there. A few years later he had changed his mind, come back to Thornton, met, courted and married Anne Paislow within two months and then left her for six almost unbroken years to fight the war on such fronts as Aldershot, Fort William and Llanelly. Returning, he had discovered Henry to be a major and the isolated cottage at the foot of 'The Saddle' – which Henry had found for them – to be his house. He had accepted this because Anne insisted on his doing so and now, five years after the war, just past his mid-thirties, he was convinced that he had made another mistake. He worked in Thornton – a clerk at the one factory of which, by now, Henry was one of the directors.

Anne was not yet thirty. She was the youngest of eight children; two of them had been killed in the war, another had just disappeared, the rest were married and settled at a distance exceeding six miles from Thornton and so – as far as everything but emergency calls were concerned – quite cut off. Her father – the inspiration behind Tom's name – had been a miner until his accident, when he had come to live with her; Tom could never remember his not being there. Tom was proud of her; no one had a prettier mother. When Edward had married her, the impact which her attraction had made on his vanity had been sufficient to send him leaping towards the army with the first batch.

She was a quick woman but not at all neat. All the things which feather womanly characteristics into domestic manners and preoccupations were alien to her. Her black, long hair and tightly-managed slim figure, which seemed to make her a true sister of all the good-looking wives and daughters of miners, had fused with a more solemn, country-fired grace and laziness: at times, Edward's eyes seemed to grope around her, his hands flickered to touch any part of her. Tom wished that he could wipe away all the sins he had committed and start again; then he knew that she would like him.

He had grown tired of the brasses; the first two gleamed, after that they shone less and less convincingly.

He had safely put the question away from his mind throughout the day – but now he had to think about it again; there was no solution – but it seemed that by posing it to himself regularly and frequently, its force was, at least, contained.

He had just passed his scholarship and he would have to go to the Grammar School in Thornton. This would change his whole life; already he had asked Miss Wilkinson if he could give it up, pinned his hopes on the possibility that during two days of violent weather the Grammar School might be struck down by lightning and spelled out every conceivable inconvenience of this new arrangement to his grandfather. No way out of it.

His mother had not wanted him to go to primary school in Thornton, and his knowledge of the town was limited to the road to the pictures. He went in with his mother on Saturday afternoons; she gave him sixpence for the 'Matinée': collected him with all her other parcels an hour and a half later and then they walked back home.

His school world was the village school at Wedham – two miles from the house in the opposite direction to Thornton. Miss Wilkinson was so old that she had taught Mr Farrow who took the five to eight year olds. A beck at the bottom of the schoolyard with the occasional possibility of an otter hunt. The sons and daughters of small farmers and their labourers. Tom had achieved some sort of position as soon as he arrived, being one of the very few pupils qualified to receive gifts for children whose fathers were in the war: the big brown wooden train was still on his windowsill. Only one other pupil had passed for the Grammar School while Tom had been there.

He knew the long path around 'The Saddle' away from the tarn so well that, for rose-hips, raspberries, ash branches, for wild strawberries, dandelions for his grandfather's rabbits, nests, hawthorn blossom and crab-apples, it had become his personal forage-land. In autumn he would meet Harry Warbeck, morning and night for a fortnight, dyking. Great slow horses pulled ploughs across the fields in spring; in summer, he helped Mr Lawton with the hay-making; Mr Turney had bought a noisy, clattering tractor.

He knew no one in Thornton. Only his uncle Henry who came to see them so rarely that he was always a stranger.

Quickly he bubbled his fears into panic.

He wanted to stay exactly where he was now!

'Tom?' His father's voice was quiet and kind.

The boy rushed into the kitchen.

'Come and help me with this.'

'Have you finished?' His mother was rocking in a chair with no rockers. Staring in front of her.

'Yes.'

'All clean?'

He could not tell whether his mother was serious or not.

'Yes.'

'This is how I want our garden to look.'

With this, his father pushed some papers across the table, indicating by that that Tom was to sit down.

'Your grandfather's out in that shed on his own,' said his mother.

'Look. We could take out those trees and extend it to about twice its present length.'

Tom slid on to a seat. His mother was beside the fire.

'That's the first thing. Now . . .' Edward rustled the papers importantly, completely happy.

'Don't you think you should go and look to your grandfather?' said Anne.

'His grandfather's all right. I want him to help me with this.'

'It's his grandfather that'll have to dig that new garden of yours. You'll never get off your seat to do it!'

'There are some new ideas here that I want Tom to see for himself.'

'Go and look to your grandfather!'

'Tom. You stay where you are!' Edward was tense; Anne, relaxed.

'There's no need to shout, Edward. Tom!'

His father reached across the table and took his arm. Said nothing.

Anne stood up and stretched herself with a long shudder. Then she walked slowly across the kitchen to the door which opened on to the stairs.

'Do what you want.'

She went out.

'Anne.'

Edward's voice made Tom feel ashamed for his mother. Father and son sat in silence.

'Go and see what your grandfather's up to.'

His grandfather was mending a hutch. The paraffin lamp was on the floor, throwing great shadows on to the crude-timbered ceiling.

'Why did you say that you would be left behind?'

Tom insisted. This was one of the two questions he had to ask. The old man said nothing.

'Come on, Granda. Why did you say you would be left?'

'Thou'll hear soon enough.'

'Why can't I hear now?'

'Thy mother would be after me with a poker!'

'Come on.'

Tom whined. No one told him anything. The old man grinned with pleasure in the strength of his own secrecy.

'Give me a hand with this.'

It could wait a little. He would move towards his second question.

'Come on! Hold it reet up! Just like yer father with yer 'ands. Useless.'

The hutch was moved into a satisfactory position. His grandfather immediately turned to something else; took down his gun and began to clean it.

Originally, Edward had designated the shed as his workshop. A few days of hurried clearing and weeks of planning had been

22

followed by such limited evidence of serious occupation that his father-in-law had moved in unnoticed. Now the shed was his.

It stood a little way from the house and, though it was unheated and so much more a part of the fields than the cottage that the birds and animals treated it with no more nervousness than a tree or a bush, yet it smacked so solidly of one man's character that Tom felt more comfort there than anywhere else. Rabbit-hutches crowded one wall and the prissy mouths nibbled and darted constantly. Above the door, an old harness flaunting old ribbons. On another wall a gallery of implements: a pick-axe, saw, hammer, various screwdrivers, a chisel, mallet, pincers, small sack of nails. Two highly-polished miner's lamps swung from the ceiling. One corner was crammed with tidied wood-shavings and scrap. A scarred work-bench supported a last and vice. On the floor: three threadworn car tyres, a large knot of dead wood, the iron arms of a park bench, some skins, a glass case with the glass cracked in a wavering X, one wellington, a straw mattress and, underneath the mattress, about half-a-dozen 'girlie' calendars. One patch of wall was crowded with photographs of football teams, royalty and soldiers. There was a broken concertina in the middle of one of the tyres; a Salvation Army cap rested squarely on top of it. The room was very small. Tom sat down on a tyre and watched his grandfather clean the gun.

'You know when we were coming back this afternoon?'

'Huh.'

'After Uncle Henry. You know that you said they were aw crackers.'

'They are.'

'Who?'

The rabbits grubbed almost noiselessly; few sounds reached them from outside. Sometimes his grandfather would just sit back and tell him a story without any fuss. It was a matter of luck. The old man spoke very quietly.

'Henry's father. Your father's step-father. Would have been your grandstep-father. He was called Henry – like your uncle. A big

23

fellow. Big red – face, big – horse – niver off it – big – drinker. They used to drink down where that empty place is. That used to be the "King's Head". He led your grandmother – she would have been – such a life as doesn't bear talkin' aboot.'

'What did he do to her?'

'Nowt for you to know abut.'

'Did he hit her like Mr Lawton?'

'Who told you about Bob Lawton?'

'Mrs Lawton.'

Ignoring the digression, his grandfather got back into his stride.

'Allus bawling and shoutin'. And there was never anybody took as much drink.'

'What did he drink?'

'Whisky.'

'Nowt else?'

'Nowt else. Stop interruptin'!'

The picture was clear enough for Tom to accept being silent.

'They were at t' "King's Head" one neet. Horses still outside: aw in their huntin' tackle – drinkin' and carryin' on like Old Nick. Anyway – so they say – Big Henry – they used to call him that – was tellin' iverybody how he could do this, and he could do that. There was nowt he couldn't do. They would fix him. Could he ride up t' Saddle at neet? Could he? He could do it that minnit. It was blacker than to-neet. Windy. Iverybody eggin' him on. They gave him a lantern to carry to see that he didn't fiddle it.

'Away he went. Up and up that bad bit – just underneath them rocks. They aw' blew their horns and cracked their whips; neebody was ganna hurry him back doon.

'And then t' lantern went oot. They could hear t' horse screamin' its heed off.'

He stopped.

Tom had edged forward so that he was now perched on the very rim of the tyre.

'What happened?'

'T' daft bugger had killed hissel.'

24

'When did they find him?'

'Same neet.'

'What was he like?'

The old man pshawed into his gun and continued to clean it.

'Why did you say you were leavin'?'

'Pass us that rag and shut up if you want to stop here.'

CHAPTER THREE

The flint jaws snapped together and the horse disappeared. Tom swung out of the bed. The cold lino struck the warm pads of his feet. He went to the top of the stairs.

The kitchen door was slightly open. Warmth trailed around the corner like smoke. He sat down and tried to twitch his brows so that his ears would prick forward.

He soon found his place in his parents' conversation.

'And I suppose that I could take one of my weeks off then.' That was his father.

'You would have to.'

'I did want to use that time to get all this organised.'

'This is more important.'

It was easy for the boy to imagine what his father and mother would be doing. Edward surrounded himself with an ever-increasing pile of plans and diagrams and graphs, settling among them like a bee on flowers, whenever he was within scenting distance. His mother would be locked into a ball beside the fender; a book turned upside down just beside her.

'In a way we're going at a bad time.' Edward said.

'Why?'

'Well.' He coaxed her. 'These plans *do* mean something, you know. I might have set up a nice little market garden on the side.'

'You can get an allotment.'

'Not the same at all.'

'Anyway. It's settled.'

'Yes?'

'It'll help Tom a lot, you know.'

His mother was speaking so kindly. Tom felt his eyes smart.

'I appreciate that.'

'I wouldn't move to Thornton for any other reason.'

'I realise that.'

'You know I can't stand that horrible little town. Everybody talking about everybody else. Mrs so-and-so did this – and – that – uh! I hate those those old women!'

'I agree . . . there you are.'

'Miss Wilkinson didn't care if he was late. Besides: I don't want him to start by paddling in like some savage.'

'Anne?'

'Yes.'

'About your father. Now – let me finish. You know I like him. You know that. But . . .' Edward tailed into silence. Anne paused before answering.

'Why can't one of the others have him?'

'Yes.'

'He pays his keep.'

'I know that. But – well there are the others; and – I don't know about him with Tom.'

'Tom'll find friends his own age in Thornton; and it's best that Father stays with us.'

'Now – we're just talking this over, aren't we? No argument or anything? – but, haven't you done your share?'

'I want him to stay.'

'I understand – all that "side of it".'

'I look after him. He's no trouble to you. Let's leave it at that.'

Tom had not taken in this news. He waited for them to go on – to repeat it again and again until it became more real. The backs of his hands were glazed cold when he put them against his cheeks; yet he tingled with warmth. They were moving.

'I'm off for a walk.' Anne spoke briskly.

27

'At this time?'

'There's nothing wrong with the time.'

His mother would be coming upstairs to get her coat. Tom turned to go back into his bedroom and almost screamed out in terror.

His grandfather was standing behind him – grinning, with his false teeth out and his hair all on end. The front of his pyjamas was wide open.

The boy scampered back into his bedroom. Moving. They were moving.

The dim orange light of the kitchen window illuminated his mother's first few steps down the path; and then she disappeared.

She would take the path on the side away from 'The Saddle'. His father could take the fell path. He himself would row down the middle of the tarn. He could keep both of them in sight by strapping luminous watches to their arms. They would meet each other at the other end. The fell path did not turn around to meet the other: he would put a boulder in it and so force his father to go over to the other path. Then they would be sure to meet.

His father rarely went out with his mother. Tom could not understand why she did not get scared.

'The air's best at night,' she said. 'Freshest then. It cleans everything out of your skin.'

The black air wiped her face and neck and hands, easing out every dot of dust that had settled into it.

The moon had disappeared. It was so dark that he could see nothing beyond the little arc of garden outside the downstairs window. There were no farms on that side of the house. The air was so black and heavy that he could dive into it and swim.

His knees scraped against the wooden train. He would stand until his feet stuck to the floor and his head started to spin around. Then he would be able to sleep.

His dead grandfather riding up the scree on a horse! He tried to imagine the horse to have been white – but it was always black.

The lantern clattered and bounced down the slope and into the tarn; he might duck-dive for it. There must be a name for the place at which his grandfather had been thrown off. He had never heard of one.

There was a tiny wood near the school that had never had a name. Tom would sometimes go there after school with the Turney brothers. They had discovered creepers curled around the trees and, carefully, they had unbound them. They were strong enough to carry the weight of all three of them and the wood had become a playground. Everyone swinging from one hummock to another on the long creepers. Tom had started to call it 'Creeper Wood'. The name had caught on. Now, no one would think of talking about it without mentioning its name.

If there was a rock there, he could call it 'Dagger Point'. He would have to climb up it to see. Or he could just call it 'Death Point'. Then he need not climb it at all. Or 'Horse Leap'. 'Huntsman's End'.

His room seemed to have acquired a force which pushed into him from behind and made him lean against the windowsill. He thought that he could smell apples, even though he knew that the apple room had been cleared soon after Christmas.

If his mother came back by the fell path then she would pass the place where the fox had been. What could they do with it if it had been shot? If it had been a weasel, they could have left it there for the other weasels to drag away to some spot of their own where they would bury it.

His forehead bumped against the cold of the window. He left the window and got into bed. It was funny about the weasels. How did they know?

The Indians burst in through the downstairs window. His grandfather opened his bedroom door.

'This way? Come with me!'

His teeth were out and there was spit all over his chin. Tom tried not to look at his pyjamas.

'Tom!'

29

He threw his train at the man who was attacking his mother. With his grandfather, they swung off the roof-top and on to the path.

His father had barricaded himself in the shed. Flaming arrows set it roaring like a bonfire. Edward smashed his way out of the back and ran along to them.

'To Dagger Point!'

His mother ran so hard that the trees jumped out of her way to let her past. Tess was miles ahead of them. barking at a clump of trees.

'Bass!'

'Drag them out! Drag them out!'

The horses pounded behind them. The ground began to shake and rock like clouds of thunder; they were running on corrugated iron which was going backwards.

His uncle Henry was sitting quietly on his horse.

'Out of the way!'

His grandfather shot at him. His uncle did not move.

'No! Get it away! Mam! Get it away!'

The weasel had dug its teeth into his ankle. However much he shook his leg, it just held on and swung around.

His father cuffed it with his papers.

'There you are, Tom. There you are.'

He was free.

'Criminal!'

Thornton Grammar schoolboys were walking in a crocodile along the fell path. From half-way up 'The Saddle', Tom saw the horses burst through them, shattering the line.

His mother was crawling.

'We've got to reach Dagger Point.'

'This is where I mean to put the peach tree.'

'Damn and hell! I can't shoot. Can't see a thing.'

The horses were on them. Ten yards to go. They had to touch the rock. He could not see a rock.

'There must be one.'

The horses were all around them. Tess was screeching. The hounds jumped at his father.

The rock split and a dark liquid came seeping out of it.

He woke up. The dank smell comforted him. But he had wet his bed.

'At your age!' his mother said. 'What if I tell everybody in the Grammar School about this?'

And, later that same morning.

'You were on the top of the stairs last night?'

'Yes.'

'Thought I heard you. You know, then?'

'Where are we going?'

'Church Street.'

'When?'

'Soon.'

Tom determined not to speak to anyone for a week.

He gave up after a day when his father found him in the fields near the house – chopping down one of Mr Turney's trees. Edward was kind and told the boy not to worry about anything.

CHAPTER FOUR

A few weeks of sun and the heavy cart-track kicked up dust like a Mediterranean path. From a distance, they looked like the sun-printed old age and youth of a Spanish village. The grandfather, in a rag and tattered bundle of all-season clothes, sat sideways on the cart; the grandson walking along beside the pony, whispering encouragement; the dog slumped on the back of the cart like an old carpet. Behind them, the town had already sunk to no more than a glimmer of shining roofs.

'Never mind, Toby,' said Tom. 'This is the very last load.'

His grandfather picked up the whip – the effort of which action drained his strength and it flopped back on to the cart.

Toby had compensated for a great deal. Now that its week's loan was almost up, Tom was torn between an affection which gladly welcomed the end of the pony's labour, and an even stronger affection which longed for the relationship, now established to the point of proven love, to go on for ever.

'Thou's wastin' it,' his grandfather said.

'No I'm not, am I?' A murmur.

'Leave off pattin' and pettin t' damn thing!'

Tom took his hand away from the bridle, stepped about three inches away from the pony, and continued to talk – but now, out of the side of his mouth.

The only advantage of Church Street was that his bedroom was bigger. He had plastered the walls with maps, pictures from magazines and postcards, before his mother had settled in sufficiently to stop him. The old man who had died in his parents' bedroom and left the house vacant for them had had only one daughter: she had taken almost everything that she could possibly cram into her own three rooms. Tom had rescued various items from the left-overs; among them, a vine-covered card which he had pinned over his bed. He knew the words by heart.

> *'Lives of great men*
> *All remind us*
> *We can make*
> *Our lives sublime.*
> *And, departing,*
> *Leave behind us*
> *Footprints*
> *On the sands of time.'*

There was a Man Friday footprint at the bottom.

The cottage already looked desolate. No curtains, garden gutted, gate flapping open; had those tiles just fallen off the roof in the past few days?

He slowed down so that he would not have to think about it.

> *'Up there the sun, like a big yellow duster*
> *Polishing the blue, blue sky.*
> *And white fleecy clouds in a cluster*
> *Hanging on the breeze to dry,'*

Internal humming with an American accent.

'Do you want *me* to git off?'

'Eh?'

Galvanised by the will to make someone else work, the old man shook out his whip at the gate.

'Open it!'

'Sorry.'

Tom ran to the gate.

'Thou'll be sorry thou walked doon a well one o' these bright mornings!'

The procession tugged over the last small field. Toby was making too much noise. They must be quiet – kick open the door – lob in a hand-grenade and retire behind the shed. He would put candle grease on the shafts: his own face should be covered with boot polish.

The farm was absolutely still. The sun struck it square in the face and Tom's eyes smarted when he looked at it.

Green slime would be dripping from the walls, the spiders hanging across the corners like great bats, weeds and nettles splitting the floorboards and a suffocating poison reeking out of the yellow and black flowers which pushed out of the mould on the walls. Long raw-skinned red worms squirmed about the kitchen, in the sink, in the lavatory, everywhere.

Tom was not going to go in. His grandfather could bring out the washtub by himself; he would got to the shed for the mangle.

They went around to the back.

The Brinns rose to receive them like beggars at the gate. Two of their women came out of the kitchenette.

Tom took his cue from his grandfather and said nothing. The old man pulled the horse up, got off the cart, stretched, walked a few paces in a circle, said nothing.

As dumbly, the Brinns regarded him. A boy of about five scrambled across to someone's legs and wrapped himself round them.

The Brinns were squatters. There were about thirteen of them. They always moved in a herd. They had no right to be at the cottage and no right to stay there, having been caught by Tom's grandfather. They had no rights at all.

The old man spoke very carefully, very precisely; his words gave his filthy clothes the appearance of being far superior to the filthy clothes of the squatters.

'And what, exactly, do you all think yer playin' at?'

'Mr Paislow.'

The oldest man nodded a greeting.

'All of you! What is it, exactly, yer up to?'

They stood quite still in the positions they had assumed at the old man's first word. 'Stuck-in-the-Mud'. The silence that gathered around them made them – in Tom's eyes – neither more dignified nor more powerful; only more guilty.

Suddenly,

'There was some wire in this garden! Where's it 'at?'

It dropped from a hand. Mr Paislow went forward, bent down, picked it up, and returned to his position.

'T' war's finished.' his grandfather said. 'Long since.' He paused. 'Do you know that?'

They did now.

The old man broke away from his stance and stamped around, chuckling loudly, appealing to the air with his hands.

'Yen minnut,' he said, gleefully. 'Turn me back for half-a-blessed-minnut – and they're in like a bunch o' crows! Not a thing to say for thessels – not them – o, no – ower much trouble, talking is. Just – zip – in; in you go me boys! Theer's a hoos. Folks is cleared off. Zip! In you go me boys! He! You bugger. They're a grand lot round 'ere!'

The Brinns stayed quite still. Tom could have searched them for hidden weapons and they would not have moved an inch. The women's cheap cotton dresses hung limp at their ankles.

His grandfather was now wound tight with delight. Hopping from one leg to another in a kind of soft-shoe-skip-and-jump – he bounced around the statues, singing his head off.

> *'Good-bye Dolly I must lee-ave you. Skee-dum.*
> *Though it breaks – nits! – my 'art to go – go – go – get out!*
> *Something tells me I am neee-ded – tiddly-om!'*

His thumb and forefinger clicked out of time.

> *'Will you stop your ticklin' Jock!*
> *Hoy!*
> *O'er the hills to fight the foooe'*

He leaned into a sprawling fat woman's ear.

'Git away!'

'And see how them soldiers boys are marchin'

He coughed and spluttered, tacking about the Brinns like a broken clockwork doll.

'See! the soldiers boys are marchin'

'Got to git it right, eh? Deafy!' Right in someone's ear.

'And I can no long-ger staaay!'

He stopped.

'And I can no long-ger staay.'

'Are you going when I ask you or do I have to fetch somebody? Eh?'

There was no answer. There never would be an answer. The squatters stood on.

Tom's grandfather had not touched any of them.

'Tom! Come with me!'

He went into the house with his grandfather. On their way through the kitchenette, the old man kicked a few alien pots and pans so that they scudded and clattered against the wall.

He led Tom upstairs into what had been Tom's parents' bedroom. The window looked out on the front – towards Thornton. Everything had been cleared from the room, but the old man pottered about, tapping walls, picking at the plaster, rubbing at the dirt with his finger.

When they came downstairs about ten minutes later, the Brinns had gone.

'What's wrong with the Brinns?'

'Everything's wrong wid them.'

36

Toby had been allowed to pull the cart along at a brisk pace. The old man yanked the reins to indicate that less speed was required. Tom was sitting beside him to get his information. The sink and the mangle pressed down the back of the cart so much that the boy felt that he was balanced in mid-air on one end of a see-saw.

Mr Paislow could not wait to spill it all out. Tess was away out in front of them; he called the dog back so that the pony would not be encouraged to go faster.

'Tell us just one thing,' Tom demanded.

'They haven't a hoos.'

'I know. Another.'

'They'll niver hev one.'

Tom kept on pestering. After a short history of squatters in general and the Brinns in particular, his grandfather came to their true distinguishing characteristic.

'They're aw muddled up,' he said. 'Naybody knows who belongs who.'

'What do you mean?'

'Well . . . there's a fellar theer – a father 'til his own wife; and a woman that's a niece 'til her own husband.'

Sometimes his grandfather would set him trick questions like this. Tom concentrated.

'There isn't a man in Thornton could sort them oot! And naybody imagines what goes on – I bet they've niver hed mair than one bed a'tween t'lot!'

'Did their grandmother get married twice like mine?'

The relationship of his father to his uncle Henry – that of stepbrother – had been explained carefully to Tom when he had demanded to know why two brothers did not have the same name. In spite of Edward's pains, Tom had had to think it over for weeks, to reassure himself that it could work. The Brinns might be more complicated – but, by now, he had no fear of incomprehension.

'You see,' his grandfather said, 'they'll be folk that's niver had nowt. They'll niver hev learnt owt and if anybody's telled them any – bit – thing that wasn't for their bellies – then they'll have forgot it.'

37

Tom pursued his point.

'Did their grandmother marry twice?'

'Not once. Isn't one of them been near a church barrin' funerals.'

Tom panicked.

'How did it happen then? How can a father be his own wife's niece?'

The old man shook his head. Tom was stranded with his problem.

One bed. He felt sorry for the Brinns. He had felt sorry for them while his grandfather was singing. There was no need to throw them out. His uncle Henry had told his father that he was going to keep the cottage unoccupied.

'At least for a year or so. Might need it for some sort of stabling – riding – school; I dunno. It's too much trouble to fill it all up again.'

A staccato of pips woke him up.

'You gonna tek every inch of this road?'

They had joined the road just a few hundred yards away from the town.

'It's Norman Dalton.'

'In a hurry.' The little black tin-lizzie bullocked its way forward, horn pipping furiously.

His grandfather cursed back good-humouredly and pulled to one side. As soon as Mr Dalton had drawn up beside them, he slowed down to a crawl and leaned out of his window.

'Gettin' on?' said Mr Paislow, admiring the battered car.

'She'll do for a start. That Annie's boy?'

'T' same.'

'He'll be maister o' you in two ticks. What's yer name?'

Tom's tongue stuck to the top of his mouth. He could not answer. Mr Dalton's stern, furrowed face split into a great reckless grin which embarrassed the boy even further.

'Cat got yer tongue?'

His grandfather banged him with his elbow. Tom shook his head.

'Fine lad is he?' asked Mr Dalton.

'When he keeps his mouth shut.'

The old man buckled at the mouth in appreciation of his own joke.

'Fine enough to be a farmer – eh? – mouthy? That right?'

Again Tom was stuck.

Mr Dalton revved up his car. It shook, like a leaf in a gale.

'An' how's Edward then?' he barked.

'Same difference.'

'A good man, your father!'

A nod at Tom and he was gone. Tom watched the car right into the town, until it turned a corner and disappeared.

'Farmer,' his grandfather said. 'Friend of yer dad and mam's. Lives two miles yon other side of Thornton.'

Toby had to be walked back to the baker who had loaned him to them. Tom stuffed the pony with sugar and received some alleviation of his pain when the baker informed him that he could come and repeat the feeding whenever he wanted to.

The evening was light with the moist sweetness of the end of a Northern summer day. Tom, dressed only in a shirt, short trousers and sandals, walked down High Street looking for something to do. He knew nobody and so went into the house.

His grandfather was helping his mother to strip the hall. In the kitchen – much smaller than the kitchen at the cottage – his father had managed to establish his own little corner of comfortable untidiness among pails, bare floors and stacked-up furniture. Tom watched him light the gas mantle with proprietorial satisfaction.

His father was a good man. Helping him with his plans, he saw evidence of this goodness in every movement he made. He was reluctant to leave him to go to bed.

From his window he could see only roofs and sky. Open countryside was about six streets away and beyond that – 'The Saddle'. For a while, he just stood and looked at all the lighted windows; wondering what people could be doing at that time of night.

The Brinns would have put their one bed in a field and all

thirteen of them would now be sleeping in it. His uncle Henry should give them the house. Yet again he tried to work out what his grandfather had meant. All he could think of as an answer was the smell that there must be with thirteen people in one bed.

Toby would be asleep – he would go round and see him in the morning.

He bit his lip as a punishment for being so daft in front of Mr Dalton.

The cottage was far away – unreachable: besides, he was too scared to go there on his own.

PART TWO

PART TWO

CHAPTER FIVE

'Dare you climb that wall.'

She stuck out her arm so high that her short frock tilted way up over her knees.

'*That* one,' she repeated.

He wanted to go into the house he had built for them to settle down in. The bowels of a bush, brown earth damp-baked, soft and heavy smelling, leaf-laced walls branching a perfect dome; this the cave which he had carefully laid over with short, prickly handfuls of sweet-mown grass, sealing and hiding their house from everyone.

'And then you'll come into t' den?'

'*That* one!'

'You will come?'

He was already moving towards the wall.

'We'll see,' she said.

Slight lisp – he wanted to catch it and plant it and watch it grow into a beautiful flower. 'We'll see' – so tickling sensible and proper – but her pout was an iron gauntlet. The white smooth arm – always an inch behind the sun so that the heat never burnt it but let it bathe in shadow – this flung out so that he would have raced into hell's furnaces if the fingers had pointed there.

He hitched up his trousers – showing white above the sun mark which, with the white below his knees – so frequently met by tight woollen stockings that they looked lonely without them – made his sun-burn look like a fanciful splodge of brown paint. The trousers immediately slipped back into their working position.

It was a high brick wall which ran all the way around the garden in order that Mrs Falcon and Catherine should be kept safely in, and everyone else kept safely out.

Tom had first climbed it two weeks before the beginning of his summer holidays. He had met his cousin Catherine some time before then, been told that she was nearly six and rather delicate – but that had been in a street full of Saturday afternoon monsters; and once in his uncle Henry's room, crowded with so many breakable things that the route from chair to door was a high-wire tight-rope.

'I'm your cousin, Tom.'

'I know.'

He hung from the top of the wall by his fingertips and dropped down beside her.

'Can I play here?'

'As long as you're not rough. If you are, my daddy will kick you up the backside into kingdom come.'

'I'm not rough.'

His affection for Toby flicked out like a light.

On his third visit, his aunt Catherine had caught him.

'Does your father know you come here?'

'Yes.' One lie.

'Do you know that you shouldn't climb that wall?'

'No.' Another.

'Let him come in through the back gate then.' His aunt nodded to her husband.

His uncle Henry Falcon had suddenly appeared behind his aunt Catherine. He was bigger and broader and finer looking than Tom's father – but, through his kindness, Tom, for the first time, saw a likeness between the step-brothers. This warmed him so quickly that his stomach – which had frozen solid at his aunt's first word – melted sufficiently for his heart to slip back down his throat.

Some sort of fidgeting went on between his aunt and uncle.

Tom knew that his aunt Catherine did not like him. She spoke in a completely different way from his mother and never wore any clothes that she could have worked in. Tom was afraid of her; he knew that she would send him away. Catherine sidled across to her mother and looked at Tom mistrustfully.

'He can come whenever he wants!' His uncle Henry glared at everyone.

His aunt Catherine turned her back to Tom and the boy heard only the fierce edges of her whisper.

'For God's sake, Cath, let the girl have one playmate who isn't made of plaster!'

Tom had left – to come back the next day and find Catherine waiting for him.

'Mummy says if you swear – you've got to go home.'

'Cross my heart and die.' Tom spat on the back of his hand.

'And you have to be careful not to hurt me.'

Tom's hands grew even larger and more clumsy in front of him. He put them behind his back and shook his head.

Catherine then uttered her final word.

'It's only because you happen to be my cousin that we can even talk to each other.'

Tom nodded. He understood perfectly.

'Let's build a house.'

She immediately agreed and directed Tom's labours.

They crawled into the house – the 'den' – very rarely; the main concern was to make it comfortable and defend it against possible marauders. Soon, however, Tom's one aim was to manoeuvre Catherine into the bush; once there, he would do no more than play fight with her – timidly, for he was terrified of hurting her – but this fragile tapping in the musky cocoon drove such a powerful excitement through him that he became asphyxiated with the heavy memory of each time he had touched her arm.

She would squat comfortably and play with the doll's house cups and saucers she had brought from the house. Tom had to lie almost curled around her as the area was so small. The only light came from the little funnel which served as the entrance. He toppled Catherine over – very gently so that she would not hurt herself, and then he made an elaborate business of straightening her to make sure that she was all right.

He did not know what to do.

Catherine gave orders, repeated her parents' words and watched him carefully to see that he behaved himself: little else.

He climbed the wall slowly and carefully to make sure that Catherine would see how difficult it was. It was easy. He stood on top and looked down at her.

'Dare you walk along it.'

He wanted to pickle her stiff in that position. Never to move again – either of them – so that he could always see her – fair hair, blue flowered dress, 'a little piece of china' his grandfather called her. And the luscious summer lap of the large garden nursed her like a bluebell on a soft velvet cushion.

'Make your hair long – then I will.'

He had been urging her to do that since the beginning of the afternoon. He hated her hair to be bundled up with a clip. When it fell loosely to her shoulders, he was reminded of the illustration of Alice in his school-prize book.

'Mummy says it gets dirty when it's long.'

'Make it long.'

'Dare you to walk along that wall – right to the end.'

The end narrowed to a single brick width: also, it was in bad repair.

Tom was on top of the wall. Catherine was so small that he could have jumped on her and squashed her. He could see over the tops of the apple trees to the marvellous bay-windows of his uncle's house. He shuffled his feet – pretending to dance.

'Make it long first. Make it long!'

For a few moments, Catherine said nothing. Both of them were conscious that the balance of power between them was changing.

The previous day, they had been playing hide and seek.

'I want to hide first,' she said.

46

'No. I'm going to.'

Tom had to hide first. Then, he always went to the den and waited for Catherine to crawl in and find him. Then he could bump against her.

'If you don't let me hide first – I'll go in.'

'I don't care,' he replied.

Catherine had looked at him – amazed. Tom had stood quite still, shocked to the core by such a terrible mistake.

And then, again, the voice popped out without any sort of conscious decision on Tom's part.

'I couldn't care less.'

Catherine had cried. But she had not run home. Tom had disguised her crying by whistling so that her mother would not come charging through the trees to find out what was wrong.

He had hid first and she had come straight to the den to find him.

Now, again, she wavered.

'I'll be in trouble,' she pleaded.

'It must be long.'

It had to be long quickly or Tom would forget who she was. It was bad enough when she put on a clean dress – on one such day Tom had made an excuse and ran away – peeping through the railings the next morning before he climbed the wall to make sure that she had changed back into the blue flowers: her hair had to be long.

Very carefully – with old maiden-like neatness, she encircled the nape of her neck with her arms and prised out the clips and pins which netted her hair.

It flowered down – long and fair – down to her shoulders.

'I'll walk right to the end!'

Catherine had filled Thornton so fully that Tom could not move without meeting her, would not move without seeing her.

And now, walking along the top of the wall, with his feet splayed out for safety even though he could have raced along it without coming to the slightest harm, he felt the silent, throbbing stillness of the late-summer late-afternoon town swell calmly about him.

With his extra holiday because of the Grammar School, he was one of the few free from work but as the factory let out its men, and the fields slowly emptied around the town, Tom felt that his freedom was now mingling with that of others and so becoming less buoyant; his solitude less singular, less precious. He wanted to finish along the wall and take Catherine into the den while he was on his own. There was no more time to rove about the garden on a horse or in an aeroplane working out accidents from which there was the whole afternoon to recover. Time had been squashing itself together like a concertina ever since the exact half-way point – ringed in black on a calendar – in his holidays, and now there was none left. She would be called in soon.

He ran to the end – across the dangerous part.

'Dare you jump to that branch.'

Without a word he swung himself out to it and landed in a bunch at her shiny buttoned feet. Her eyes were wide open and her mouth began to twitch into another challenge.

'Are you coming to the den?'

'One more dare.'

'No.'

'A little one.'

'No.'

Tom stood up. Towering beside her. She looked slightly scared and he was pleased.

'Come on!'

He took her hand – and it stuck fast. They walked to the den quickly. Tom went in first.

Catherine looked at him questioningly.

'Well?'

Tom was uncomfortable. The ground seemed to have grown a hundred new stones and spikes; the leaves and grass smelt sour; he was sitting cross-legged and his feet felt big.

'What do you want me to do?'

She spoke in a great hoarse whisper. Tom wanted to go out and come in and start again from the beginning.

'Take your shoes off!'

Quickly she pulled off her shoes, holding them in front of her nose in the half-light to show proof that the order had been carried out.

'Socks.'

Off in a second. Dangled in front of his face.

Tom was almost crying. He did not understand why he had asked her to take off her shoes and socks and, knowing now that she would do whatever he asked, he felt no desire to demand anything further of her. He rocked himself on his behind and nudged her; instead of rolling away, she pressed herself against him.

He wanted to go away.

'What do you want me to do now?'

Let him out. He made a tremendous effort and told her to be quiet for a minute so that he could think. She was quiet in such a way that he was more aware of her than when she was talking. He shut his eyes. A great sigh of rustling and manoeuvring came from her.

'Shut up!'

Silence.

There was nowhere to run to because he would be able to tell no one what he was running away from. He was trapped in the emptiness of his own mind which wanted nothing to happen: everything should vanish and leave everything untouched; then he could start again.

His eyes were still closed. Catherine was six and he was eleven. He almost shook with the shame of it.

'Cathy!' His aunt was there!

He bolted out of the den like a rabbit.

'Put your shoes back on!' he hissed.

He did not look at her.

Almost as tall as a tree, his aunt Catherine. The blank-faced question in a twitch of eyebrows which lit the cannons that blasted him into the sky.

'Where's Cath?'

49

'Coming out. Inside. There.'

He faced his aunt and pointed behind him at the den; hand sticking out like a tail. Catherine was only six! He was going to the Grammar School in three days.

His aunt's face tightened. Suddenly, she stepped forward and slapped Tom, hard, across the cheek.

'You little criminal!'

Catherine crawled out of the hole dressed only in her knickers. She squealed when her mother hit Tom.

'What has he done? Cathy! What did he do? What have you been doing?'

Tom did not know. The skin on his cheek smarted so stiffly that if he moved his face it would crack wide open and blood would spurt everywhere. He dared not move his head. Catherine came into his area of vision. She had put her shoes on.

If he pretended that nothing had happened, then perhaps nothing would happen.

His breakfast had been left out on the table for him. He ate it beside the empty grate.

Empty house on a Saturday morning. A clock ticking very loudly to remind him how empty it was. The two eggs had been boiled hard and he ate them like pasch eggs, dipping them in a tiny pyramid of salt.

A few weeks after their arrival in the house in Church Street, his mother had said:

'I've got no clothes. I can't look like a tramp in Thornton. I'll have to get a job. We've got to get some money with this rent.'

At first his father had argued; then hurled himself into schemes which promised him seven and sixpence for every twenty pounds' worth of knick-knacks he sold; then sulked for a few days.

She had gone to work at the post office.

'It's better than nothing and they're giving me the country round. Anyway, biking'll keep me fit.'

She started at 5.30 in the mornings and was not back sometimes until two in the afternoons. But she had already bought a new coat and a new pair of shoes.

His grandfather worked part-time in the churchyard.

Tom would have felt much busier, much more of a crowd, walking through the fields near the cottage than he did walking up Thornton's main street. He already knew all the faces off by heart – but he had no gossip or chatter or accidents or jokes to put to them. He did not even nod to anyone.

Walking in this way, with his hands bulging his pockets, he was soon out of the town which had once seemed so big that if he had lost himself he might never have been found for weeks.

He was on the road to the cottage – but it was such a different road that he recognised it with his eyes only.

Saturday. Two days to go and he would be at the Grammar School. He smarted with shame to remember that Catherine was five years younger than he was.

Lying on his back in the long grass, trying not to cry. He was always wanting to cry these days and there was no particular reason why he should.

He tried to prise the few clouds away from the blue so that he could see the sky as endless as it really was. On and on and on. Blue with deepest black and then the flash-blinding white-heat of sun and stars forevermore. Meteors dipping and racing like spitfires. Planets exploding and hurtling away into equally unconfined nothingness. He wondered why he could not hear them; sometimes, lying on or in his bed, his mind seemed to blacken and wipe itself so completely that he was sure that he heard the echoes of all those million clashes; tingling against the ribbed, narrow-fibre winnowings of sensation like light on a photographic plate. Whoosh! and he went away with Captain Marvel – away from the clockwork terror of the Boy's World explanation of it all – so exact that every calamity seemed to threaten like a triple millennium of doom – away into the gliding blackness and twinkling tinsel stars of manageable stories.

There was not a sound. Not the rough tear of grass under the leather jaws of a cow; not the grassy clomp of horses; not even the startled spluttering of a motor-car. He breathed out, loudly.

The only thing to do was to find his uncle Henry and settle it before something was let out.

Normally, he would not have dared to go into his uncle's office; had he thought about the outrageous insolence of 'disturbing' someone at their work, then he would have skirted the door as if it had been a mine.

Mr Waters smiled at him and sent a woman to tell his uncle. Tom sat on a high chair; the cold leather smacked through his thin shorts; his feet did not quite touch the floor.

His uncle's office was a brown palace-chamber. Tom was calmed as soon as he went into it. The musty smell and quietly grained lighting secured him against all the hailstones of indecisions and hopelessness.

'I've come to say I'm sorry.'

His uncle laughed – sharply – and the happy report shot away all Tom's cobwebbed miseries.

'Your aunt Catherine has a terrible temper.'

It was his aunt's fault!

'I won't play with Catherine again.'

'You have my permission to do so – if you want to.'

Tom shook his head. He could not bear the thought of her.

'I'm too rough,' he said.

His uncle laughed again and rose up from behind his wide desk to come round and talk to the boy.

'Cathy needs someone rough.'

'Not me. I swear.'

'So do I.'

A wink. Tom relaxed even more.

'So you won't tell mam and dad?'

'No.'

'And aunty Catherine won't?'

'No. I promise.'

Tom sighed with happiness. Everything was simple again.

'I would like to be a lawyer when I grow up.'

'Good.' He looked at Tom with such open affection that the boy immediately put him at the top of his list of favourites.

'I didn't give you anything for passing your scholarship, did I?'

'No.'

His uncle put his hand in a long pocket and pulled out a great handful of money. Then he changed his mind and got out his wallet.

'Here's a pound.'

'I would rather have a half-a-crown. Mam'll make me save that note.'

His uncle took out half-a-crown.

'Spin you for it.'

'Tails.' Never fails.

'It is.'

He wrapped the coin in the note and handed the little package over to the boy.

'I'm glad you've come to live in Thornton.' He put an arm around the boy's shoulder.

'So am I,' said Tom.

CHAPTER SIX

The same Saturday morning. Nearly dinner-time.

He trotted up the street to look for his father. The house had still been empty. He had hidden the pound note behind the quotation above his bed. The half-a-crown swung in his trouser-pocket like a lump of lead.

He knew where to go and he padded through Duke's Lane, past the Primitive Methodist Church and the pawn-shop to the Temperance Billiard Rooms.

His father was in his usual corner. Inside, day turned into night and the great hooded lights above the green tables lit up the white balls as if they were luminous. The cues slid rapidly along the rough hands and cracked sharply against the balls. The windows were church-pointed, clotted with grime from having been left tightly shut since the place was built. The air was so still that the cigarette smoke hung thickly, just above the table – drifting away only when a low murmur pushed against it.

'Hello, Tom. Sit down. Just finishing these figures.'

Edward had taken the job of bookie's runner. He ran for Mr Carlin whose kitchen was his office in an alley beside the Friends' Meeting House. Tom was aware of the dangers of the job.

'If they catch me running at the factory, they'll fire me,' his father had told him. 'You're not supposed to do any extra work. And the police could stop me on the street any time they wanted. If they searched me, I'd be up.'

Tom scanned the room from underneath his eyebrows. He could always buy a shoulder holster. Then his father would be safe.

'Check these.'

He passed Tom a list of bets. Edward made the most beautiful lists: five columns: name of staker; time received money; horse; meeting; amount and construction of bet. Tom raced through the amounts.

'Three pounds, nine and three.'

'Correct!'

Edward scudded the money across the table top with two trotting fingers, spilling it, accurately, into a little blue bag. He put the columned sheet into a large diary.

'Now then,' he said, 'what have you been doing?'

'Nothing.'

So his father could not have heard about it.

Edward was in no hurry. Racing did not start until 1.15. He put his arm around Tom and drew him into him. One or two of the men who were waiting for a game drifted into their corner.

Tom was glad that his father was wearing a suit. He did not like it as much as his uncle's, but at least it was a suit, with a white collar and tie. Everyone else wore old jackets and mufflers jammed into their shirt-fronts.

Edward was proud of his son and he sat back comfortably – happy for the two of them to be seen together. Tom realised his father's thought immediately and wanted to show off.

Edward gave him the opportunity.

'Jack. Who do you fancy this afternoon?'

'At Brunton Park? Ah'll tek Wrexham.'

'Carlisle's nut worth a luk in,' another man. 'They niver war worth followin' and they niver will be.'

'Whoa plays for them now?'

A nudge. Tom rattled off the team: declared them unbeatable. His father slapped him on the shoulder.

The men liked somebody who could answer questions. They pumped him about teams and club records for the next five minutes.

'He'll tell you,' said Edward. 'Knows a damn sight more than I do.'

Tom sat on the edge of his seat: scared that he might be caught out.

'Nobody'll beat Frank Swift. Manchester's bound to beat them.'

Edward laughed. He had marked the game down as a draw. But he hoped that Tom was right.

The men went over to one of the tables. Occasionally, the door would open and the bright morning could be seen standing outside; never coming in. Tom felt as though he was in the dressing-rooms at Brunton Park. Outside, the crowd were shuffling on the grandstand and their feet were a roll of drums preceding his entrance. He picked up the brand-new ball.

'OK, lads. This is it.'

And out they went. The cheers could be heard a mile away.

'We'd better be off.'

A hook over his head in the opening minute. Goal!

'Do you want to carry the diary?'

He decided to walk alongside his father. It would look too suspicious if he ran on ahead to look around all the corners. He tried to keep in step with Edward and walked down the street in a sort of goose-march.

If they were stopped his father could always say that he carried his money – his own money – in the blue bag. What could he say about the list? The diary slowly melted away his hand until it was supported on nothing but sweat.

A second goal! He trotted back to the centre-circle.

'I don't know how your mother manages this sort of a day.'

He could say that he had copied it all out for a bet! That would do it.

'Ten miles. It would kill me.'

His father nodded to most of the people they passed. Tom did not like him to draw attention to himself but nevertheless, he included himself in the nod so that he could nod on his own the next time.

'That's Edward Graham's boy.'

'Would you like to bike ten miles?'

Or he could say that he was practising his writing for school. In two days. They turned into the alley beside the Friends' Meeting House. On the gate was a hoarding. The top part was bombed houses and broken aeroplanes; the bottom half was a fist with the index finger stuck out in front. 'War in the World – or Peace in your Heart?'

'Three pounds nine and three-pence!'

'Close the door. Not so loud. Sit down. That your boy? He can stand. He don't mind?'

All spoken in a monotone.

Mr Carlin was so fat that Tom could think of no comparisons that would not get his father into trouble.

'He knows? Of course he knows. Everybody knows. It's a comedy. Where's the list?'

His belly started just underneath his last chin, swelling in a smooth, stiff arc, to come to his body again just above his knees. His V-necked jumper was no more than a large bib; his shirt was open at the vital buttons; a thick yellow vest encased the growth.

'Shall I go to the Hare and Hounds?'

'You've not been. I knew you wouldn't. You'd forget. Dick went. He was mending the car but he went.'

'Sorry.'

Grunt. Mr Carlin replaced himself, above the money and the list – now on the table. He was so pink. His fingers were pink, his head was pink, his eyes were pink, and his chins, like careful, chunky blanket folds, were clean pink, smooth and dry.

'Correct.'

He looked at Tom. The boy wondered if his feet were fat. He could not see them because the trousers were so wide that they hid his shoes. Mrs Carlin was cooking something which required a large block of lard. Her cooker was next to the telephone and she had not once turned around. It would have been difficult as the room was no more than six feet wide. She was also fat: her behind spread the width of the cooker.

When he looked back at Mr Carlin he saw that he had been watching him watch his wife. He blushed.

'Can I bet?'

His father had been sitting on the arm of the settee with his face as respectful as a waiter. He jumped up at Tom's suggestion and picked up a paper.

'I'll put something on for you.'

Mr Carlin said nothing. Perhaps his fat had clogged up his body and stopped him. His position was unchanged from minute to minute. Tom picked out the best name.

'Striding Eagle.'

'100–8. Winchester. Third race. Good stable. How much?'

'I've got some money.' Tom's hand slammed into his pocket.

'Who gave you that?'

'Uncle Henry.'

His father took a small bunch of change from the ticket pocket inside his jacket.

'Put a shilling on the nose,' he said.

'Take it out of this.'

'Keep that.' Edward ruffled his hair.

Mr Carlin picked up a very stubby pencil and bent over to the table very slowly.

'Thirteen and six to come,' his father said.

'If it wins.' Tom was cautious.

Mrs Carlin bobbed, slowly, and reached out her left hand to take a large dinner plate. Mr Carlin looked at Tom.

'You didn't see anything. Your father is just a friend of mine. Nothing happens here. Ring through for the course prices.'

Edward went over to the telephone.

'Go and find your grandfather.'

Tom went out.

The Rev Pursur was in charge of the Anglican church – the Church of St Mary – in Thornton – and he had appointed Tom's grandfather to a post:

'Looking after the churchyard. The job will only take up your time for three afternoons a week – and even if it takes more, I'm afraid that the Parish Council will take those three afternoons only into account in the finding of your wage.'

'No overtime!' his grandfather said.

'We'll just have to tell everybody to hurry up and die,' replied his daughter, when they talked it over at home.

'I think you should know, Mr Paislow,' the Rev Pursur had said – sensible of the repercussions which would inevitably follow from such a choice – 'that if a member of my regular congregation had been either able or fitted to do the work – then there would have been no question but that the job would have gone to him. However . . .'

'None of them's daft enough for it,' said Anne.

'You may grow into the congregation.'

'He didn't exactly say that I'd got to go to church,' the old man said.

'You should,' said Edward.

'He won't.' Anne.

'At least, once or twice.'

'Mr Waters, our chief churchwarden, will help you. You can call on me, of course, whenever you wish.'

'As long as you don't put them in upside down.'

'Ah 'ope they keep up in that hard weather.'

Tom was still rather afraid of the back streets and so he went out into the High Street and turned into King Street and came to the church by the main road.

It stood as the fourth side of a little square. Opposite was the 'Lion and Lamb', flanked by tall, narrow-doored houses. To the left, a row of shops – always more shut than open – a leather shop, an old shoemaker, a failing cake-shop, a wool and patterns shop. To the right, a wavering rank of low-roofed cottages two up, one down – with a hole blasted in the middle for the road to go through.

Two children were pressing their noses against the shop windows. Three women were clustered around one of the cottage doors, smoking, talking. A car drew up outside the 'Lion and Lamb' and everyone looked at the young man who climbed out of it to go into the pub.

Tom hoisted himself on to the wall and whistled. One of the children outside the shop whistled in reply. Tom forbade himself to look around and dropped into the churchyard.

Little of the day's heat got in there. The flagstones and yew-shadows cloistered the long grass and held in all the damp and cold that there was.

'Granda!' And another whistle. Tess, at least, should respond.

He wandered around the dry green-slimed gravestones, his feet twitching on to and off the little hummocks beside them as if they were live electric currents.

'Granda!' He whispered his call, out of respect.

At the bottom of the churchyard, a tree had fallen down, pushing some of the headstones sideways. Someone had been lopping off the branches; the axe had been left in a log. His grandfather must have gone for his dinner.

Tom decided to risk returning home by the back way. Church Street should be just around the corner; he had seen one end of it in the church square.

The tree had broken the wall down. Beyond it was a wide side street which led away from the auction. He came out into the sun. The cottages were whitewashed and the glare lifted as a haze above the road. Open windows included him in a record programme and the high-speed clatter of knives and forks. He did not feel hungry.

He walked uncertainly to his left – hoping to hit the main street once more. He kept looking over his shoulder to make sure that Church Street did not suddenly appear behind him.

Around the corner, a boy of about Tom's age was playing with a tennis ball; throwing it against a wall. The wall spread a clean black shadow over the area in which the boy was playing. The ball hit the wall, bounced down on to the ground and then up into the boy's hands. He did not move more than a step to his left or to his right.

Tom waited for him to miss it.

The ball donked the high wall – between two cardboard-shuttered windows, floated down to the smooth tarmac, and lifted into the boy's hands. There were no target marks either on the wall or on the ground.

Tom walked over to stand just behind the boy; just out of the shadow.

The ball floated up to the wall and donked the ground which hit it up into the boy's hands. It lifted high off the ground so that, each time, Tom was sure that it was going to bounce over the boy's head and run free. But, always, its flight dipped and the boy caught it in both hands.

He threw with his right arm, snapping his wrist like a fan.

Dipping and bouncing and floating, the old, worn tennis ball curved parabolas from hand to wall to ground to hand.

The shadow edged out and tipped Tom's feet. He stood back.

On the boy's left was another wall; none of the bottom windows had been repaired.

The boy took a pace to his right, collected an errant return, moved back to his original position and snapped his wrist to send the ball curving up to the wall.

Tom must have stood there for some time. When, finally, he pulled himself around to go away, the shadow had covered his feet. He jogged to shake off the cold.

He did not look over his shoulder. The regular beat of the ball was enough.

Tom was glad to see the tramp because he knew him. He slowed down to be recognised. He had seen him with his father last night.

'What did you go back to him for?' he had demanded.

'Never mind.' His father had grinned down at him, happily. Tom clutched his arm and jumped up and down beside him. No. one was on the street to see him.

'What for? What for?'

Edward jumped into a little trot and Tom clung on to his arm until he slowed down.

'Did you tell him something?' asked the boy.

'I did. But he didn't hear.'

'Why not?'

'He's deaf; he can't speak either.'

Tongue sliced off on the galleys by a great, brutal ganger with a sharp, slitting knife. Ugh! Blood-filled, spurting, clotted mouth and a fin of a tongue wavering like a stumpy tail. Tom licked his palate. The cannons boomed, cracked, crashed in his ear, bursting the drums and they rolled out like peas.

'Or they say he can't.'

'What happened?'

'I don't know. He gets around to Thornton about this time every year.'

Where did he sleep? What did he eat? What was there in his sack? How did he not get knocked down? There was something more important to ask first.

'What did you go back for, then?'

His father laughed. Tom laughed with him – his father looked so pleased.

'To give him a shilling.'

A lump of admiration formed and grew inside Tom's chest until it clogged his whole body with a desire to sacrifice himself in some way for his father. He hovered around him for the rest of the evening . . .

If the tramp had been doing something, he had stopped by the time Tom got near enough to see. He might have slid into a squat, but his clothes were so numerous that the outer layer was connected in no direct way with the movements of his body, and so the boy could not know for certain.

Tramps were common enough around Thornton; but, like gipsies and tinkers and long-staying strangers – they were curious and endlessly fascinating.

Tom began to speak and then he remembered, stopped and blushed.

The tramp's face was brittle red, caking with flakes of what might have been sweat, too often gathered to be brushed away.

He might have been eating. No one else was in the street. Tom blushed even harder to think that he might be butting in.

Three jackets, all frayed, frayed, frayed! Old boots no laces

Tom wanted to rage and cry and dress up the tramp like his father, and shave him and cure his deafness, teach him to speak deaf and dumb language, get him a job. The sun first leaned against, then weighed on the back of his neck.

Poor old man. He could not turn away; he watched him for minutes, murmuring tears to himself.

The tramp never moved.

And the half-a-crown grew colder and colder against Tom's leg. Through the thin lining and against his leg. It was too much!

The red face offered itself blankly to the sun; a saucer of milk looking into a cat's face.

He should have asked his uncle for some change.

He was preventing the tramp from doing what he wanted to do. Quickly, he twisted the coin around and around between two fingers. Then he spun into the sun and whipped it out of his pocket.

Heads!

He kept it.

He turned around slowly to face the tramp. He might have moved. Just an inch.

For no reason, Tom lost interest and looked back the way he had come. The boy had disappeared. He could see the main road in the opposite direction. Miss Ivinson's sweet shop just across it. He knew where he was.

Walking towards it, he felt very tired. It was blazingly hot. The road was slightly sticky under his feet. The houses on either side of him, two uninterrupted façades of regular windows and grey cement, two slow-trailing ribbons of baked gloom, two strong, hairless caterpillars shrugged their way past him with every drainpipe passed.

He turned, sprinted back to the tramp, held out his half-a-crown, saw, with relief, a gloved hand rise up to receive it, and blew back, bowling back, lightly howling and dancing back down the street, like a bounding, feathery leaf. He still had the pound.

His grandfather was just shutting the door as he arrived home. Tess, tail drooped, moved at his feet.

'Thou'll 'ev te meck thee oan dinner!'

Tom accepted that. He wished that his grandfather could be with him while he ate it.

'Can I come with you?'

'No!'

The quality of Tom's love for his grandfather was absolute obedience: the black mine shaft gulped down the candle and remained black.

'Where're you goin'?'

'Where you would be eat-up for breakfast!'

His grandfather glared at him. His face was as shiny as a brass knob.

'See if you can hit us! Come on!'

He stiffened his shoulders and held out his left arm as straight as a rod.

Tom sailed in, arms flailing. His grandfather's fist stuck against his forehead. Whichever way Tom dodged, the fist was there, knuckles pressed against the plate-bone of his forehead.

'Come on! Come on!'

Tess lifted her tail and burrowed her nose to within inches of the old man's heels, attacking a wish of a bone.

'Let me in! Let me in granda!'

The fist lifted away and Tom shot forward, to be pinioned and hoisted by great arms whose muscles worked into his own arms like smooth-bulging vices. He was hugged against the old man's body and shaken up and down like a sack.

'Ah-ha!'

His grandfather spread a reek of beer all over him. Tom could not move. His stomach was flattened against the old man's chest. From there upwards, the boy arched himself back like a swan's neck.

'Ah-ha!'

Another heave up and down. Another hot blast of wet beer.

'Whose lad are you?'

'Let go!'

'Whose lad are you? Eh?'

'Yours! Let go!

'Want a shave?'

'No!'

Tom screamed out loud. His grandfather smiled widely and moved his chin forward.

'No granda! Please! I like you best!'

'Grrrhh!'

The old man rubbed his bristles against the boy's smooth cheek. Tom screwed up his eyes in horror. Then he was dumped down to the ground.

'Thut hurt?'

Tom nodded. His fingers were as delicate as petals on the roughened skin.

His grandfather grinned.

'Your mother should be back soon,' he said.

Tom held the tears, stuck on to his eyeballs.

'Can I come?'

The old man laughed, proudly.

'He likes his granda, doesn't he?'

Still laughing, he turned and went up the street and around the corner.

Tom did not run after him. He knew where he was going.

CHAPTER SEVEN

He had watched the clock for five minutes and they had not mentioned it. Watched the clock without looking at his mother or his father or his uncle Henry, his aunt Catherine or Catherine; watched the clock in a still prayer of waiting. And they had not mentioned it. He had heard everything that they had said – but he was in a corner and so he need not answer. The clock was five minutes fast, anyway.

He was safe.

Catherine beamed at him when he looked up. Her hair was up, she wore a short, wine coat with a black lapel and she sat on the kitchen chair like a little doll. Tom shuddered.

'It won't be long,' said his mother. She glared at Edward.

He looked embarrassed and spoke apologetically to the whole room.

'I had no idea how late it was. When I met you, Henry, and we thought it would be a good idea for you all to come and see us – I had no idea how late . . . I should have come back right away.'

Anne moved around like a cat. Her black hair was shaken loose and thick, way down over the collar of her tough navy-blue uniform. Tom thought she looked like the captain of a ship. With her wellingtons and jacket and great baggy trousers – side-striped with red – her legs clonking heavily because of the long encasements below the knee – 'duck-nebbed lankeys', his grandfather called them – she was a dark pirate's girlfriend who took over the ship.

Edward went on.

'Anyway. Here you are. That's the main thing. Isn't it, little Cathy! Isn't it? His niece ignored him and continued to smile at Tom. 'You know where we live now. It's about time they came to see us – anyway – isn't it, Annie? We're neighbours now.'

His wife said nothing but her hands executed him time and again. Strangled him in the sugar basin which she put on the table; chopped off his arms and legs and then his head as she placed the best knives, carefully, beside the best plates.

'Don't rush for us,' his aunt Catherine implored her.

'It's not a bad place,' Edward went on. 'A lot more space than you can see from the outside . . . shall I take them to see the sitting-room?'

'No carpets,' said Anne, quickly.

'Sorry . . . But they won't mind, will you?'

His sister-in-law moved her neck to the left and then to the right again; several times.

'Of course not.'

'It's airless!'

Anne placed a large plate of sandwiches in the middle of the table and looked, smilingly, at her husband.

'Well,' he said, 'we're comfortable enough here.'

Henry, so largely sprawled that the large chair was obscured, waved one hand, like a policeman starting to give the 'Stop!' sign and then changing his mind. He had only spoken about six words since they had come in. Six people in a kitchen built for a table, four chairs and the undernourished.

'Can I help you?'

Anne turned to Catherine and smiled. Tom felt as secure as a drifting boat which has moved on to shifting sands.

'I don't think so,' she replied. 'But thank you for the offer.'

And the tea built up even faster on the table.

Little Catherine could be silent no longer.

'Are you coming to play with me again, Tom?'

Anne looked at him, enquiringly. Edward splayed out in a great guffaw.

'Well. Well. Well. What have we here?' Imitating a popular radio comedian.

Tom burned and looked at his feet and mumbled something But Catherine wanted a much more positive declaration.

'I'll let you take me into the den,' she announced. 'Whenever you want.'

Tom groaned.

Again his mother said nothing, but asked him everything with a very ordinary glance. Edward saw a new bond.

'Our Tom and your little Cathy, eh? Well, now, Tom. You never told anybody about this.

> 'Oh! Good Gracious me,
> What is this I see?
> A little boy
> Full of joy.
> Oh! Good gracious me.'

And he rocked in his chair and laughed again. Tom hated him.

Henry was also laughing – but not outwards; he laughed to his shoes. Tom was afraid that he might tell. His uncle was so big. He was afraid of him.

Catherine persisted.

'Can I sit beside Tom?'

'No, dear.'

Her mother laid an arm across the front of her chair; like an iron grill.

'Why not?'

'Because your aunt Anne wants to have room to move in.'

'It would give her more room if I sat with Tom.'

Her mother laughed, lightly, at this difference between them.

'You just sit where you are, dear.'

'You said aunt Anne could move on a sixpence.'

Her father twisted his head and glared at her.

'Catherine! Sit where you are.'

His daughter whimpered into silence.

Tom's hands were locked together. But they had not mentioned it. The kettle whistled. Edward jumped up.

'Tea. Catherine, would you like to sit here next to me? Little Cathy can sit next to Tom.'

'I think that she had better be next to me today. If you don't mind,' and his aunt Catherine pushed her daughter, pram-like, in front of her.

Henry placed his daughter firmly between himself and his wife.

And the tea came clear and brown out of the large cream pot, the cups and plates clattered with use, hands laced a may-pole across the middle of the table, reaching out for sandwiches.

There was no centre. Tom bumped himself first against one, then against another. He was afraid of each one of them.

They talked about Thornton. His aunt Catherine said that it was a dreadful place to live in. She had come from the north of Lancashire. The people were, she hated to use the word, more pleasant somehow in Lancashire. She had always been going out somewhere with her brother. In Thornton, she did not even care to walk.

Henry hunted – but he had been born here of course.

'And it suits me well enough,' said Henry.

He was just contradicting her. She knew that from the number of times he had told her how stifled he felt in such a small place. She would agree to leave any day.

'She thinks you can get up and go like a blasted gipsy!'

However, there was no denying that the countryside was lovely. No one could deny that.

'I've never seen better,' Edward agreed.

He was like Catherine though. He would leave Thornton any day. It did not do to talk about it in public – but he had quite a number of plans for leaving Thornton.

'Changes are nearly always for the worse,' said Anne.

And she said no more.

An exclusive dialogue developed between the step-brothers on the making of money. Tom wanted Edward to win; knew that Henry would.

'If I had something behind me,' Edward said, 'it would all go into a hotel. There isn't a decent hotel in the place. And people are going to start coming to this part of the world for their holidays – you mark my words.'

If they did come to the Lake District, said Henry, then they would stay further south, beside the big lakes.

'What would bring them as far north as this?' he asked.

'Privacy,' said Edward, with certainty, 'and a good hotel.'

Anne was up and down; up with empty dishes, plates, cups, fruit-bowls, down with full ones. Silent but for nudges and stirrings and occasional murmurs of 'would-you-like?' and 'are-you-sure?'

When, as often, the words failed to cover the wide silences, widespread between the members of the teaparty, Tom wanted to say something, to start building another dam – but he realised that the less attention he drew to himself the greater the chance he would have of keeping his secret.

'I love that uniform,' said his aunt Catherine.

Henry paid very particular attention to the sandwich he was about to eat. Anne laughed and Tom knew that she was happy.

'If it's good enough for Nasher, it's good enough for me,' she said.

And they all laughed at Nasher – The Galloping Telegraph Boy – sixty, sixty times – never out of Neville's, the barber's, where he looked at the dirty pictures until word had got around who the telegram was for and they would come and find him.

The door banged, Tess ran in, boots scraped hard on the rough strip of coconut matting, a blast of beer heralded the arrival and Tom's grandfather shouted:

'Aah's back! Anybody in?'

And he clumped the three paces from outside door to kitchen door as if he was bent on a ten-mile hike.

'Whoa back there!' he shouted, standing steady at the door – with his arms pushed against the frame on either side to give him the central impulse which his next move would obviously need

– blazing out at the crimp-cramped all-set-at-table bone china kitchen.

'Whoa there, boy! Company!'

The company leaned back on their chairs to welcome him.

'Don't get up! No fuss! I'm a ghost!'

And, for a second, he pulled his arms away from the door frames, to flap them up and down. Anne jumped up, led him to the armchair beside the fire and supervised his sitting-down.

'Are you not all cold in 'ere?' he demanded.

Anne had put on a small fire for the evening – because the house was in the shade all day. Her father built it up with a great, scooped armful of logs.

'Bit uv 'eat.'

He pushed his cap back on his head. His muffler had loosened at the knot and Tom could see the collarless rim of his shirt, a stud stuck through the top hole tapping against the large adam's apple whenever the old man jerked forward. His hands were thrust deep into his pockets and his legs were splayed out across the fender.

'Posh tea today, eh?'

Anne brought him a plate of sandwiches and a cup of tea. Tom noticed that his aunt Catherine was trying to stop her daughter staring at the old man by pulling off her rings and showing them to her, one by one.

'Aah'll sit here,' the old man announced, his legs and arms lifting up one after the other. 'Don't bother yoursells about me. Just you keep on wid what you were doing. I can sit here, all right. There's no doubt about that. I can sit here.' He realised that he was shouting. His voice strained itself into clouded respectability.

'Aah'm all right. Per-fect-ly – okey-dok-ey!' And the plate slithered down his thighs to be caught, just in time, by the quick snap of his knees. His mouth gaped a crumb-smeared smile to one and all.

'I think we might go,' said Tom's aunt Catherine. 'It's after five.'

'Five o'clock!'

Edward sprang across to the radio, picking up his pools' coupon in mid-flight. The last chord of the Sport's Report signature tune announced the presentation of the football and racing results. It was unthinkable that Edward should be disturbed by ceremonial leave-taking at such a time.

Anne began to clear the table.

'Let me help you,' said aunt Catherine, reaching into her handbag for a cigarette.

'Fine,' said Anne. 'You can dry.' And she held out a tea-towel.

'Ssshh!' Edward hissed.

'League Division One.'

With great difficulty, Catherine manoeuvred her way over to the kitchenette.

Old Tom wolfed his food and began to take an interest in his great-niece. First he made faces for her, quitting this turn only when she turned away in terror and grabbed her father's hand. Then he began to slap his knees – having taken the precaution of putting his cup and plate beside the now blazing fire: this was accompanied by a great chucking and sucking at the mouth – supposed to encourage confidence.

'Cum to Granda Paislow.'

Henry hardly noticed her burrowing into his side. He was smoking. Tom was afraid that he was angry. Henry looked at Edward without blinking; stared right at him, and then he would seem to catch himself doing so and inhale a long draw of smoke. Tom saw his face change only once; that was when Anne came in to take up the table-cloth and they both looked at the old man and laughed. Tom laughed with them: he did not know why.

'Manchester United 2. Arsenal 1.'

'Tom was right,' he said without looking up.

They would soon be gone and then he would be able to organise himself for the new school. His stomach tightened at the thought of it. He would know nobody. Already he had been up to his room several times and laid out his new blazer and grey short trousers and stockings, shirt, school tie, cap, satchel and fountain pen; laid them out on his bed, neatly, wondering how he would look in

them, trying to cheer himself up by pulling on his blazer and showing off in front of the mirror. If only his mother would say
something that might cheer him up. He hung around her, waiting
for her to smile, waiting for her to tell him that everything would
be wonderful, that he would soon get to know everybody, that
nothing mattered as long as she loved him. His father told him
what a wonderful opportunity he was to have – but that only made
him feel more lonely.

Soon they would be gone – Catherine – aged six! – would be
gone with them and he would run a mile before he ever saw her
again.

'A biscuit. Come to Granda Paislow for a biscuit.'

He held it out waveringly. The little girl stared at him, terrified.

Tom's mother and his aunt came back into the kitchen which
had shrunk to handkerchief-size since everyone had stood up. His
mother pushed her father's legs out of the way and stood with her
back to the fire.

'She doesn't like me,' the old man said.

'And now, Racing.'

'Henry. We really must go. I'm sure that Anne has a great deal
to do.'

'Winchester.'

'Sssh.'

Tom tried not to listen so that he would not spoil his luck. Little
Catherine was staring at him again; his grandfather was staring at
her. Tom hitched his nose; a new smell had got into the room.

'Barney's Boy. 3.15. First. Striding Eagle 100–8.'

'He's won!'

Edward jumped up and barged his way over to Tom – to stop in
front of him without knowing what to do. Thirteen and six; what
he could buy with thirteen and six!

'Oh my God!'

Anne jumped away from the fire. A thick grimy smoke streamed
up from her wellingtons. Edward ran into the kitchenette. Tom did
not move. Suddenly, Henry was there beside his mother, pushing

her on to a seat and pulling off the wellingtons which stunk to heaven. He had them off into two seconds.

'Are you all right?'

'Yes.'

'There's some water.' Edward with a pan in his hand.

'Are you sure?' Henry persisted: still kneeling in front of Anne.

'Yes.'

Henry had been brushing her legs with his hands. Without looking up, he said:

'Cath; make some tea. She's had a shock.'

'I'm all right. Please don't bother.'

Catherine hesitated and then stood quite still where she was.

'I'll get an Aspro.'

Edward ran into the kitchenette.

'Got you!'

Taking advantage of the mêlée, Tom's grandfather had crept up on to the little girl. Now he caught her around the waist and swung her into the air. She windmilled around the kitchen like a puppet, screaming her head off, screaming even louder than the old man who bellowed a nursery rhyme as accompaniment to his swinging.

'Ride a cock horse to Banberry Crost – wheeee!'

'Henry! Make him stop! Make him stop at once!' Henry glared at his wife savagely. Then he stood up and began to move in.

'When she got there the maiden got lost.'

A tall, shapeless 'Brought from Morecambe' flower-vase caught a foot which kicked it half-way across the room.

'Dad, put her down!'

Anne was furious. The old man slowed down immediately and set the little girl gently on the ground. She ran, howling, to her mother who gathered her daughter to her side and moved right next to the door with her back to everyone.

'Sit down!' Anne said, quietly this time. 'And stop making a fool of all of us.'

The old man sat down on one of the hard kitchen chairs.

Edward was standing in the doorway of the kitchen, glass of water in one hand, Aspro strip in the other. He looked so unhappy that Tom was not surprised when his uncle went over to him and patted his shoulder.

'Don't worry. She's all right.' He went over to his daughter whose screams burst out afresh at the sight of a new comforter.

'Give dad the Aspros,' ordered Anne. It was done.

Somehow, the Falcons left.

Edward picked up the wellingtons from the table and took them into the back-yard. Tom's grandfather looked scared. His mother had leaned her head right back so that she was looking straight into the ceiling.

'Are you hurt, mam?'

'I'm all right,' she said, without looking at him.

When, at last, she did look down, it was her father she looked at, not Tom. He was huddled on his hard-backed chair; immobile.

'You have to be careful, dad, you know that, um?' she spoke softly.

The old man nodded.

'You mustn't get like that. It's no good. Whatever happens – you mustn't get yourself into that state.'

His grandfather looked at the ground. Anne leaned back again and gazed up at the ceiling.

When Tom managed to find the courage to break the clamp of embarrassment which seemed to have locked his chin to his chest – he saw that his grandfather was crying.

'Sorry, Annie,' he kept muttering. 'Sorry, Annie. Sorry, Annie. Sorry.'

Tom was lonelier than he had ever been in his whole life.

The basis of his calculations was that ninepence would take him to Carlisle by bus. That was eighteen miles away. Thirteen and six would take him 162 divided by 9 multipled by eighteen miles. He scribbled it all down on a piece of paper. 324 miles! Unhurried, he flicked through his atlas until he came to the map of Great Britain. Laying his ruler down it, and trying to allow for the wiggles in the road, he saw that he could go to London or John o'Groats. He preferred London. He could be sure of somewhere to stay there. The pound note should keep him going for quite a long time.

SOS messages sung along the telegraph lines. 'Tom Graham. Age 11 (nearly 12). Last seen boarding a bus in Thornton.' His mother would give up the post to sit at home and wait for news. 'His mother says that she is sorry if she did anything wrong. All she wants is for him to come home.' And he would slip into alleyways in London, avoiding the police. 'Here is a personal message.' His mother's voice: he looked closely at the map to hide the tears which suddenly started in his eyes. 'Please come back, Tom, Please.' She would have to come and fetch him.

She came into the kitchen, changed, a new dress on, beautiful, Tom thought. Edward looked up from his book.

'Is he better?'

'He's asleep.' She sat down on the edge of one of the chairs, first tugging her skirt up carefully and then crossing her legs She looked at Tom.

'He's even more trouble than you are.'

He would stay in London until he died of starvation and all they found was a 'a pitiful skeleton of bones' with his mother's picture beside him. That would make her realise!

Edward was back in his book.

'Don't you ever get sick of that stuff?'

He husband looked up absent-mindedly, smiled just at the sight of his wife being there, and dipped into print again.

'That a new dress?' Tom asked.

'I'm still mad with you,' she replied.

She had made him tell her all about Catherine and then told him – forced him – to promise that he would never go to his uncle Henry's again.

'Let them invite you properly or don't bother with them at all.'

She was still mad with him. Whatever he did in the future, she would always be mad with him for this. There was no way of

76

cancelling it out. Tom started to feel that he was choking. He must not tell her about the pound note.

Anne stood up and paced the small area of the kitchen several times. She stopped in front of Edward.

'We need never have left that cottage for all the good we get out of Thornton.'

Edward held tightly on to his book and refused to look up.

'Well? Does reading make you dumb as well as deaf?'

'I thought that we had settled in quite nicely.'

'We've settled in concrete.'

He put the book to one side – still refusing to look up.

'Do you want to go out?' he asked.

'Where?'

'Anywhere.'

'That's the only place you know.'

She swirled her skirt in his face and sat down again. Edward looked at her nervously.

'We could go to the "Lion" for a drink.'

'With that lot? No thank you!'

Silence. A thick woollen muffler forced itself between Tom's teeth, into his mouth, filling it with the warm, suffocating pressure of water. He swallowed quickly to try and chase it away.

'I don't know what you want.'

Edward stared into the fire.

'And all I know is that you don't want anything.'

Tom started to cry. He could not stop himself, it was the only way to melt away the thick mist which was smothering him. He put his head on his hands and cried, cried like a baby with his face twisted in an agony of relieved pain.

For a few seconds his parents looked at him without moving.

'What's wrong?'

His mother's voice was kind but unanxious. Sniffling and sobbing, Tom tried to give some sort of answer – but this only made him cry even more. His father looked bewildered. Anne began to smile. She moved over to sit beside him.

'I'm not really mad with you, you know?'

Tom looked at her. She was laughing at him. He prayed for a bomb to drop on the house.

'You shouldn't be crying,' said his father. 'You've won thirteen and six, after all. I'll collect it for you on Monday.'

'What's the matter?' She tried to prise his head off his arms. 'You'll have to stop crying.'

Tom was afraid that he would end up dead like the man who had killed himself because he could not stop laughing. He gulped hard and slowed his tears down.

And then his mother put an arm around his shoulders.

He told her that he did not want to go to school, that he hated Thornton, that he knew nobody – moving into the crook of her arm for warmth.

'You'll be all right,' she said. 'You'll be all right.'

Edward came across to join them. He stood in front of them, not knowing who to talk to.

'Mr Carlin says that you're better at arithmetic than anybody he knows,' he said, eventually.

How did Mr Carlin know that? He had never added up in front of him. Tom closed his eyes and pressed his head against his mother's shoulder. She hardly ever kissed him; his father would come to his bedroom some nights and kiss him on the brow when he was asleep – this he knew from the number of times he had been awake; but his mother had stopped kissing him years ago.

Her cheek was so fresh and furry smooth; white and slightly red; clean-smelling and soft. But he had not the courage.

To excuse his behaviour, he sat up and told them about the pound his uncle Henry had given him. When he came back downstairs with it, he was startled to see that his mother had put her coat on.

'Spend it, this time,' she said.

Edward looked at her and then looked at Tom, but said nothing. 'Back soon.'

And she went out.

His father examined the pound note carefully. Tom felt cold.

'Your mother misses her walks,' his father told him. 'It isn't as easy for her to go for them here. She's better when she has them.'

Tom nodded. Sometimes, if he was still up when his mother came back from her walks, she would joke and play with him until he became so swollen with happiness that he floated right through the ceiling and into his bed.

Edward put his arm around his son's shoulders and pulled him close to him.

'She has a hard life, your mother,' he said, quietly. 'You understand that, Tom?'

Again Tom nodded. His lips were trembling too much for him to speak.

He understood. He would wait up for her.

CHAPTER EIGHT

'But I've told her you're coming.' Tom was almost whining with frustration.

'I don't want to be late home.'

'But she'll have done all sorts. You've got to come! I've got a present for you as well!'

'I mustn't be late . . . what is it?'

'What?'

'The present.'

'Oh! A book.' There was a pause. Tom sorted out a book he could give.

'I can come but I can't stay.'

'But you'll come. I've a pile of comics you can have. You know that big catapult – you can have that as well.'

'I'll come – just for a few minutes, though. I mustn't be too late.'

Tom wanted to freeze him for a moment and thunder home to tell his mother. She was not expecting them. But he could always rush upstairs and grab a book – and his comics – and his catapult. His mother would be nice. She had to be. Philip was coming at last.

It was because of Philip that he had joined the church choir: because of Philip that he wore his battered school blazer buttoned with three buttons: because of Philip that a medal display of pen-tops – some without any foundation – bristled along the top of his front pocket. Because of Philip he would endanger this whole, tenuous, feather-fabricated, marvellous friendship – because Philip had to come to his house.

The two boys moved away from the front of the church. Other choristers passed them – and all of them bade good night to Tom's friend. Tom shouted out his good night, uncalled for.

It was nearly the end of winter, but the cold had bitten so deeply into the ground, so completely commanded the air, that the boys moved against it quickly, in spite of their coats and gloves and long scarves. The street-lighting was no more than a lantern line of feeble, smudgy blobs of sickly yellow colouring, marking out the occasional shapes which shuffled through it.

The town was still. During the practice, Tom had worried lest 'The Sands' gang might have ridden down the street on their boots and clogs, waving their chair-legs, looking for any gang that might stand up to them. The Sands were near Tom's house; two rows of double-backed terraces slammed up to serve a seam that had run out in eighteen months and left them sitting on the raped ashes of what had once been a large field. But they were safe. Philip would not have to fly home. The town was still.

'We'll get you some warm cocoa to warm you up.'

Tom mothered him. Philip was so dainty, slight and serene and slenderly formed that his friend warded off every imaginable harm in countless hairsbreadth dreams: and now he could actually do something real for him. They met so rarely at school. Philip was a year older than he was and in Form 2. Not only was he top of his own form but also, just a few weeks ago, he had beaten everyone in the whole school at recitation. He was so neat that his blazer could have been resold as new any day. His mother brought him sweets on Fridays and he rationed himself throughout the week. His stockings never slipped down. He collected stamps. On Sundays his parents would take him out in their car for a run around the Lake District. His father was a doctor.

'I've got some stamps,' said Tom.

'What sort?'

'Big ones.'

81

'I mean – what country?' Tom reacted quickly against the contempt.

'Africa.'

'Where in Africa?'

Tom considered. Then he took the risk of winning through ignorance.

'I don't know.'

It worked. Philip smiled with that tight-bowed arch of his top lip which Tom so laboriously imitated – and then proceeded to talk at length about recent African issues. It was the longest conversation they had ever had. Tom would build a treasure house and fill it with stamps, cars, new pens, books, silver pieces – reaching his hands into it every day to haul out great heaps of gifts for his friend whose pale, composed face would break into the smile that Tom wanted but never saw; and so, as master, he would serve his debtor.

Tom kept up the talk as best he could – but his mind flickered violently, working out the movements of all the people who could appear in the street and break up this walk. For Philip had his own circle, boys slightly older than he was, but all – so it seemed to Tom – favoured with some gift of grace which could compel Philip's attention far more successfully than all Tom's careful plots. Boys with names like Roger and Paul and Peter; and with second Christian names that rolled their identity in a rounded phrase; all of whom lived in large houses, turret-like, along the western boundary of the town.

Philip stopped.

'How much farther is it?'

Tom answered immediately.

'Not far. Around the corner.'

Philip swung out his left arm in an elaborate hook. Tom knew that he could beat him in a fight any time. The giant wristwatch shone luminously.

'They'll be expecting me in about quarter of an hour.'

Three minutes to reach home. Four minutes for Philip to get back to his house. Eight minutes together – at least. He dared to say nothing. Someone walked past on the dark other side of the street and Tom prayed that it was good luck.

'I would just have time to pick up the things,' said Philip, firmly.

Tom stood still and let the tears inside him race down coldly into his stomach and compress it into a tiny knot.

'That's OK,' he replied.

Philip replaced his wrist in his sleeve and his arm beside his raincoat pocket.

'We can walk quickly,' he said.

They jerked off again.

Soon – Tom was sure that it would happen soon – they would go for walks together – visit churches, or something like that, talk and argue the way Tom wanted to. He wanted Philip to share his wonder in the romances of history he was reading; in the patience and genius of King Alfred, the courage of Strongbow, the unhappiness of Harold, the wickedness of King John and his treacherous acts against Robin Hood. But not now. He had tried, before, to talk to Philip about the subjects which attracted him, but Philip always said:

'What were his dates?'

Tom did not know. Or

'Have you seen the new heavy bomber?'

Or

'I can't see why you read such stuff.'

He had even showed him the illustrations, magnificently coloured in forest greens and blood-reds.

'My father has a set of encyclopaedias with 300 coloured plates in each volume.' That had settled Tom's history book.

They reached the bottom end of Church Street. Tom had brought Philip the long way round – by the main road – because he was scared of whom he might meet if he walked the whole length of the street. His house was number nine, around the first of many twists and turns which led the street wriggling from the main street to the church like an artificial snake.

'This is it.'

No light in the front. He knocked, loudly, always keeping an eye on Philip as if to make sure that he did not look anywhere he shouldn't.

This was it.

Tom held back his pain as if he was afraid that its impact would crush him.

He knocked again and then – as if to prove that he was well aware that mere knocking was useless – immediately stood back and bellowed:

'Are you in?'

But the house was black.

Without daring to look at Philip – Philip standing quite still and saying, doing nothing, a thick shape in the velvet-grey, pale, moon-lit street – he ran across to Mrs Blacklock's house.

'I know where she'll be.'

Knocked on another door.

'This is where she'll be.'

'Come in.'

Kitchen-cosy voice a hundred miles away.

He could not go in. Philip would disappear.

He thundered at the door with hoof-knuckles.

'What is it?'

And the door flung open with a great intaken gape.

Philip's house would be well-lit and warm with Father and Mother in proper armchairs astride a fire at a constant, proper level of heat, 'Hello, Philip, dear, we were just beginning to worry ourselves about you.' Cocoa on the table and the welcoming rustle of crisp book-pages – his father must know a lot – and the clean smell of big rooms.

'Where's mam?'

Voice from inside.

'Who's that?'

And Mrs Blacklock actually turned around – before Tom's eyes – and took up hours of time by answering the stupid question!

'Tom Paislow . . . young Tom.'

'Have you seen mam?'

'Have we seen his mother?'

Again her big fat head turned in retreat to the kitchen.

'What does he want her for?'

Repeated.

Tom shook his head.

'You haven't seen her?'

Mrs Blacklock considered the enquiry with her head bowed.
She had come out from a chair to the door and did not wish to
waste the move on brevity.

'I saw her earlier,' she said, cautiously.

'When?'

Philip was moving away.

'When?' Tom bellowed his question for the second time.

'When did I come down from upstairs?'

Tom turned to go. She had to tell him.

'You never were upstairs.'

'When?'

It was almost a whisper.

'Yes, I was,' Mrs Blacklock replied. Again her head turned away.

Philip had turned the corner.

Tom bolted after him.

'What is it you want to see her about?'

There was always the cottage. His uncle Henry had not sold the
cottage and the Brinns had not come back – so his grandfather told
him. He could have got five hundred pounds for it. Tom had hoped
that he might be invited up there. They could build huts, climb
mountains on which he would save Philip's life, miraculously, sixty
times a day. He hated his mother. Philip was just in front of him.
They would find him at the cottage wrapped in old sacks for
warmth. Hated her. He slowed down. He could walk behind him
for a while – catch him up later. Hated her for ever.

Philip was so neat and precise and he need never tell lies. Tom
felt poisoned with the secrets that gathered and spread inside him.

He could not imagine Philip ever having to tell lies to anyone. Cut Tom open and there would be lies yellow as pus, stinking him to hell. Philip did not look back – even though Tom clomped his feet like a giant – Philip kept right on busily walking up main street. It was a wonder people could not smell how full of lies he was.

His filthy, dirty, rotten mother – always, always out. He could invite nobody to his house – nobody at all without knowing that he was breaking some Great Law and sinning so deeply that the wound would never be closed. Philip would never be bothered with anything like that! He had seen *his* mother, in a nice hat – *his* mother never wore a hat – going into that sweetshop for the weekly sweets. His father was just as bad. And he saw little of his grandfather these days. He would never be able to talk to Philip again; how could he get through another five years of school without ever meeting him again? He would have to. This time he would really go away; overseas. Where was his mother?

Where the main street forked – going left to the church and straight on to the houses along West Road – there was a huge marble monument which functioned – once upon its time – as a fountain. As a mark of respect, it was guarded by iron railings, and superintended by four flickering street-lamps. Now the fountain began to swarm with scuddling boys. Tom shut off the noise in his mind so that he could listen. Both Philip and he stopped dead.

It was the Sally Army gang. There was Speedy Walker in his white polo-neck. They were in retreat. Tom watched them rush towards him. Their only sound was leather on pavement. Some of them were still carrying cornets from the band rehearsal. Bulleting down the street like a horde of black umbrellas caught in a gale. They were almost up to him.

And sweeping around the corner, like a great, drilled cavalry brigade, clogs stamping their power on the bare street, came the great Sands gang. Their chair-legs were waving in the air like black swords. The poor light picked at their faces in panic. And as they turned the corner of the fountain and straightened lines to charge down main street, their great song spurted and drummed out above them.

> *'We – are*
> *The chair-leg raiders*
> *We come from*
> *No – where*
> *For Sally*
> *Ar – my.*
>
> *'We – are*
> *The chair-leg raiders*
> *We come from*
> *No – where*
> *For Sally*
> *Ar – my.'*

And a howl went up that rattled the windows. There was Blos and Vic and Screw, Mutt, Tint, Knocker, Nobby, Twin, the other Twin, young Masher, Reg Patt, Fatty Burns – there was everybody that Tom would walk a mile to miss. And they came on down the street, rolling down the street, shouting out their song.

'Philip!'

They rushed into an alley and ran hard. Tom knew that the gang would split up opposite the end of Church Street and go out looking for people in small groups. Thornton was riddled with black back-alleys.

They came out in Tickle's Lane.

'Hide behind the Fire Station!' Tom shouted.

'No.'

'Come – on!'

He grabbed Philip's arm and began to pull him there. But perhaps it wasn't a good place. They would be sure to look behind the Fire Station!

'Up to the auction!'

'They're coming!'

> *'We come from*
> *No – where*

For Sally
Ar – my.
Aaaiiiee!!'

'They're coming!'

They ran up Tickle's Lane and down the alley that led into Water Street. Philip was holding on to Tom's arm.

'We'll be OK,' Tom said.

They popped out of the bottom of the alley.

'Oh!'

Two boys were round the corner. Tom and Philip stopped.

'Who is it?'

No answer. Then Tom heard a sniffle. The Sands gang would not cry. He peered at the boys.

'It's us.'

Two Salvation Army junior bandsmen. Younger than Tom. One with a tambourine, another with a cornet.

'Shut up!' Tom hissed, in a whisper.

Philip tugged at his arm. Tom listened hard and heard feet and shouts in Tickle's Lane.

'Can we come with you?' one of the boys asked.

'No,' said Philip.

This time, the boy with the cornet burst into real sobs.

'Shut up!' Tom was frantic.

'Come on!'

Philip was away.

'Let's come. Please!'

Tom grabbed one of them by the shoulder.

'Down there,' he said. 'Mason's Garage. You can hide there.'

And he raced after Philip. After he had gone a short way he heard the jangle of a tambourine disappearing in the other direction.

They squatted in the corner of a sheep-pen. The wooden bars all around them cut the faint moonlight into narrow dim stripes. It was cold. They had been there for hours.

'What time is it?'

Philip rustled to release his arm and look at his watch. Tom stopped him just in time and made him turn the other way.

'They'll see the luminous bits.'

Philip hunched and trundled his way around.

'Twenty past eight.'

He was whimpering. He had been complaining ever since they had arrived – and yet every time that Tom had suggested a move – he had refused to budge.

'Seven minutes,' Philip announced.

'What?'

'We've been here for seven minutes. I looked at my watch when we got here.'

'Oh.'

'I'll be late home.'

The town was quiet. They had heard one or two shouts – once someone had belted past the end of the auction and they had stopped breathing. Now it was quiet again. It could have been midnight.

'It's too – quiet,' said Tom. 'Let's move.'

'We're safe here.'

'We've got to keep moving.'

Tom was too scared to stay any longer. His legs were cramped so tightly that the blood seemed to have run out of his bare knees. Anybody could be creeping around them in the dark. He stood up.

'I'm going.'

'No.'

Philip grabbed his coat.

'You can't go!'

Tom turned on him.

'I'm not going to sit here to be caught by that lot. We could shout all we wanted – nobody would hear us.'

He moved across the pen on his own. Philip had caught up to him by the time they got on to the road. They went down the

Baths' Road. Tom was making for the front of the church. They cut into Meeting-house Lane. There were three alleys which led off from this and came out in the church square.

Tom chose the right-hand alley. It was as dark as an old chimney – and about as narrow. Tom walked in front.

Vic, Twin and Reg Patt were waiting for them at the bottom.

'Who's that?'

Tom said nothing. The three Sands boys were standing under a street light.

'Come over 'ere!'

They went over. Philip started a dry coughing which sounded near enough to crying.

'Thowt you'd git away, eh?'

Twin was cross-eyed. His blond hair stood up in a brush. They all wore long pants. He did all the talking.

Tom kept his mouth shut and his eyes on the chair-legs held in each hand. Suddenly, Twin came forward and knocked Philip on the shoulder.

'Thou'd doctor's sun?'

Philip began to cry properly. Tom edged back, towards the alley. Twin poked out his chair-leg and caught Tom on the chest.

'Hoi!'

Vic planted himself in front of the alley. Reg Patt stayed under the light, keeping look-out. Twin patted Philip on the arm with his chair-leg.

'Bugger off!' he said and stood to one side.

Philip ran – clattering away like a mad cockroach.

Twin came close up to Tom. His squint eyes glared all over Tom's face.

'Aa've got to decide what to do wid thee.'

Vic and Reg Patt laughed, together. Encouraged, Twin went on.

'Thou in't Sally army?'

Tom was going to say nothing.

The butt of the chair-leg knocked into his stomach.

'No.' he said.

90

'Liar!' Twin screamed. And then he butted Tom again and laughed like a hyena.

Tom had pressed himself to the wall. He could feel the cold stones on his back. Twin marched round in front of him, thinking out his next move. Tom heard noises nearby. More of them were coming. If he screamed, they would kill him. And no one would hear. All the blinds were drawn and the front doors bolted all over town.

Twin stopped.

'Thy grandfather dig t' churchyard?'

This time he really would say nothing. Again Twin came up close to him. He smelled of chewing-gum. Setting his features in a grimace, he pushed his head right into Tom's face.

'Answer!'

Tom clenched his lips.

Twin took one pace back and spat at him.

'Coppers!'

Reg Patt ran out of the light and into the alley. Twin hesitated for a second, banged Tom on the knee with his chair-leg, and followed.

'Aa'll git thee sum-time!'

They rattled their weapons against the close walls of the alley and made it echo like a catacomb.

Tom dare not bend his knee. He was sure it was broken.

The policeman came into the light.

'All right?' he said.

Tom nodded. He wanted to cry. He wished the policeman would go away and let him.

'Who was it?'

Tom shook his head.

'Don't know,' he said.

CHAPTER NINE

The summer had been long and damp. He had become obsessed with a girl called Gladys Wallace, after seeing her doing upside-down swings on the parallel bars in the park with her knickers showing so many holes that their function was strictly token. They had gone into the field beside the park, among the bushes which grew out of the roots of dead trees and there he had sat on a stump and she had taken off her knickers, and set her bare behind on his bare knees. For days he had a lump growing inside of him so painful that it could be eased only when this was repeated.

He had longed for her through every drizzly day of his summer holidays. He had practically ignored the fact that he was growing taller; he had refused an offer from Mr Lawton to go and 'live in' with that family and help with the harvest; had not even considered an invitation from one of his aunts on his mother's side to go and spend a fortnight in Workington. On the days he did not see Gladys, he would go down to the park and swing backwards and forwards on the parallel bars, looking up every second to see her tilt back, legs gripping the bar, skirt flopping on to her face, a gap above the tight elastic of her knickers which suffocated his eyes. They were green.

If he was not in the park, he was in the bathroom combing his hair.

Sometimes he went for walks by himself. He had started going to church and he liked to find village churches and sit in them for as long as he dared. If there was someone else there, he would not go in.

He had helped his grandfather in the churchyard once or twice – but now the old man would either give him all the work to do and come back hours later with his face purple with beer – or he would swear and curse until Tom was forced to go, if only to allow the dead to be left in peace.

Gladys would sit on his knee, and stare out in front of him and rarely say a word. Sometimes he would fiddle with the button on her blouse aand then her brown eyes would sway around to him like brown lanterns and he would stop.

He liked her to sit on his knees – especially when they were cold – but after about three weeks he began to fidget. He was sure that he could be doing something else.

One day he took off her blouse without looking into her eyes at all. She had nothing on underneath but somehow it was worse – not better. Then he took off her skirt, and everything, and she sat on his knees wearing nothing.

They had to be very careful. That part of the river was not popular, but they – or rather, Tom, because she did not seem to worry – had to be very careful. He would get up every other minute and go and look to see if anyone was coming. No one ever came. Occasionally she talked. Tom remembered only one thing that she said:

'Can't we change places sometimes?' He refused.

Now that she had nothing on, Tom began to enjoy it less and less. He felt frustrated. He made her lie down in the grass. Even though it was nearly always wet, she did as he asked. First she lay on her back; then she lay on her stomach; arms up or arms down. It made no difference. Tom was losing interest.

He asked Albert Grainger to come with him. Albert used to play on the parallel bars – he used to do nothing else – until one day he had lost his grip when he was hanging upside down, fell, and cracked his head open. Tom struck up a friendship with him just for his own purpose. Albert did not talk much.

Together they watched Gladys lying in the grass with nothing on. All ways. Tom watched Albert for his reactions – but all he wanted to do was to go and raid an orchard.

After that – although Tom had been reluctant to give up the pleasure he gained from having Gladys sit on his knee – somehow it became less and less fascinating. At the very end of the summer holidays, he went down to the park no more than once or twice a week.

Apart from that, nothing happened in the summer and Tom had been glad to get back to school. He would draw the blinds in his bedroom when he was doing his homework so that it appeared darker than it was. He was glad when the clocks were put back. His father had given him a new wristwatch for his thirteenth birthday. He stayed up until midnight so that he could put it back at the proper time.

School started. The holidays had driven all affection for Philip out of his mind, and he met him with the innocence of a stranger. The name, 'Philip', which had once been suckled in his mouth, now dropped from his lips dryly, almost contemptuously.

Tom's position in Thornton was that of a guest. He knew everyone, said 'hello' all the way up every street – but he had not the settled feeling which Fell Cottage had given him. The others seemed to be uneasy as well. His father was still doing most of Mr Carlin's running – but he seemed to do more work for his money every week. His allotment scheme had not even got under way; and one long period of debate as to whether or not he should buy a local sweetshop had ended with Anne telling him that nobody would ever lend him the money. Anne herself was quickened by the exercise and contact which she got out of her post round, and the house was now far too small for her; Tom felt that she would break down the walls; some evenings, she would dress up and look wonderful, and then sprawl, black hair loose, in a chair in front of the fire, resisting all Edward's invitations to go to the pub or the pictures, seething with waiting for something to happen. His grandfather had started to dribble, to forget to fasten his fly-buttons, to let his pipe ash collect on his clothes in little grey heaps, to pretend to a deafness to cover the fact that he never listened. The

94

only times at which he was as strong as he had once been was when he went out shooting.

Now, in the autumn, Tom liked to cut himself away from the town completely and drift around the countryside. He enjoyed the cobwebbed loneliness of the old cottage, sitting in his own room, wondering how he had ever got all the furniture in. The Brinns had still not come back – but he saw them once or twice each month, trudging around in a herd, with or without the cart and mattresses, always with a pram full of wood or potatoes.

He cushioned himself around with emptiness. The further he was away from people, the more he liked them. He was convinced that he could think of nothing at all for days on end. He had stopped flopping against his mother; at first consciously out of hurt and revenge – and then out of habit. For now, however much he felt about her, he was locked out. He was on his own.

Spreading, as it did, into all his activities, this feeling seemed to be his whole character. Everything that had gone before was slotted into a pattern which led to his being three miles outside of Thornton at six o'clock on that Saturday afternoon when it was already getting dark.

He loved walking back on his own. He had gone along Low Moor Road and up to Speedgill and he decided to follow the river back into the town. The darkness clustered around him gradually; millions of speckles of dust slowly slipping out of the sun's path and shading to blackness. He could see them whispering down to the ground. It was cold, but there was not much wind; the sky had been a sprawling billow of thick clouds all day and now they, too, settled into the night – spreading across the whole arch like mighty black drapes.

Every so often, he would stop and look at the silhouettes of the hedges against the sky. Or he would listen to the noises which rustled and gathered around him until the whole earth seemed to be trembling with muted battles of passion. He wanted to grasp the blackness with both hands and tear it and nurse it and let it settle into him until he, too, died into the night.

He walked beside the ebony river and matched his own humming to its endless gurgle of spray; he passed over fields of black ice, skating on the dry rustling grass which swished against his feet, against his feet so far away that they walked a path of their own; he nuzzled against the tangy freshness of the quiet, hidden ground. He walked in aimless exaltation.

Turning on to the road which led him the last quarter of a mile into the town, he met the ugliest woman he had ever seen. He stopped.

'I've been waiting for you,' she said.

This was not true. She was sitting on a bench put there out of respect for some half-way point, and she was waiting for anyone.

'Waiting for you,' she repeated.

Tom believed her. Now that he was near to her, he recognised who it was. The darkness had confused him. Old Sall – she was called. Tom never knew whether this was her proper name or whether it had been given to her because she was always trailing around after the Salvation Army band. She wore slippers, and many pairs of stockings collected in two bulging heaps around her ankles. As usual, she had a slack coat on, fastened by one button at the top, spreading wide across her body to reveal an apron which covered several thick skirts.

Her face was terrible. It had turned inside out. Her lips curled back on themselves so far that her mouth was a horrible smudge. Her eyes had slackened so much that the eyeballs were suspended in a shuddering mess of veins and red jelly. All her pores were wide open and almost furry with splotches of tissue endings. There was a large boil near her chin.

Tom was not frightened – but he was powerless. He stood and waited for her to have done with him.

'Graham,' she said. Her voice was the top edge of a great asthmatic wheeze. She knew him.

'Yes.'

'You're on your own,' she said.

Tom nodded. He wanted her to start to sing, to rave, to dance, to do something awful: to do anything that would make the meeting a joke – on her – which he could dimiss as such. But she sat on the bench immobile, a great shadow in the darkness.

'I knew your grandmother,' she said.

'Which one?'

She wheezed loudly and for a second Tom shrank back, thinking that she was going to get up.

'Your mother's.'

'What was she like?'

The question was unanswered.

'I knew the other one as well.'

'They're both dead . . .'

'I know that.'

She paused for such a long time that Tom thought that she was not going to say any more. It was nearly a quarter to eight by his watch. He had to get back home.

'You don't know who your grandfather is: I know that, as well.'

'Yes, I do.'

'I mean the one that's dead.'

'He was a bank – something or other – he worked in a bank.'

'No, he didn't.' Again, the words plopped out like mothballs of mystery.

Tom asked her what she meant, whom she meant. He tormented her with questions – but she just kept saying:

'You don't know. You don't know.'

She repeated it again and again like a child. Once, Tom moved right up close to her to force her into some clear admission. But he retreated as soon as he saw her face.

The old woman was 'The Saddle'; and, like the mountain, out of sight, out of harm. So Tom dismissed her on the final lap to his house. She had brushed into his consciousness like a jellyfish; stingless, because he had not been sufficiently afraid of her to believe her. He was very careful about what did and what did not make him afraid. He had stopped – out of curiosity. Old Sall settled into the fattening, lazy background of his mind.

He did not tell his mother until the next day. He had come back from church and, as was happening more frequently, he wanted to throw every possible shade from his thoughts so that they might be completely clean. And so he told her.

His mother turned it from an incident into an omen.

She screamed at him.

She forced him to repeat, word for word, again and again, what the old woman had said. She broke off after each word – every time – and made him swear that it had not been qualified in any way.

She scared his grandfather so much that he hung in his clothes, breathless.

And then she began to curse Old Sall. A gossip, a lunatic, a filthy old woman, a black-tongued, sour-faced, ugly-faced, rotten old slut, a crazy old carcase that should have been carted away to a madhouse years ago. A woman who could talk about nothing and no one without making the subject as dirty as she was, a liar, a woman who would talk about no one if she had any sense at all because there was so much, so much that could be said about her. A criminal liar. A bitch! A smelly, ugly, filthy disgrace!

The words hissed and splashed around Tom like boiling muck.

And then his mother slapped his face for believing such terrible lies.

The November of that year was bitter. It snowed so hard that it soon stopped being fun and became just a nuisance and then a torment. Tom would refuse to go out. He had built a tunnel for himself, raced around with mittens full of snowballs, made stockpiles at strategic points all the way up Church Street; but no one else wanted to play as long or as hard or as often as he did – and so he gave up.

His mother seemed to enjoy it. Her post round took twice as long, but she came back blazing-fresh, with white petals of snow gleaming and melting in her black, tossed hair, and if he were lucky, she would tell him of some fight she had had with a particular drift or a lane or a field. Old Sall was never referred to after that Sunday.

He was invited by his uncle Henry to go and build a snowman

for Catherine – but he refused to go. His father – who took the bad weather badly and coughed a great deal – was angry with him for this. His grandfather – out of work with the hard ground – offered to go instead of Tom, but Anne would not allow it.

Tom went to sleep, shivering, and woke up with his fingers and toes stiff with cold.

The snow battened down the town, snuffing out any flicker of resistance with a heavy fall of thick flakes. People walked silently along white-carpeted streets, or sloshed quickly through brown, running mud.

The north wind began to rise – rise until it blew down the street like a great mountain draught. The snow covered itself with ice; the mud stiffened into glass pools. No one had ever known such a wind; it hurled out November and blasted, icily, into the last month of the year as if it were determined to freeze and wither the whole of the winter. Coats were piled on coats; gloves doubled; socks knitted thick and uncomfortable. But the wind cut through everything.

Anne told Tom to go out and walk himself warm. To stump through the fields in his wellingtons until he sweated so much that he would not mind taking off all his clothes and rolling over and over on the crackling top of the deep snow. She sometimes felt like doing that herself.

He would not go out. Sitting inside the house, he looked out at the slate sky and the slate-coloured houses. Anything that stirred was out of place.

The wind would never stop. And everyone said that – even if it did – it would only be the beginning of real trouble.

PART THREE

CHAPTER TEN

'And they heard the voice of the Lord God walking in the garden in the cool of the day: and Adam and his wife hid themselves from the presence of the Lord God amongst the trees of the garden.

'And the Lord God called unto Adam, and said unto him, where art thou?

'And he said, I heard thy voice in the garden, and I was afraid, because I was naked; and I hid myself.'

And Tom's voice left him and took the first lesson right through the church on its own. He was not frightened; he knew the passage by heart; he waited until he should be nearer the end so that he could then join up with his voice once again and they could move, together, back to the choir stalls.

It was Christmas and the service of the nine lessons and carols. His lesson, the choirboy's, was the first. He had to remember to turn over the pages when he finished and leave May Stoddart's place open. That was all he had to remember.

The church was full, and the yellow light warmed the solemn faces of the congregation until they looked relaxed and sympathetic. They would all have a good view. The Rev Pursur observed what was referred to as 'High Church Practice' and the choir sang the nine carols from nine different points in the church, including – to the delight of the choirboys – the gallery – 'In Dulce Jubilo' – which was unsafe.

The Bible rested on a great brass eagle which sparkled and winked most light-heartedly at the candles which were set on either side of it. Behind Tom were the brown stalls; boys in front, girls in between, men at the back. The great tenors and basses flung out their harmonies at each other across the black-velveted, dipping heads of the sopranos and the plastered mops of the trebles.

And behind them – the altar rails and the altar itself – blazing its Christmas colours, bearing two long candles and a shining cross that might have been gold – set underneath the three windows of coloured glass – illuminated by the sidelights – which, in the centre, showed Jesus in a church not unlike Thornton's own, both arms full of children, feet resting on the words: 'Suffer little children to come unto me.'

'And the Lord God said unto the serpent, Because thou has done this, thou art cursed above all cattle, and above every beast of the field; upon thy belly shalt thou go and dust shalt thou eat all the days of thy life.'

His voice rejoined him. He finished. 'Here endeth the first lesson.' Then he turned to May Stoddart's page, took two shaky steps backwards down the steps, swung around, bowed deeply to the altar, and went to his seat, his face steaming above the white frilly collar and surplice. Arnold Jackson knocked him in the ribs with an encouraging elbow. The Rev Pursur took up the service.

'Christmas was an old pagan festival which the Christians took over. The pagans used to eat up all the meat that would not keep through the winter on that day. Did you know that?'

Tom did not know. But this was only one of the things that the Rev Pursur could tell him.

'Prayer is not concentration, Tom, it is relaxation. We must give God an emptied mind to do with as he wishes. But some of us have to concentrate to relax, eh?'

That was more difficult to work out. But he understood. The Rev Pursur told him that he was considering whether or not to train him as a server. Tom went to church three times every Sunday.

'Consubstantiation, transubstantiation and commemoration – those are the three terms to remember.'

The vicar was tall and his voice was very educated. He lived alone in the huge vicarage with only Mrs Thompson to look after him. Sometimes he walked down the main street – in all his vestments – carrying the communion to someone who was sick. At Tom's communion, he had given everyone a book – *Prayers for each day of the year* – signed, 'To Tom Graham from Andrew J. Pursur.' – The Trinity: three in one and one in three. Father, Son and Holy Ghost. Three spirits in one body or three bodies in one spirit?

Tom had joined the Anglican Young People's Association so that he could hear the vicar speak on Wednesday evenings. Anything that voice uttered was true. The sound of it sent Tom into a dream of cornfields and small village churches, singing hymns in front of giant candles, praying all night on soft marble floors.

'If a doctor, a teacher, an engineer and a priest were up in a balloon and it was decided that only one of them could stay in it or they would all be killed, who should be allowed to live?'

Tom racked his brain. He could find good excuses for all of them and, as it was his turn, he defended each, in turn, as best he could. This sort of argument never happened at home or school. He was always inclined to make a great number of allowances so that the vicar could stay in the balloon but, to his bewilderment, the Rev Pursur would always oppose them. And then he produced his final verdict.

'The vicar should stay,' Tom announced, 'because, without him, there would be no one to look after people's souls and no one would get to heaven.'

'But a soul is no good without a body,' the vicar replied. 'The body is its testing ground.'

No one could beat him in argument. The vicar ruffled his hair.

The Rev Pursur had corked up Tom's depression and thrown it away. The boy had swerved away from his family and from all other interests and dedicated himself to the church. He prayed morning and night. He had only to step into the church to feel the bells of centuries of cloistered monastries ring out for him. The Apostles were examined, cross-questioned, almost daily to test their loyalty to Jesus. Jesus himself was a flaming white fire, pointing, away at the very top, to endless blue. Tom began to check all his actions in terms of Christian purity and find sin creeping its temptations before everything he said or did. Sometimes he felt so guilty that he would pray for Sunday to come quickly so that he might be absolved after the general confession. But to ask the Lord for selfish ends – that, too, was a sin.

Tom began and ended every other sentence with the vicar's.

'It's the Rev Pursur this, the Rev Pursur that – you haven't to believe everything he tells you.' Anne was in a bad temper.

'But the Rev Pursur said . . .'

'Does he never stop?'

'I think Tom's right to go to church,' said his father. 'He can represent all of us.'

'As long as this Rev Pursur doesn't expect to be believed by all of us!'

His grandfather woke up and repeated a question which seemed to have been troubling him a lot lately.

'What are you going to be when you grow up?'

Tom decided that he could not lie – even to his grandfather.

'A boxer – or a vicar,' he replied.

They would not start to move until after the third lesson. Tom waited patiently. He loved the processions. First Willie Irving carrying the cross – he was a senior server – then the two oldest choirboys with candles. Then the choir – boys, girls, men, nearly thirty in all, followed by another two servers and all led, from the back, by the Rev Pursur who was as tall as the cross at the front of the procession.

He was still too excited to concentrate on the service, and too exalted, too dizzy with the fuzzing effect of golden walls, the crushed glow of darkened stained glass, the shimmering whites and soft felt blacks of the surplice and cassocks to pass the time – as he often did – by sending messages across the chancel steps on his fingers in the deaf-and-dumb language.

He looked around the church. The fortress was complete.

His grandfather had crept into the church one evening – right at the back, nearest to the door – in order to discover the weight of his tacit obligation and, encouraged by the revelation that nothing more was required of him than a gentle rhythm of standing up and sitting down (he did not kneel, being in the back row), he now came every Sunday evening – whether it was Christmas or not.

Sitting next to him was Anne. She had put on her black suit.

'Just to hear Tom read,' she said, warningly.

His father stuck the tie-pin into his shirt front very carefully.

'I think that I'll start going every Sunday,' he said.

Tom had achieved his first conversions.

'It is often the case that the best work a Christian can do is to serve his family,' the Rev Pursur had said.

And, for months, Tom had nagged and begged them to come to church. His mother was boiling in hell, covered in serpents, surrounded by fire and brimstone, shackled by iron chains which clanked every time she lifted up her hands to heaven. Tom could do nothing to save her if she did not come to church.

'Speak out,' she said. 'I'll be at the back with your grandfather.'

His father was half-hidden behind a pillar.

Right at the front sat his uncle Henry, his aunt Catherine and little Catherine. In all these years she had not changed one bit. Tom wriggled in his long pants and sweated at the memory that he had once wanted to marry her. He could not even bear to look at her for more than two seconds. She might start talking to him. His uncle Henry and aunt Catherine always came to church when there was something special on: it was about the only time he ever saw them. His uncle had not come to their home again: Tom did not know why.

Philip was there, of course. His voice had broken, but he still came, wedged between his plump parents like a broken matchstick, between two thumbs.

Tom was glad that Mr Tate – his English teacher – was there. He had tried to make Tom go into one of the school-plays and, although he had refused, he had been flattered. Besides, he was good at English.

Mr Waters, his uncle's partner was there; had to be: he was a churchwarden.

Mrs Blacklock sat somewhere in the middle: the Turneys had come in all the way from their farm for the service. 'Tosh Glaister who worked on the post with his mother was there in a suit that was sufficiently like his uniform for Tom to recognise him without much difficulty. Miss Windle, with whom he had taken piano lessons for three months, was sitting in the very front pew, and her sister was sitting directly behind her in the next pew. The Brinns, the Sands gang, Mr Carlin, Old Sall – none of them had come – nor would they have been let in, probably.

But of all the congregation, Tom was interested only in one person: the girl who sat at the end of a row near the back. She had long black hair and her face was almost brown – even in the middle of winter. She wore the smartest blue coat Tom had ever seen. He was sure that he recognised her father – it must have been her father sitting next to her. He tried to relax so that he could concentrate on discovering the name.

The first procession started. The choirboys popped out of their opposing stalls and met on the chancel steps, bowed, turned inwards, and walked down the nave singing *O come all ye faithful*. The second verse was sung by the trebles and sopranos on their own – in Latin. Tom knew the words by heart, and so devoted himself to keeping his feet away from the bottom of his cassock – which was too long – and to measuring out the distance between himself and the girl. At the correct spot, his head lifted up like a bird's beak. She was looking at him! He blushed crimson and bellowed 'Deus et Deo'.

Mr Dalton! She had met him on the road with his grandfather when they were moving. That was his name. 'Old friends of your mam and dad.' Mr Dalton!

'The Lord be with you.'
'And with thy spirit.'

'And the blessing of the Lord God Almighty, Father, Son and Holy Ghost . . .'

If he did not hurry up then he would miss her. In the church, they would already have finished their last dab of prayer and be going out. And she was near the back.

Sometimes the vicar talked to them in the vestry after the service.

'Amen. The singing was beautiful tonight.'

'Thank yous' growled around the tiny room. No move yet. He prayed.

'And all the lessons were read very clearly.'

Tom wanted to be singled out – but he wanted, much more, to be left alone. His hands worked furiously underneath his surplice and undid the nineteen buttons of his cassock. He crept his fingers up to his throat to unbutton his collar.

'Thank you all, very much,' said the vicar and turned away. Willie Irving followed him into the vicar's vestry with the cross.

Tom's peg was in the corner. He threw his things on to it and belted out yards ahead of the field. Usually, the vicar was first so that he could get to the west door and shake hands with as many people as possible. Tom beat him there by the length of the church.

The congregation spread out from the church door in a widening funnel. The edges were always breaking away to go home but, as yet, they were always replenished from the church.

Tom saw his aunt Catherine standing near the door, not moving, one hand holding Catherine, the other waiting for a shake. He put down his head and trotted past her.

Mr Dalton would be near the back. He pushed his way through the crowd. He was already taller than some of the women.

'You were lovely!'

A hand, the weight of an axe, hit down on to his shoulder.

'Lovely! I didn't know you could read . . .'

Mrs Blacklock, from across the street!

'Like that! What will your mother think of you?'

109

She bent her broad-brimmed head in thanksgiving. A bunch of red cherries swung up from the back of her hat.

'Thank you, Mrs Blacklock.'

When she looked up to continue, he was gone.

He ducked to avoid Mr Tate, and again to miss Philip. The light from the open church-doors lit up everyone so clearly that it might have been day. He saw girls in every colour coat except blue. No one spoke very loudly; in fact, the whole square was a black-coated, slowly shifting mass of whispers – scared to speak normally in case the earthly remarks should beat the prayers up to heaven. Tom thrashed around silently. The Rev Pursur was now at the door, shining in his gaudy clothes like a gipsy at a funeral. Mr Dalton was not in the cluster around him.

He saw his father looking around for him and dodged behind some women. A car started up, bursting into the Sunday silence like a thunderclap. Others, now given the excuse, joined in and Tom sprinted over to the car-park. White lights from large hand-lamps hit him in the face and he stepped to one side to let them pass. She was at the window! He ran after the car and caught up with it as it slowed down to pass through the crowd and on to the road. Mr Dalton and his wife were in the front. The girl was behind them, hunched forward over their shoulders. She must have seen him. Quite powerless, he walked beside the gently-nosing car, discarding every idea of gaining her attention as soon as he thought of it. All he could do was to relax to concentrate on her so that she would *know* he was there.

The car came out of the crowd. He would not be able to keep up with it for much longer. It could have a crash: Tom tore away the burning wreckage and hauled her out, gently saving her life by artificial respiration. Mr Dalton said that he could have anything he wanted.

'What is your daughter called? I've got to know.' That was all he wanted.

The car pulled away. She had not looked around. Maybe she had seen him at first and then turned away.

'Who were you talking to?'

'What?'

'Pardon! What's rude. Who were you talking to?'

It was his mother. He decided not to tell her anything.

'Nobody!'

'You'll end up like your grandfather.'

She looked around. Tom could sense that she did not like being there. Her face was stern and he dropped all expectation of a compliment being given him for his reading.

'You read very nicely.'

'Did you really think so?'

'Yes. Have you seen your father?'

Tom's eyes flicked over to the only source of light.

'He's with the Rev Pursur.'

'Well he should hurry up.'

Tom took a huge breath.

'Why don't you come and meet the vicar?'

His mother paused before replying. Tom looked around with her and saw the streets already draining away the church-goers – turning back to its normal appearance with the few groups of loiterers thickening across the pavement at the usual places. His mother shuddered slightly.

'Are you cold?'

'Let's go and get your father and get back home.'

His grandfather had already disappeared. Tom did not need to ask where, the 'Lion' frowned its secrets behind tight curtains and the puffy squeeze of its accordion tainted all Christians, except these who, like his grandfather, saw both sides.

There were very few people around the Rev Pursur now. His father was talking to him.

'He did well, didn't he, vicar?'

Tom squirmed for his father who, thinking that he had spotted modesty, put out a hand to ruffle his son's hair. Tom dodged as if it was a blow.

'He's too shy. Not at home, though, eh? Anne? Anne – I would like you to meet – you haven't met him properly – have you? – the vicar. Vicar – my wife. Tom's mother.'

'I saw you,' said the vicar, shaking hands, lengthily, 'at Tom's communion.'

'Yes,' said Anne. 'I came to that.'

The Rev Pursur looked down at Tom and said:

'You have done your duty very well tonight.'

Tom understood. He hugged the secret achievement in his heart and looked at his parents indulgently.

Edward worked away at the conversation.

'It was a very nice service, I thought, very nice.'

'I'm glad that you enjoyed it.'

'Oh I did. In fact, I'm thinking about, about . . .' – 'coming again' would be too crude – 'what Tom was telling us.'

'And may I ask what that was?'

Anne had been hopping from one foot to another. They were the only people left with the vicar. She cut right across Edward's talk.

'We mustn't keep the vicar.'

'I'm glad to talk to Tom's parents.'

Edward caught his wife's irritation but in him it panicked into nervousness.

'Of course he does. Cigarette?'

'I don't smoke. Only a pipe.'

'Sorry.'

Edward stuffed the packet back into his overcoat pocket.

'Well,' he said, 'we'll be going.'

'Good night, Mr Graham. Good night, Mrs Graham.'

'Hope to see you again, sometimes.'

'Good night.'

'Good night, Tom.'

They moved away. Anne's heels rattled on the paving stones like drumsticks. Edward lit a cigarette. They were silent all the way back to the house.

Over supper, Tom's father went into a long and uninterrupted

112

description of the Rev Pursur's virtues. He ended up with a warning:

'Don't you ever do anything to upset that man, Tom. He's a good man, and he likes you. He could do a lot for you. Don't you go and spoil it.'

Tom let this pass over him. He was waiting for the right moment to ask his question.

At last they settled down. His father was reading; his mother in a sort of sleep. Listening to the wireless. It had to be done before his grandfather came in and broke everything up.

'Mam. D'you know Mr Dalton?'

Anne sat up in her chair as if she had been flicked with a whip.

'Why do you want to know that?'

'I just wondered.'

'Why?'

Edward had been wanting an opportunity to speak again.

'Yes. Your mother and me know Norman Dalton very well.'

'Why do you want to know?' Anne demanded.

Tom's courage melted back into his mind. He picked up his pen and started to write.

'Why do you want to know?'

Anne had stood up. Tom had to answer.

'I met him once with Granda.'

'Where?'

'Near the cottage.'

'When?'

'When we moved.'

'Oh!'

She sat down, her body stiff as a trunk. Then, quite suddenly, she relaxed.

'I see,' she said. Tom trembled.

'What?'

Edward was curious. Tom felt afraid, seeing the outlines of fear beginning to appear on his father's face.

'Never mind.' His mother looked at him, steadily.

Tom was ashamed that she had found out so easily.

'You're far too young for that sort of thing, Tom. Keep away from her!'

Tom ignored his father's bewilderment and, in spite of his nervousness at being exposed, he blurted out:

'But you said you knew them – him, anyway.'

'Neither your father, nor I,' Anne spoke very deliberately, 'have seen Mr Dalton or anyone concerned with him for a very long time.'

'But you knew him once!'

'That's enough!'

Edward made as if to attempt to catch up on the conversation but sank back when Anne switched off the wireless and indicated that it was all over. She was even more fidgety than usual; Edward more silent.

Tom looked at the piece of paper on which he had been scribbling. It read: 'Mr Dalton', '– Dalton'. 'Dalton'. 'Tom and – Dalton'. He had to discover her name.

Tom pulled the lever into low gear and his ankles flapped around like windmill arms on a windy day. The wind flattened his long trousers against his legs and slammed his blazer against his chest. The wind bent back the hedges on each side of him and swayed the leafless branches of trees with long, silent strokes of power. The wind whipped back his long hair and smacked into his face like water. The grasses on the verges were tossed back to their roots, and when he reached the top of the hill and looked down on the tarn, he saw the windy ripples chasing each other furiously across its surface; as if a whirlpool had been turned inside out. As hard as he shouted – and he bellowed for there was no one to hear him – his voice was whipped past his ears so quickly that he hardly caught a sound. The clouds bounced and tossed like dirty grey sheets let loose from all the back gardens of Thornton, of Cumberland, of the whole of England!

Betty!! Her name was Betty and he was going to see if he could see her. He pushed his bicycle downhill, into the wind, clicking into middle gear, shouting back at the hollow blasting wind with all his flattened breath. Betty Dalton!

It had been very difficult to discover her name. Finally, after innumerable 'white' lies, he had been told it by Mr Lawton who used to be his neighbour at Fell Cottage.

'Betty. She looks just like your mother used to look.'

'Did you know my mother that long ago?'

This both got him off the subject and opened up the possibility of satisfying his endless curiosity about his parents.

'Everybody did.'

'When she was my age?'

'And younger.'

'Was she like me?'

'No.'

'Not even in her ways?'

'Nowt like thee. She was like that Betty.' Mr Lawton paused. 'That Betty that thou's be interested in!'

Still, he had found out. His religion did not weigh delicate balances between ends and means. He was safe. He wanted to be safe.

He was safer in the church than he had been anywhere. The previous winter, when the weather had been so violent and the floods so damaging, he had felt desperate. After the incident over Old Sall, he felt that he could not tell his mother anything without getting into trouble; while his father's attentions seemed so soft and messy that he cringed away from him as from a sweet, sticky snail; and his grandfather hardly counted any more; everything he did was an embarrassment or a nuisance to everyone. Tom had fled from the house.

And then the Rev Pursur had begun to take special notice of him at choir-practice. Tom had rushed into the church, raced into its regular services and easy-to-learn hymns and psalms and names of kings and prophets, walked through all its demands in the space of one year so that, at the end of it, he was set to be a server; above all, avoided women and raced to his bedside one night to lug out the bamboo and string cross and stay on his knees until his back properly ached and his mother came into tell him that he should have knocked off the light long ago if he was doing nothing – and all that because he had tried to drag a fatter, unwilling this time, Gladys on to his knees one dust-still and cloud-feather summer night. It had taken the place of everything that had had no place before; it told him his guilt and twisted his mind into fantastical convolutions of self-examination in order that he might see the scorpion's tail behind every lamb's coat – and it made him sweat in his bed to think of those gates being clashed together in front of his nose with the word 'Closed' hung up outside them and no alternative but to march along Longthwaite Road to Hell; and then, after the General Confession, it filled up his black, squeezed heart with holy absolution so that it sponged into a dream of eternal comfort for a few minutes before the service caught up with him again. It mothered and fathered and brothered and sistered him into its hard-seated lap of brown-stained choir-stalls and gathered him into its ultimate demands.

'Looked like his mother.'

All the better. There was no one – of her age – who could ever hope to look like his mother. The biggest compliment that Tom could – privately – be paid, was to be told just that.

The tarn was about the same size as the one which had been near his cottage, and he bent his back like a horseman's and paddled against the ripples. The two tarns, one on each side of the town, were like the balances on either side of the figure of justice. Tom was Libra. This morning, it said: 'Avoid all unnecessary encounters. Remember that friends remembered are better than friends newly sought sought out. Lucky number – 17.'

Seventeen more trees on his right hand side and he would be next to the farm. Everything but himself had been swept off the road by the wind: he rode in the middle, tyres faltering from side to side on the smudgy white line.

'Gent-le bree-zes soft-ly blow – from out – the sew-ers overflow!'

Sixteen seventeen? At the end of the next seventeen trees. Still on his right hand side. No cheating.

Eight. There it was. A slate-green, open-sided, square of large-stoned, tiny-windowed farm buildings. And behind it, immediately behind, a fell ran up in a swift curve, divided between two men by the squat wall which lined its centre and vanished over the top.

Following his plan, Tom biked right past it. Round a corner, he turned and bowled back again, free-wheeling in the following wind. No one was about. He repeated his manoeuvre several times. He could not expect her to appear immediately. He went past the farm as slowly as he could. The yard was cobbled and weedless: clean and empty of any gusted fragments of paper. The house itself might have been empty: there was no way of telling.

He stopped, right outside the gate, and turned his bicycle upside down. It was a risk, but he had his excuses all lined up. To make it look realistic, he took the small yellow tin of mending gear out of his pouch and tapped the back wheel with one of the spanners. At first, he worked with his back to the house to arouse less suspicion.

'Trouble?'

Tom jumped around and threw his spanner on to the ground. It was Mr Dalton.

'Fixed it,' Tom replied.

Mr Dalton's black hair blew about in the wind. He must have come just to see Tom. He was wearing a waistcoat but no jacket.

'What was it?'

'Puncture!' He made it white. 'Suspected, anyway.'

'Good machine you have there.'

'Yes.'

Tom hauled it back up on to its wheels. His hands were trembling. Mr Dalton stood and said nothing. Tom spent as much time as he could in gathering his mending kit together.

'Oot on a ride?'

'Yes.'

'Like this part?'

'Yes.'

'Must do. You've been backwards and forrads like a windscreen wiper.'

The farmer's face was hard.

'I didn't know whether to go on or not,' Tom replied.

'Do you know now?'

'Yes.'

'Right then.'

And Tom hopped along with one foot on the ground, swung his leg over the cross-bar, and let the wind push him down the road.

He felt sick at not having seen Betty. But he could think about her any time. Why had Mr Dalton not recognised him? He had not changed all that much – and he must have seen him reading the lesson. The last time they had met, Mr Dalton had wanted him to talk.

Tom went back into Thornton feeling shaken. He would have to work out some foolproof excuses for going back to the farm.

CHAPTER ELEVEN

'Tom Graham?'

'Yes.'

'Tom Graham, is it?'

'Yes.'

'Come in then. Don't stand out there. I'm very sorry.'

Bemused by the unassociated nature of Mrs Thompson's apology, and a little bewildered by the bulk of her black plumage, which gave her the appearance of a stuffed umbrella turned upside down, Tom lifted his careful feet over the entrance to the Rev Pursur's almighty vicarage – and felt the double honour of being allowed into such a house – and of being trained as a server. The great bell crashed ahead of him and the vicar popped out of a tall door at the clang of the latch at the front.

'Tom Graham, Vicar,' the grey bun bobbed at this announcement. 'Annie Graham's boy. Such a pity.'

The vicar looked for an explanation and then, as though fearing it, he reached out for Tom and said:

'You seem to have a gift for making mothers. Come in.'

'I'm very sorry for him.'

She expressed this sorrow by shielding Tom from the affliction of her expression by a broad, unquivering back. Tom wanted to examine the facts behind her accusations of grief.

'Mrs Thompson is sorry for everyone.' The vicar leaned forward and almost licked Tom's ear in confidence. 'Perhaps it gives her the opportunity to be so sorry for herself.'

Selfishness! Tom accepted the vicar's daring analysis, man to man. They swept past Mrs Thompson and into the drawing-room.

Two of the other elective servers had been to see the vicar over the last fortnight. After a struggle, Tom had decided that the vicar had done it that way so that his favouritism for Tom would not be so glaringly patent. For it did exist.

'When I think of a choirboy, I think of Tom,' he had once said – to Miss Windle, the one who did the flowers, in the boy's hearing.

But it was more subtle and more profound than that. It was the sympathetic, silent look that shared a common feeling, the extra impositions whose severity proclaimed affection, the references which only he could be expected to catch, the occasional revelations of a private pleasure which was now shared for the first time.

Now, the vicar's drawing-room became, immediately, the dreamt-of setting of every upper-class novel Tom had read. There were the hunting pictures and the spindle-legged, burnished brown wooden chairs, the fraying carpets in what his mother would have called 'quiet' patterns, the dishevelled, brown-bound rows of gold-titled books, the high, moulded ceiling, and the long velvet curtains which pleated down to the floor like a careless cloak.

'This is where I write my sermon.'

Tom took as his text: 'God spake the word, and the word was made flesh.' 'And the blessing of the Lord God Almighty . . .' Pause to wait for the rustling to stop. 'In this century, science has shown us many things. Acts which would have been accounted miracles are now a part of our everyday lives. Words – sound-waves – can undoubtedly create matter. But the question behind the act remains. Why, ladies and gentlemen, why?'

'Sit down.'

Tom flopped into an armchair which surrounded him like a tent. 'The question behind the act remains.' He began to remember that the vicar had asked him to come to discuss 'the personal problems of being a server'. He waited.

'Now. I don't want to teach – or preach! – not tonight. You've had about as much of that as you can take this week – I know that you've been to Said Evensong every night, so far, since Lent began and don't think that I don't appreciate your effort – it's a good one! – but tonight – if we can, I want the two of us, together, to talk not about the church, not about Christ, or me, or being a server – but about you. About the way you feel, about the things that you feel about!'

He pushed a large, curving pipe between his teeth and began a great business with an enormous tobacco pouch.

'Think about it.'

Tom watched the large, stately face grope towards a position of dignity which would accommodate the wooden wedge comfortably between its teeth. When this was found, both of them relaxed. Tom let himself float around the room, appreciating every distinguished fray-mark on carpets and furniture. At home, the furniture was either new or old; they never bought this ageless, wearing stuff.

'Difficult, eh? I believe in springing it on you.'

And the vicar pulled his head into the large back of the chair and sucked hungrily on his pipe. Tom smiled at him. Nothing stirred in his mind.

'Let me bowl first then.' The vicar's face was obscured by smoke for a moment and, when it lifted, Tom could see that it had clouded his features into seriousness. He continued:

'What I want us to talk about now are all those personal things that you never get off your chest to anyone. There is provision in Anglican practice for confession, you know, and I want this to be a sort of confession. If you are going to ask the Church to take you seriously by making you a server – then you must take the Church seriously by making it a full confession. I know it isn't easy: that's why I am asking you here – so that you can take all the time in the world about it.'

Tom was stumped. His guilt, he knew, was an ever-increasing debt which was gradually jamming the whole of his action, clinging to each gesture like ineradicable dye. The only way in which he could live with it was by pressing prayers out of his mouth as often as possible – especially in church, into which he sometimes went even on a weekday morning, in order that the still, glass-softened silence of the huge building might neutralise the frantic twitchings of remorse

121

which sparked through his head like broken saws on tight wire. The preoccupation with his sin exhausted and so absorbed him. It was equalled in the strength of its fascination only by Betty – on whom it fed avariciously, feeding her, in turn, as it did, by the glamour of temptation. But all – all that he did, was brought out in his prayers. He told the truth about his acts to the point of investing them with significances which they had never, originally, had. There was nothing that he could tell the vicar that he had not already told God.

But one of the aspects of character which Tom had been able to develop – for the first time – since meeting the vicar, was that of 'being obliging'. He did not want to disappoint him now and so, after a good deal of clumsy exchanges about 'What do you mean?' 'I mean the things you know about but never talk about – never even think about; the unconscious sins; those that are the most poisonous.' 'Not like swearing or – even lying?' 'Nothing like that!' – after some minutes of this, Tom launched into the problem of vanity – explaining, with extensive circumlocutions, the fear he had of earthly pride on account of always glancing at shop-windows to see his reflection. The vicar listened carefully.

This was the hub of Tom's affection for the Rev Pursur. At home, his statements were listened to – or not – as the mood of his parents might be; he was encouraged, occasionally, to rhyme out some story – but only, so it seemed to Tom – if he mimed and clowned and imitated voices and made it funny. Whereas the vicar made him feel serious and important by treating nearly everything he said as being interesting. With him, Tom took the first steps towards an appreciation of the significance of his own views – and so to the realisation that they might be enlarged.

After vanity, he turned to greed. He was sure that he was greedy – but his examples seemed to fall flat and so he hurried on to envy. Here, his sin was retrospective – for he now believed that he had envied Philip his possessions – but nevertheless – as eternity stretched backwards as well as forwards, and as all time was just a blink of sunlight to God – it was still something for which he had to be forgiven. Again, however, the vicar's passive acceptance of his crimes made him move on to others, rather quickly. In order to give full measure, he went into lurid descriptions of his hatred of different people: but again the vicar seemed impatient. Eventually, Tom would up with a general confession of constant and complete unworthiness.

The vicar was silent. Tom was conscious that he had failed to satisfy and, though an instinctive explanation of this lay on the tip of his subconscious, he felt disappointed. He also felt uncomfortable. This was the first time that the vicar had taken everything from him without return. He was on his guard.

The vicar allowed the silence to mount. To begin with it was no more than an acknowledgment of a long effort. Soon, however, it began to thicken with distrust until, finally, it was solid between them: an accusation. Tom would not understand why this had happened – but the silence was, by now, such a physical power shutting him off from the vicar that he sat absolutely still and let his mind work over everything he had said. It seemed that, in a moment, this silence had suffocated all living contacts between the two. Tom was alone.

'You haven't told me everything.'

This vicar spoke rather cattily. This sort of tone was used at school too often for Tom to feel anything but the reflex action of contempt. He said nothing.

Suddenly, the vicar was furious.

'I cannot have my servers concealing things from me! I cannot have those with whom I enter the altar unwilling to tell me the truth about themselves! I'm sorry, Tom. I expected more of you. Much more.'

His sins must have been very bad. Perhaps he should not have told him about hating Mrs Blacklock; or about Philip.

'I'm sorry.'

'No, you're not. You haven't told me what you really should be sorry about!'

Betty! The vicar knew – how? – about Betty! Immediately Tom knew that he had concealed her throughout his confession. He blushed.

'What's that?' he asked.

'*You* must tell me.'

123

'I don't know what you mean.'

The vicar had been quivering in his chair like a great lizard. Now he jumped to his feet – his cassock-tail smacking the carpet like a whip, and from his tremendous height, he glowered down at Tom's huddle in the chair.

'I'm serious, Tom!'

How did he know? How did he know? How did he know?

Tom's voice became gruff and obstinate.

'I've told you everything.'

Poised like a black eagle, the vicar made as if to sweep down on the boy and shake him. Then, with obvious control, he pulled himself into a very stiff and rigid stance.

'I – could – smack – you – over – the – head. You have told me only those things that I knew already.'

He had seen Betty only four times. Nothing had happened. She had only spoken to him once. It was all dreams – thrashed out in furious wishful planning and scheming. The vicar could not know that. Tom set his shoulders in imitation of the vicar's own straight-panelled back.

He jerked his head up to look at the Rev Pursur – but said nothing. Betty was private. He worked out the situation in his bedroom-prayers, even sometimes in church – though he had half-decided that the mere thought of her name inside a church would bring him eternal damnation – but he could not talk to anyone about her.

'You're not going to tell me?'

'Nothing to tell.'

For a second, Tom thought that the vicar was going to stalk out and leave him. Then he gathered himself up into a great puffed-up balloon of black shoulders.

'Girls!' The word deflated him. He sat down – once more creasing his long bones in criss-crossed angularity.

'You must think of girls!' he said, quietly this time. 'And you must tell me what you think.' The vicar fixed him with an unbreakable stare.

Did he or didn't he know?

'Which girls?'

'Any. All.'

'Think what sort of things?' Tom played for time.

'That is what you must tell me.'

He did not know! He was bluffing.

'Well,' said Tom, with relieved jocosity, 'I do think about them. Everybody does.'

'*What* do you think?'

Tom knew what was required – but he had not even formulated clear symptoms for these feelings – let alone words. But he knew that the dark, excited stirrings, which the smell of Betty's name brought to him, were evil. So evil that the vicar had to be told nothing if he was to be made a server. Tom combined truth with caution.

'I don't know. I just think about them.'

And then, the vicar relaxed. His face flowed back into the pleasant lines that Tom trusted. He began to fiddle with his pipe once more.

'Sorry I was so rough with you, old chap. I knew I had to be. Never have got it out of you otherwise. Sometimes we are called on to help the suppliant, you know, to force them to tell us what they have to. Better for them in the long run.'

Tom watched him closely. He could not pull himself out of his trenches so easily. He wanted more proof.

The Rev Pursur now spoke as gently as a whisper.

'Nothing wrong with girls, of course.'

Tom was quite sure that there was, and he suspected a trick.

'Nothing at all,' the vicar went on. 'It's just that – it's difficult to explain to a lad of your age – I know that – but let me try . . . Here goes! You see, Tom, being part of a church – a real part – as you would be, will be, when you become a server – this takes much more out of you than you might think at first glance. Now: I want you to understand that I'm speaking to you like this because I'm interested – deeply interested – in what becomes of you. Now, let me put it this way: I know all about it. Remember that. I know all about it. I know the feelings a lad like yourself must have – I know why they come and I know that – on the whole – they are good

125

feelings. All this, I accept. But – and here you must let me be the vicar once more – I also know that these feelings must be controlled – if, and I say "if", if you want to be a real part of the living church. For, in the end, they will set up a conflict. They will institute a division of loyalties which – if they have not been controlled – will always result in a defeat for the church. And that defeat will be all the heavier, the more important you yourself are to the church. So: it is to protect the church – to protect you in the church and the church in you – it is for that reason that I must ask – I needn't ask, I can take it for granted, but you have to tell me of your own free will – it is for that reason that I must ask you to consider these feelings very carefully – and to weigh them against your responsibilities and obligations in other directions.'

Tom was unmoved. Not only would he refuse to say anything about Betty, he would certainly – now he knew – refuse to give her up. She blazed in his mind – no longer a secret – but a triumph.

He wished that the vicar would stop fiddling with that great pipe. He filled it in such a disorganised way that Tom could not trust him.

'Of course,' the vicar shook his head, sadly, 'this is something that you have to work out for yourself.' He took a fireless suck at his pipe and the tobacco lifted like dust from the wide bowl. 'I had to. Everyone has to.' He hurried on. 'I'll tell you something that helped me at that time – and – I don't know – might help you. I don't know, of course. It might. And . . .' he smiled right across his teeth, 'and it is on the basis of that possibility that I offer you this advice!'

Even though the vicar was talking non-stop, Tom felt something akin to the strength of the silence which had existed between them grow up again. He was dry and light: ready to spring off in any direction.

'You see – I was very much like you.' The vicar leaned heavily on the words. 'We are – very much alike. And – when I was your age – I, too, had these feelings – nothing definite, just, like yours, feelings. And then I secured help. Not from my vicar – because, as it happens, I went to a school where they kept us there all the time – a public school – and it was my – housemaster we called him – who helped me.'

This elastic tension between Tom and the Rev Pursur suddenly twanged, harshly. Tom found himself listening to his own breathing. The vicar put his pipe to one side and limbered himself forward in his chair so that he hung half-out of it, almost touching the boy.

'And he helped me in a very simple way.'

The eyes. Tom was riveted to the vicar's eyes – the more he looked at them, the more his body seemed to draw away, leaving only his glance to defend him. But he dare not look away.

'All that he did was – rather like you and me now – to ask me to study and talk. We talked about everything. There we were – man and boy – as I then was – together – just talking.'

'Yes.'

Tom had to say something or he would be sucked into those eyes. The vicar's voice grew more urgent.

'And it was his help which made me realise how short-lived – how superficial and how really unsatisfying such thoughts can be compared with the genuine friendship which man and boy can experience. A friendship that is based on the same hopes, and works towards the same end. A friendship that does not depend on some nasty sneaking feeling at the back of the mind – but one which can develop on any level, at any time and not be confined to some – terrible sort of physical thing – only.'

'Yes.'

A dry tongue trembled quickly around the inside of dry lips. The spring evening had darkened and the vicar was dusky in the shadows of his own room.

'After all,' the vicar was never going to stop, 'all through history, men have done their best work with other men. They have fought with them, sported with them, learned and taught with – other men. This relationship – this real friendship between . . .'

'Would you like some coffee?'

The vicar's hand shot across to Tom's knee in irritation. Tom himself jumped back in his seat. Mrs Thompson followed up her enquiry by the snap of a switch which wiped all darkness from the room.

'Yes.'

Tom barked out his relief. The vicar jumped up and glared at his housekeeper.

'I knocked,' she said, 'and then, I knew you were in.' She stood at the door.

'So you came in without my permission!'

Mrs Thompson was not to be shouted at.

'I'll go out again if you feel like that!'

The vicar twisted himself into an attitude of acceptance.

'No, no. Tom would like some coffee – and so would I. You're very kind.' He waved his right arm in a broken blessing.

She nodded her acknowledgment of his apology and went out. Slowly, the vicar walked across the room and hauled the long curtains together. He walked back directly towards Tom.

'I had it all ready.' She swayed in carrying a small tray in front of her. 'It's late, you know. Annie Graham'll be wondering where the boy is if I know anything about her.'

Tom accepted this general rule about mothers with gratitude – even thought he was not sure how it would stand the test in his own particular case.

'She will,' he said. He looked at his watch with a large display of dumb surprise. 'It's very late.'

'It's cool enough to drink right away.'

Tom bolted it down and, within a few minutes, he was out of the vicarage.

He walked down the long drive without once looking back. Closing the gate behind him, he exhaled lengthily, and then turned to peer across the lawn at the great Georgian frontage which had come to represent all that he could aspire to: almost invisible, except for the glimmered traces of one light; it looked more like a prison.

Every week at first, and then every day, he went up to the vicar's house for talks.

'I'm very sorry. Have some coffee.'

Mrs Thompson led him into the Sermon Room and Tom sat beside the vicar. They wrote the sermons together. A word each.

'Real friendship is silence – like this.'

Tom nodded. His own face was black. It was hooded with a monk's cowl.

'Man to man.'

He dare not look up. Betty's face would be at the window. White: cut into little squares by the wooden frames. Never able to find one pane big enough for Tom to see the whole of her face.

'I never go with any girls. Never go with any girls.'

'I'm sorry.' Mrs Thompson brought in his surplice and covered the coffee tray with it.

Betty's face would be at the window. Cut into pieces. Her black hair flew all around her and darkened the rest of the glass.

The vicar put his arm around Tom's shoulder.

'I want you to pour water over my thumbs before I take the wine in the chalice.'

He was certain to forget that.

Every day, every week, every month. He saw no one except the vicar. The house was blown up. The window smashed in. Betty's face was still there. Rat-tat-tat-tat! German machine-gun fire! The face was untouched.

'My permission!'

Every day!

'Shout!'

Betty's face.

The cowl crept around his mouth and nose, suffocating him.

Betty!

The vicar smiled across all his teeth and walked slowly towards the curtains.

Tom wrote down every sin he could think of.

'Christ have mercy upon us.'

Lord have mercy upon us.

Christ have mercy upon us.'

Swish! Swish! The curtains were drawn. Betty vanished.

Gently, nervously, small from the quiet and still back of his mind, two words floated up on to Tom's tongue . . .

'Piss – off.'

He woke up. It was morning.

It was terrible to say that!

And then, the next day, the words came back. As hard as he tried, he could not get rid of them. At first they stayed small, and then, gradually, they grew louder until they clanged in his temple like great bells swinging madly against each other.

'Piss – off!' 'Piss – off!' 'Piss – off!'

He could not destroy them. Those bells.

He did not want to destroy them. Let them peal.

He liked to hear them.

The evening after his visit to the vicarage, Tom was sitting in his kitchen doing his homework. The bells were dying down – but their sound had imprinted an attitude on to his mind which made sitting on a hard-backed chair, supported by an oil-clothed table and superintended by a newly and clumsily bespectacled father, appear loudly ordinary.

Normally, he enjoyed homework. Not the sort of enjoyment which demands regular and consistent nutrition – for it was always one of many alternatives, sometimes more, sometimes less attractive than the others – but the enjoyment that comes from a battle – even if it is lost. The knowledge of achievement. Coupled, always – in Tom's case – with some new revelation as to his own capacity. For, besides being something to be visibly shifted away – like a pile of sand moved from one side of a road to the other – his homework was a standard against which he could test himself. These tests could be tests of speed – the commonest; of memory – the easiest; or of perfection – to be perfectly honest in putting down everything that the question or problem might, under every known circumstance, require: this was the most difficult – and yet it was this very difficulty which made it the most exciting, and – surprisingly perhaps for someone who would still have been deeply insulted had he been called a 'swot', moved, indeed, to his knuckle-tips – far from being the least common. For in this exercise, Tom felt most definitely that he was two people: the cajoled, threatened, despised part of him, that lump of uselessness which frittered away his work or his dreams – these came in the same second – and that other part which fought with his imagined wonder-self to settle on top of each pinnacle it admired. The kitchen would sigh at his grunts.

But – on this evening – he was doing his homework to camouflage the trembling vacancy which promised to disrupt into some masochistic explosion should it be left uncovered. Had his mother been in, her very presence would have set off that silent, physical tension which had lately begun to grow between them – and that might have relieved him. As it was, she was out on a walk with one of her sisters, who had missed a bus and determined to use the time both to see her 'family' and, with part of that family, to make contact with an old friend.

Tom did not want to talk to his father. He found it easy to imagine himself confessing all he felt to him – and occasionally this stuttered into brief reality – but there was no subject sufficiently buoyant to keep their mutual interest engaged for more than a few seconds. Besides, Tom had grown out of the football-teams, great athletes, and commercial dreams stage – at least, before his father who, however, had not yet recognised this. So Tom said nothing. He played, idly, with the observation that his mother's sister looked exactly like his father and not at all like her own kinswoman – but there was little nourishment in that.

Tom was all feelings – all too passionately broiling for thought. Outside, it was becoming dark, and the restless settling of the spring night touched on Tom almost painfully. He, too, could not bear to store himself away for hours on end. He, too, rested himself as energetically as possible. His grandfather was out again, always out these days, drinking. The old man had scattered himself around Thornton like a handful of corn. And nothing had grown except his own addiction to the pubs. He still cleaned his gun once a week – rarely used it now – he had no shed of his own.

131

Tom felt sorrier for his grandfather than he had ever before felt for anyone. He would watch him slope down the street with his knees-bent plod, shabby in country-rough clothes, stopping to talk to anyone and everyone with a word for him: on his own. And Tom would want to run up to him and wash away the wrinkled and battered face, smooth out and whiten the limbs into youth, breathe freshening air into the mouth and – let him start again: give him another chance. He walked after him and they talked – but Tom had grown too big for the happy-tough mauling; besides, these days, the old man only exploded in rancid smells of tremblingly fragile violence which resembled madness. A quarter of the house was sinking.

So he sat, and mused over *The Cloister and the Hearth* – for Mr Tate. Expected to know all the answers by Mr Tate – his English teacher – he usually enjoyed testing himself in advance. But tonight, he was not interested.

Apart from those two words which had worn their meaning deep into Tom's mind, he had thought little about the Rev Pursur. That whole evening had been pushed away as being too important to be considered at the moment. If its reverberations did touch on his mind, a shudder of distaste would send them scudding away before they could strike any sympathetic chords.

Neither Tom nor his father had displaced their positions by more than a few inches when Anne, unburdened of her sister, arrived. She entered as she always did – with a singing flourish that brushed away all claims to the house except her own. Husband and son were included in the spell which brought everything in those rooms, at some time or other, to her accounting.

'Where's father?'

The words were flung across the small kitchen as the coat was flung across the chair. Edward rustled like a spikeless hedgehog, drawing his shoulders around his head.

'Still out,' he managed to say. He was desperate to cling on to the umbilical chord which piped him into forgetfulness in his book.

'Tom? Do you know?'

'Still out,' he repeated.

Tom, too, roused himself resentfully. But whereas his father retreated immediately and for good, Tom half inclined his voice and gesture to counter-attack.

'Well?' Anne demanded.

Well, what? Well, what? Impossible to be other than left unsaid.

'Well?' she smiled and pirouetted, relishing the action which would follow her command.

Instinctively, Tom surveyed his books and pens and timetables – all neatly laid out on the green-squared oil-cloth; he would have to collect and re-dispose of them quickly if his mother was not to shuffle him out of the house with the promise that *she* would 'put them away': he hated her to touch his books and paper: she gathered them like an armful of laundry and dumped them on the nearest flat place.

'I'll go and look for him,' Tom volunteered.

'I knew you would,' she said. Then, to make Tom as confused as he always was in front of her, she added, with real kindness, 'You're a good lad. You look after him. I know that.'

Tom reached out to screw his pen into its cap.

'I'll do that.'

Her arms shot under his nose and surrounded the tiny army.

'No!' he appealed. 'Let me! Please.'

She grimaced and scooped her hands backwards and forwards across the table as though she was hugging and shaping a great mass of pastry. Tom stared at her in terror. Then she stopped and straightened up. The books were untouched.

'All right,' she said.

Tom cleared them away.

Outside, there was hardly a sound. A pair of heavy boots walked steadily up the other end of Church Street – but Tom could not identify them. On the main street, one or two quickfooted bundles of coat tap-tapped along the dry pavement, hurrying to be swallowed in a brick box. The mountains seemed to grow lively again with the end of winter; and whereas, in that season, they had menaced the town and been ignored on account of the threats they held, now they sent in their soft winds like heralds to the besieged city, with their streams and pleasant laps promising comfort throughout the summer, adjoined with the town once more. Tom smelt the country's surge and thought of 'The Saddle'. More than anything else, the thought of that fell could bring back the smell of the sweet, heavy fields which flowed from its feet like a train. Yet he had to be careful about allowing himself to think of 'The Saddle', for its flint jaws could turn his mind to a flash of white and sear his thoughts with trepidation: it was the touchstone of his guilt.

But now, he could think of it – and of the cottage – as he walked up the street to find his grandfather. It was a pleasant pain. The feeling that it could, in some way, harm him, mingled with regret that he could never be near enough to it to allow this to happen, suffused his mind with a clouded sense of sad-sweetness which protected him against all other thoughts.

This searching for his grandfather was becoming habitual. As a habit, it wove a ritual around the act, giving it an importance in Tom's life which far outweighed its inconvenience. It was the one time at which he could, patently and realistically, be of help to his grandfather – and as the instinct towards helping him had grown so strong in Tom's mind, these night excursions gave him the strength which came from doing what he wanted to do and, at the same time, doing something to another's benefit.

His grandfather would not be around the 'Lion and Lamb' in the church square. A few months previously, he had called in there with his gun after a successful afternoon's shooting – and then – in some way or other which Tom had never clearly discovered – he had been led on into a description of how he had once shot the fox. The incident had not resulted in their being regarded in Thornton as village idiots – as Tom had feared it might – but, nevertheless, its history had occasionally menaced his security: even though, in Thornton itself, where some of the huntsmen lived and Tom actually passed them in the street, daily, he was much further away from the hunting world than he had been in the isolation of the cottage. The result of this provocation had been – according to the landlady of the 'Lion' – 'disgusting', according to Mrs Blacklock's ancient, unmarried son and gossip string, 'fair trouble', and according to Mr Carlin 'nasty'. His grandfather had been banned from ever entering that pub again. Edward, after two days of distressed cross-examination in which he had been constantly reassured by his father-in-law that 'nowt happened – just a bit of fun', had promised to go and straighten things out; but he had never done so. Old Tom had shrunk a little more at this disgrace.

So few cars passed through Thornton after six o'clock in the evening that the street-lights stood as a token to progress rather than an aid to it. Tom imagined some giant paw ripping away all the roof-tops and revealing all Thornton in its hidden third of life, yellow and shadowy in the weak-bulbed light. At the edge of The Sands part of the town, one of the houses had been demolished, leaving, stuck to the wall like so many pasted mementoes, a fire-place, wallpaper, mantelpiece and the jagged white scab of a staircase. The sight had fascinated the boy and given him a strange but compelling feeling of pleasure. Everything would be revealed.

By this time he had reached the 'Crown' – but his grandfather was not there. He went on up the street to the 'Vaults'. After visiting three other pubs, Tom decided that his grandfather must have gone to find somewhere quiet in order to sleep off his drink without having to stand up to his daughter's increasingly frequent harangues. He always protested that he was 'all right'. 'All right', 'All right' – he slumped against the cold walls and held off the enemies who did not even bother to approach him. He was wilting into the terrible waxen feebleness which presses on some old men all the lacks and weaknesses of their life until they become the image of everything they had avoided.

Tom went up an alley which had once led him into the cross-eyes and chair-leg of Twin. This time, without fear, but with a pity which was almost as crushing. He had not begun to define his thoughts on the position of man to man in society, and so his sadness had not the sharpening, relieving point of anger to it: it lay on him as it was – an incomprehensible and unhappy responsibility.

Tom came out near the Fire Station. Whenever he stopped to listen – all the sounds around him seemed to stop at the same time. The night had finally tightened its short hold on the still town.

He walked around one side of the building. The station was raised from the ground; the engine went in and out on a ramp. Tom was sure that his grandfather was huddled underneath it somewhere. But whenever he stopped – all the sounds stopped. He began to call out 'Granda'; softly always, and, though his impatience to consummate his pity hurried him towards petulance, he restrained himself and cooed out the word as gently as a whisper. A clumsy rustle convinced him that he was near. He bent almost double and crabbed his way along until he discovered a large pair of boots which twitched under the building as soon as his eyes rested on them.

'Aa's all right.'

'Come on, Granda.'

'All right.'

'You'll be cold.'

'Ah can sleep here.'

'I know. But come and sleep at home anyway.'

A pause. Both knew how the affair would end. Neither of them could keep up the play of persuasion and resistance for very long – and yet Tom felt that his grandfather had, as his due, to be coaxed.

'Come on . . . Mam's expecting you.'

'Aa'h all right.'

There was no force behind the voice: none at all. Tom wanted to help his grandfather in his own conviction and, for a second, wavered over his own position. Perhaps he was happier under the Fire Station.

'I can't leave you out all night,' he said, eventually.

'Why?'

'I would have to stop out with you,' said Tom, 'and I wouldn't want that.'

'You gan back.'

'No.' And the boy sat down.

Neither of them were very good at holding out a silence – but Tom was determined not to be the first to break it.

'Budge over.'

Tom got up.

Feet first, his grandfather pushed himself out from underneath the Fire Station.

Tom helped him up, and, immediately, his sympathy changed to direct concern as he inhaled the great wave of beer which panted into his face. He was sure that his grandfather would die of drink. He took the old man's arm and they walked off.

Tom was too preoccupied with keeping his grandfather upright to say anything and the old man was too shaky to start a conversation.

They came out on to the main street.

Tom's head was bowed; his total attention was given to his grandfather's feet. They trailed through some imaginary slush.

Tom watched for their first weakening.

Suddenly, his grandfather stiffened. Tom looked up.

The Rev Pursur was in front of them.

Tom brimmed full with a tight, bottle-necked blush.

'Good evening,' the vicar said.

They made some sort of reply.

'I've been hoping to see you all day,' he said to Tom.

What had he done?

'Aah's all right,' the old man said.

'I meant Tom.'

His grandfather coughed – nastily as though he was reaching for phlegm in his throat. Only Tom could have known that this was a laugh.

'Aah's Tom!' – his grandfather shook himself into trembling glee at his joke.

The vicar leaned down, tall, from another race.

'I meant your grandson, Mr Paislow.'

He must have smelled the beer. Tom's arm stiffened in the crook of his grandfather's elbow, and he pulled him, urgently, to be quiet.

'Beg pardon.'

The old man's head flopped down again.

Tom waited for his guilt to be announced.

'You didn't attend Evensong.'

'No.'

That was it!

'I'm not blaming you for it. I'm just remarking on it.' The Rev Pursur hesitated. Then, evidently considering Tom's grandfather to be too drunk to matter, he went on:

'I wanted to talk to you about last night.'

'Last night?' It could not be so near. It had been months ago.

'Yes.'

The vicar came forward and stretched out a hand towards Tom's shoulder – withdrawing it before it reached its objective. Then he spoke very quickly:

'Yes. I was too hard on you. I shouldn't have gone for you like that. Knew it was on your mind – bound to be – but I was rather ruthless. We always are with those we – expect the most of. But I made you suffer for a great deal that you had not done.'

Tom waited for the explanation. As far as he was concerned, the vicar had the right to say and do anything in the world he wanted to. But the affair was at an end. The vicar moved to the outside of the pavement.

'Good night.' Then he looked at Tom's grandfather. 'By the way, Mr Paislow, this is becoming a habit, isn't it? I'm not saying anything – but, you know . . . Good night.'

He left them.

Tom did not look after him. Something in the tone of voice he had used to address his grandfather had started a tiny needle of fury inside him.

'Come on.' They went on.

And then, small from the quiet and still back of his mind, two words floated up on to Tom's tongue. Terrible words.

'Piss – off.'

His grandfather laughed – and joined in.

CHAPTER TWELVE

Tom now went to Said Evensong as a matter of superstition. All traces of enthusiasm and even duty had long since vanished. His attendance was due solely to the terrible consequences which would inevitably follow should he fail to keep the promise he had made to himself of going to the evening service at least three times during the week.

He could not understand his own state of mind. One thing alone was certain. He could not bear the Rev Pursur to come near him. He shrank away, physically, from any suggestion of contact between them. It was as if his whole mind – once saturated with the warm-wine affection of a disciple for his master – had suddenly soured, so that its vinegary tang repelled everything it had once loved. Yet he still wanted to be a server. He could not give up now. Besides, he had promised that he would do it in his prayers.

He was at Evensong. There were very few others in the congregation. Mr Waters: one of the Windle sisters – they took it in turn through the week – Alan Richards who also wanted to be a server, about four old ladies, one of them with her husband, and Willie Irving, who came to church whether he was carrying the cross or not. The spring evening light shafted through the windows in broad, clean beams, each one an unbearable reminder of the freshness and adventure outside in the town. Tom was finding it more than usually difficult to concentrate. If he relaxed – as the vicar had told him – then his thoughts flew away immediately and fastened on to guilty subjects, each of which would need a whole service to itself to bring about its absolution.

Previously, with the quiet, closing words of Evensong, the more solemn for being uncoloured by music, lifting plainly up the fluted pillars with serious Christian purpose, with the unaccustomed holiness of weekday church and the fenced serenity of the short service, with the monk-like austerity of the vicar's few movements and his own attention the more clearly held, being one of ten as against one of two or three hundred; and again with the altar clearly in front of him, not waiting for attention from the corner of one eye as it did when he sat in the choir stalls – with all this, Tom had felt a barely-concealed exhilaration which had taken him into those garden-fresh and innumerable services of the medieval monasteries. He was bound to the church and would serve wherever a demand was made.

But now he was in church for no reason; chanting a liturgy which silted his throat with the hypocrisy it made him feel; submitted to a vicar he feared. It could not be over quickly enough.

The first sign was a bang which came through the still windows like a loud, sudden snapping of glass. But the windows were unbroken. Tom thought it was a tractor backfiring. He could measure the length of the service by comparing the time before the bang and the time after it.

The Rev Pursur continued uninterruptedly. People had walked out of his sermons, ill (once, a Mr Wolstonholme), and he had not broken off for a second. The Miss Windle of the evening tightened her coat around her as if to keep out the bang with everything else. Only Mr Waters registered concern; he had to: he was the churchwarden.

And then an uproar broke out – it must have been in the churchyard itself. No one could ignore this. There were two more shots; shouts – words which closed the ears of the congregation as if a hood had been settled on all of them – banging on the walls and then – Tom froze—

'Paislow! What do you think you're up to?'

The vicar had mumbled his words quietly to hear what was

going on; now he turned up their volume and raced towards the end of the service.

The congregation knelt.

Bang!

Tess was barking.

The congregation stood up.

'Lighten our darkness we besecch Thee, O Lord . . .'

Mr Waters slipped out.

A motor-bike revved up, and up again.

'Through Jesus Christ, our Lord . . .'

There must be half of Thornton outside.

'Amen.'

Down on your knees. Last prayer.

The vicar's white surplice fled up the nave.

Tom followed.

Outside, the noise blasted right into him, making him pause at the church door as though pressed by a wind.

People everywhere: on the church wall, behind it, on the gravestones, right in the churchyard, one girl up a tree.

The vicar walked down through the tombstones to a great cheer. Mr Waters was already near his grandfather. He fell flat on his face when the old man swung around with his gun. Tess was uncontrolled, scudding around a headstone, worrying a bunch of flowers. The vicar walked straight on. Tom could see his grandfather's free arm whirling around like a piston. He was going to have a fit. In spite of his shame, Tom began to move forward. He could hear the people hissing him on.

The vicar reached his grandfather and the old man was still. The crowd grew silent to hear what was being said. Tom turned around. Mr Lightfoot, the policeman, was directly behind him.

Tom had not looked into the vicar's face once. He had missed the morning service deliberately, knowing that something like this was bound to happen. His father would not let him miss Evensong. Last to come in; first changed after the service and then:

141

'Vicar says stay behind,' Willie Irving.

The vestry had emptied around him – gurgling out and away with the miserable carelessness of ignorant indifference.

Of course the vicar had told him that his grandfather had had to give up his job.

'For his own good, Tom,' the vicar sat on the edge of the table, his cassock hitched half-way up his legs. 'For his own good. You're old enough to understand what was wrong with your grandfather and we're both educated enough to realise just exactly what it means.'

His grandfather said he had seen a rabbit. Tom had believed him all the way home and all the way through that crowded and embarrassed fussing over the old man – now perfectly sobered – believed him and thought it not at all strange until his mother had said:

'And I'll have that gun. That's the last you'll see of it! You'll kill somebody next!'

And then, more quietly, to his uncle Henry – who had come in with the commotion—

'He said he saw a rabbit. He's not right. He's just not right.'

What did the vicar want him for?

'I want to tell you – not to tell you, that would be the wrong word and I don't want to *tell* you anything – I want, rather, to discuss – talk over – because nothing has changed, nothing *basic* has changed – *that*, above all, you must realise—'

What did he want?

'To – where was I? – you,' he rustled on the table and Tom immediately felt its ruled-edged hardness on his own behind, 'know, you remember how we used to talk – I want us to go on as before. I want you to be aware – not of my position in relation to your grandfather – but of my position in relation to you – because I know that you understand – don't you? – that I didn't *fire* your grandfather – in fact, constitutionally, I was no more than the messenger to the chorus of the Parish Council – eh? – anyway, I needn't go into all that—'

What then?

'My position in relation to you;' he stood up and spoke in his church voice, 'that of a vicar – in relation to – one – of – his – imminent servers. I don't want that to suffer.'

Tom waited to go. The two words did not come up in his mind. He felt neither sin, nor guilt, nor shame. He was, suddenly, unconnected with the vicar in any way. Blackness closed in around him – and he did not resist it.

'It doesn't matter what your grandfather does – what your father does, or I do, or anybody does – you just keep on in your own way. Nobody's going to help you – so let nobody stop you. You just go on and do what you want to do.'

At another time, his mother's direct interest might have pierced his armour and flattered him into the temporary belief that she really was the image which he had carefully closeted in the back of his mind.

Now – it all meant nothing. For a week, he had moped. He had succeeded in convincing himself that even Betty did not matter. Nothing did. Opening his school-books was like turning the gluey pages of a foreign dictionary. He had not gone outside – in spite of the fine weather – except to go to school and come back home.

His grandfather moved from his bedroom to his kitchen armchair – collapsed in all that had once held him so strong. Sometimes, he even had to be fed. His father strayed around restlessly. Tom saw his worry, was surprised at his irritability but – attributing it all to 'that day' – attempted no further analysis. He was not interested.

As the one fixed point in the house, Tom became at once its stumbling-block and its point of relief. Advice, imprecations, explanations, suggestions, orders – all hailed on him without any visible effect. He could make no effort. He could not understand why he could make no effort. He could not understand why he could not understand why he could make no effort. But he would do nothing: just sit.

143

His mother started up again:

'Everybody's for themselves in this world. You'll learn that sooner or later and if you've learned it now then maybe it isn't such a bad thing.'

His father was quite still – staring at Anne viciously. Tom observed it without a trace of the usual tremors felt at any indication of his parents' disunity. He had lost all his faith. 'Why don't you go and see Andrew or Jimmie or somebody you know and do something?'

His grandfather wore all sorts of clothes all over the day. Pyjamas in the afternoon, slippers in the morning. He was an invalid.

He must go over it again; and again and again and again for the eight-hundredth time. To prolong it and start from the very beginning. His toes were pointing straight up to the ceiling and they tickled the thin sheet which was all that covered him on this hot night. It was the first time he had slept naked.

Now.

Finally, he had decided to go to see Betty. He tried to remember as much of the ride out to the farm as he could – to spin it out – but he was there in a flash. And there, also, was Betty – with no pause for the tacking and trailing around which had almost driven him away. His bike was against the hedge and they were talking together through the field.

The warm, suffocatingly sweet and golden smell of the corn swept into all his pores until his body breathed out its scent and his skin burned with its rasping freshness. They had held hands at first and then he had put his arm around the thick, black elastic, gold-buckled belt which marked out a two-inch width of waist and drawn her so tightly into his side that her breast had pressed him. Now, again, he felt for the mark; just below his right shoulder; it would always be there: the soft, yielding force of her breast.

Mr Dalton was not around. Both of them had to make sure of that. They were near the tarn. Safe.

Her black hair was hot and it shivered in its warmth as his

144

mouth pressed against it. Tom felt his skin go brown against the starched white of his shirt.

The tarn shimmered in the heat: the haze from the water drifted up the side of the fells so that they, too, were unclear. Only Betty was clear. Her long bare arms were brown from fingertip to shoulder. He pressed her body against his and at first they sat on the grass and then lay back on it.

He clung to her until their clothes became so damp with sweat that they might have been naked. He trembled in his bed with the joy of that thought. They held long kisses, which started on the tender outside of their lips and bit into the hardness of their mouths. He stroked her hair, her arms, her face. They rolled over together – arms around each other as if in danger.

And then. He paused and scratched his bare thighs with his fingernails to make sure that he was tinglingly awake to enjoy the climax once again. And then, from somewhere deep in his stomach, a careful fist had tightened and screwed him into still delirium; forcing its way down into his groin and out like an ice cold rapier withdrawing from boiling honey – releasing everything in great spasms which threw him away from Betty, on to his back with his face straight up against the sky, one hand kneading her arm – wondering what the hell had happened to him.

He could not be a server now. He was glad. He need not go to church so often. He was glad. He would come out and see Betty again the very next day. Nothing mattered – except Betty and that feeling.

He lay wide-awake. Even the single sheet was too hot. He threw it off and lay completely naked. When he had taken his clothes off before bed – some ears of corn had fallen out of the creases. He could smell them.

Now.

He must go over it again.

A few weeks later, Tom felt himself to be settled in a new and strong pattern – and he waited to go back to school with that mixture of dread and impatience which indicated how important he knew it to be.

For, now, he had found a legitimate reason for a split in his character whose friction provided the dynamo for him to go on.

For a long time, Tom had been no more than a receptacle – filled out or coloured by whatever force or influence was nearest. He had always been acted on, and always been given and asked for no explanation of this invasion of himself. 'The Saddle' had scared and spellbound him without his ever provoking himself into any action against it; the Brinns, the Sands gang, even Mr Carlin and Old Sall – all had been authorities whose power he might escape – but not contradict. This had been especially true in his family – and, within the family – most particularly true of his mother. She was a blackness which smothered him whenever she wished, and an enigma in whom he could discover and confirm nothing. He loved her – but that love could show itself only by waiting unquestioningly for a lead from her which would fulfil his action. The greater part of his time was spent alone – with things. At best, with others, he was in a position of being a cadger.

Then his position had gained strength. At first, with his grandfather, he had overcome, even reversed, their previous relationship as the old man's weakening had gradually aroused his pity. Slowly, this pity had given him the knowledge of his own superiority. In a way, his great sympathy for his grandfather had a touch of the attraction of newly-discovered power in its composition. By being sympathetic, he was being himself.

He had begun to feel some concern for his father, as well. Previously, Edward had been the misty back-drop of rarely expressed goodness. Now, Tom was beginning to discover for himself proof of his father's qualities. He admired, for example, the way in which his father accepted without bitterness or humiliation the drastic disparity between his own position in Thornton and that of Henry, his step-brother. And, as an admirer, he was already more than he had been.

He kept his feelings for his mother so tightly locked away in the back of his mind that it was almost impossible for him to prise them out – even if he wanted to. Now – older – he saw how beautiful she was. He saw that she was more beautiful than the mother of anyone else at his school. He was jealous when other men looked at her and embarrassed when – as happened occasionally – his father tried to kiss her in full view. He watched her.

Yet, even though he had raised himself up to a position of some relevance in relation to his family – his attempts to strike out on his own, to impose his character on someone else – as with Catherine, or Philip, or even the Rev Pursur – these had all led him into an uncomfortable situation in which he had been swaddled almost to smothering in a fastidiousness or delicacy, or alien set of values which had, in the end, either thrown him off or been thrown off by him. Even so, he needed the social or intellectual ascendency which these people represented in order to fix rules of perspective into which he himself could be accommodated. He needed a confrontation to make him realise what he could stand for. With Gladys, there had been no response, no challenge, stalemate.

Now, however, the church and his school had helped him to develop within himself the two personalities whose interplay was essential for any forward movement. And this, he demanded. Now, some things were bad and some good: one part of him was lazy, another hard-working; one was ambitious, another careless. In his black periods, he was preyed on by everything and nothing, as before; but now, he could mark all this part of himself down as the useless part, to be cancelled out by those times of sustained effort and progress which filled him with such strength that he could tackle anything.

And with Betty as his girlfriend – everything was settled.

Except for the one scare which pricked against his mind like a Chinese torture – sometimes searing it with terrible madness.

He would see himself drift away. He would be in front of the mirror, or lying alone in bed, or even out in the country on his bicycle – and then, his mind would go away, everything about him would soften into the air around it and float up to the ceiling; all that would be left would be a hard edge of terror, trembling to keep still and hold out until he came back together and calmed down. He could see himself – like a tree-trunk – or a tap, or a window. He had no feeling of central existence. His atoms interchanged with those around them – threatening disintegration even on that one, tiny part of him which stayed firm – however tossed about – straining to pull back all that was lost.

He could not explain this. Sometimes it slipped in and out like a loose knee-cap and was no more painful. At other times, he had to scream out loud to bring life back to his body.

He would pass a window and wonder what would happen if his hand suddenly smashed through it. See a car approaching and have to hold himself back from throwing himself under it.

He pushed all this as far away from the front of his mind as he could. When such a state was on him – he accepted it or fought it – as his strength might be. Otherwise, he refused to acknowledge it.

PART FOUR

CHAPTER THIRTEEN

By now, Tom knew the road to the Daltons' farm so well that he could cycle there while being totally preoccupied with something else. Two things worried him and, knowing that, while both were unanswerable, there was one which could be eased in the very act of being rehearsed and one which could not, he decided to test himself first on the easier problem.

This was his failure to become a server. They had received their crosses in church the previous week – without Tom. Although the vicar had tried, on many occasions, to discover why Tom had suddenly stopped coming to the classes, Tom had always managed to evade him – or to evade giving a direct answer. The reason seemed simple to him: it was what he had done while with Betty; that could never be explained to anyone. Underneath this, however, was the repulsion he felt towards the vicar's voice, his face, his gestures – above all, towards any gesture which might result in their being in any sort of contact. He could not pin this down – although he was sure that it had something to do with his last visit to the vicarage – but its effect on him was as particular as a cut.

Yet, he had failed to become a server. His efforts had had no effect and he had again, he knew, given in: allowed others to influence something which should have been his decision. He had failed to work his way through on his own. During that service, he had felt that everyone was looking at him with contempt, knowing all about his failure; then, recognising pride, he had felt despair; from that, the only release had been a twisted howl of protest which had brought his mother hurrying upstairs to see what was wrong.

The revising of all this loosened the impaled position it had acquired at the back of his mind. The other worry clouded everything he did – and it could be aired as often as Tom liked without its weight decreasing by one ounce.

He had never repeated his feat with Betty. For one thing – in spite of the injustice of it – he had never again had the length of time with her under such ideal conditions. He was still the clandestine raider at the Daltons' farm. Mrs Dalton 'knew about it' – having met them once when Tom had decided to take the enormous risk of going right into the farmyard because it seemed empty – except for Betty: Mr Dalton knew nothing at all. Tom had not found it difficult to assume the measures of a poacher. These fitted in with his idea of himself as two people; but, far more basic than that, they were enjoyed as the reality of many a dream.

He was very good at it. It was only rarely that he drifted past the farm like a distress signal. He approached it from every direction in the guise of ambler, church-hunter, bird-nester, local historian, daydreamer, cross-country runner, swimmer, fisherman, collector for the overseas mission fund. Always, he had a sentence of surprised greeting ready rehearsed, on the tip of his tongue; always, he had clearly-defined excuses with which his assumed character would baffle any attempt at uncloaking by an unexpected Mr Dalton. He could even conduct a dialogue – given the guarantee of Betty's silence – in which he would converse quite casually about everything irrelevant to his main purpose. He had it all worked out.

But circumstances were out of sympathy with his plan. Instead of that previous afternoon being merely the overture to a grand symphony of love with Betty – it was at once the first and the final chord, or so it seemed. For they never again met in such freedom. And in the worried minutes they spent together, Tom was too hot and Betty too cold, or vice versa, or neither of them were really ready for anything more than the broken-hearted mutual reassurances that they would meet again as soon as possible. For Tom had never repeated his experience. He ached to do so. But the only way to achieve a similar result was, he thought, to re-enact the previous situation as closely as possible; and this had proved impossible.

Yet he still went to see Betty as much as he could. Even on a day such as this, with the sky a tight sheet of steel grey, and the east wind, a spiteful discomforter.

This time, he had chosen the plainest disguise of all. He had merely decided that he would go out for a bicycle ride and – as he wanted to go to Bothel, it was therefore necessary to pass by the Daltons' farm. If Mr Dalton should find him sitting on a dyke a quarter of a mile beyond the farm, then his second excuse would come into operation in the shape of a drawing-pad and a set of coloured chalks which had been carefully placed in his saddle-bag. Mr Gate – the art-teacher – had given them 'a country scene' as homework (and this was true – even though it was four months out of date). If Mr Dalton should catch Betty and himself talking, then this would be demonstrated as the natural occupation for two people one of whom knew the area, the other wishing to know it.

'I was asking her where the best place for a broad view was. Do you know?'

If Mr Dalton mentioned that he had been seen in the area more than occasionally, then Tom's answer would be the church at Bolton-Gate, on which he was making a special study as part of a book which his form were writing on the local history of the area. (Also true: Tom knew from his reading and the pictures that the nearer a liar was to the truth, the more successful he was bound to be.)

He felt secure. He also felt quite light-hearted – for none of his prepared alibis contradicted the truth in that painful way which made it so physically distressing for him to tell a lie.

He free-wheeled down the hill.

Perhaps it would happen today. He tried to call up the drum-roll of tinglings in his stomach – but it was too cold.

He slowed down. And then he stopped.

He looked over the bicycle carefully. It was a post-office bicycle

– ladies' model. It could belong to any one of six postwomen. Tom was certain that it was his mother's machine.

It was a measure of his confidence in his own plans that he never considered for a moment that his mother might be suspicious of his being there. Since the reading of the first lesson and its aftermath, Tom had not once mentioned Betty to his parents. Having no clues to his action on such days as he went to see Betty, his mother could draw no conclusions now – and he decided immediately that he would use her as an excuse to get inside the farmyard . . .

'I was just going to Bothel church to get some notes for Mr Tate's book – not his book, really, ours, but his idea – when I saw your bike and thought I'd come in to say hello.'

His mother introduced him to Mr Dalton.

'I've seen this lad before,' said Mr Dalton – but he ruffled Tom's hair in a way which assured the boy that he was referring to the time when he had drawn up beside his grandfather and himself as they were carting their last possessions back from the cottage.

They chatted about things in general.

And then Betty came out. Quite naturally, Tom was introduced to her. His face betrayed not the slightest expression. All four of them chatted together.

Just before they left, Mr Dalton said:

'Any time you want to come along here – just drop in. I could do with a big lad like yourself to give me a hand. And Betty needs someone her own age to play with.'

Tom thanked him and said that he might well come along – he liked farming . . .

He got off his bike and propped it against his mother's much heavier machine.

She was standing in the middle of the farmyard – talking to Mr Dalton just as Tom had imagined. He was slightly shocked, however, because they were laughing; standing close to each other and laughing loudly. This threw out Tom's calculations; it gave them a strength which made the possibility of his taking over the situation – as he had to – seem very remote. Their laughter was at odds with the afternoon – ignoring its grey sobriety and bullying promises – splitting the whole hearing area around them with their own lightning crack of spring laughter. Tom was an official of the responsibilities of a dreary autumn Saturday afternoon. Also, Mr Dalton had become associated with so many well-piled defensive attitudes, that to walk up to him with the excuse that he was curious to see his mother seemed the merest pretence. Their laughter died away. He shambled across the cobbled yard.

Worse. His mother was furious. She gave him that cold look in which all the anger later to be released was clearly signalled, frightening him both in its immediate impact and in its promised sequel.

'What are you doing here?'

Tom mumbled back.

'I was just doing local-history for Mr Tate at Bolton church and I saw your bike outside as I was going to Bothel for a ride.'

'He's often round these parts!' said Mr Dalton.

Tom's confidence slunk away in shame.

'Are you?' She had turned to face him; both of them faced him, side by side, like two pillars on a wall.

'Not very often.'

'Has a great deal of trouble with his bike! No punctures this time?'

'No.'

Anne again stared at him – but, evidently, she had decided to freeze all her questions for the moment.

'Mr Dalton and I were just talking about being at school together.'

Tom nodded.

Mr Dalton winked, largely.

'Can you imagine your mother in plaits?'

'No.'

Tom felt that he was going to cry. This had not happened to him for – months at least. He was completely helpless. He had cut right into the adult world and they had cut him right out of it. Besides, he knew that his mother would cross-question him – and he had no answers worked out for *her*.

'How's old Tom?' Mr Dalton asked of him.

'Very well, thank you.'

'He's very bad,' said his mother, crisply. 'I don't know what's come over him. He can't do anything for himself. But the doctor says there's nothing really wrong with him – nothing more than should be at his age. He just won't stir himself one little bit. He seems to have given up.'

Mr Dalton's face switched to serious.

'It's a terrible thing – age.'

Anne turned to reply to him. Tom noticed how fresh she looked. If she had not been his mother, he would have said that she was blushing. Also, he felt a complete intruder in the company of his mother and Mr Dalton – shut off from both of them, categorically.

'But he was so strong. Norman! When we were at Fell Cottage – he had his turns – but even then – he was as fit as you were.'

Mr Dalton sighed.

'Ay! He was a fine-looking feller – your grandfather.' He turned, very deliberately back towards Tom, having instinctively swung away from him to face Anne. 'When these two were out together – you would have thought they were – a young couple! And that wasn't long ago. Not very long ago at all.'

'I can't understand it. He's just – broken down.'

Anne seemed to be appealing to Mr Dalton for help. Tom knew that he was getting in the way. He had no part in their conversation. He stepped back and tried to think of a parting.

'I'll come back with you,' said Anne.

Tom stopped in his movements.

'It's all right – I can go.'

'You can go back with me . . . I've finished what I had to say to Mr Dalton.'

She nodded to him and propelled Tom to the gate. The farmer followed them and waved as they mounted their bicycles and rode off.

Nothing was said until they came to the bottom of the hill. His mother dismounted and Tom followed suit – even though he could have raced up the hill in third gear. She had the great brown-canvas post-bag slung over her shoulders. Tom wanted to offer to carry it for her – but he desisted; he did not want to be the first to break the silence.

They pushed their machines up the long hill. The fields were empty on either side of them. The wind had dropped slightly – and their efforts took the edge off its impact on them. The sky was still kneaded with clouds – but they moved only slowly – as if they had been distorted and shaped long ago in another world and were sailing across Cumberland simply to show off their power. The whole day was quiet and bare – but strong in the energies it could so patiently and so quickly release.

They reached the top of the hill without a word having been spoken. Tom was out of breath. The efforts of waiting for his mother to say something; pushing his bike, trying to work out his excuses and trying to settle a specific impression of what he felt about his mother and Mr Dalton – all had combined to make him pant for air.

His mother turned around and looked at him. Tom was surprised to see that the fury had left her face altogether: nor did its prophesied return seem to threaten. In fact, his mother looked worried.

Nevertheless, she spoke with all the authority Tom needed to make him feel that he was being told something he could not afford to forget.

'I want you to promise me that you won't go near that place again.'

Tom looked over her shoulder.

'But I haven't done anything.'

'I don't care what you have or haven't done: I want to make sure that you won't do anything in the future. Never again. I want that promise.'

Tom could not promise something he could not keep to. He

looked back. The farm was hidden by a sloping corner and trees – but he could see many of the fields which he knew like his own house; he could even see that particular field – beside the tarn. Where had Betty been? Had his mother already spoken to Mr Dalton about it all?

'I didn't know that your round covered Dalton's farm,' Tom ventured.

'It did today – for a good reason. But that's none of your business . . . How long has this been going on?'

'What?'

Again, Tom marvelled that she was keeping her temper. It encouraged him to fight back.

'Tom,' his name thrilled him, 'don't play about. You know perfectly well what I mean.'

He shook his head – donkey-like.

'I don't.'

He didn't. She had not told him – and so he could not know. He was not telling a lie.

She was leaning against her bicycle. She looked tired after the long walk up the hill.

'You're lying!' The softest slap of an accusation.

'No. I don't know what you mean. Why shouldn't I – come out round here if I want to?'

'You admit that you do come here.'

'I come *past* here – to go to Bothel and Bolton-Gate – or just for a ride or . . .'

'All right.'

She started to push her bicycle forward. Tom followed her, not knowing whether to get on or not. It was stupid to push downhill.

'All right,' she repeated. 'Don't tell me . . . Just keep away from Norman Dalton's farm. I want you to keep away – and that should be enough. I can't watch what you do all the time – but I can do – other things. And I will – if you go there – if I hear of you going there again.' She stopped.

'You mustn't, Tom. I won't have it.'

Tom was too confused by the pride which his mother's possessiveness called up in him to think of exploring her reasons for the decision. Besides – he could sense that she had little more to say – and she had dropped the idea of making him promise – without having forced him to do so. He was still free.

'And another thing,' she said, abruptly. 'I don't want your father to hear about this – unless I have to tell him – so we'll keep the whole business to ourselves. We needn't even say that we met.'

He agreed. They could have met in the town – on the road – anywhere except at the farm. That was easy.

'All right?'

He nodded. She dipped her leg through the V-frame of her bicycle and spun away down the hill. Tom let her race ahead – and then he followed her.

He had not promised anything.

His mind was in such a whirl that all that he could think of was the fight: other lines of information flashed on to the front of his brain like urgent telegrams, but he would not think, he would not think of what Arnold Jackson had said. It had burned a hole in his mind and his arms flailed wildly as if to beat out the flames.

Hard knuckles banged against his cheekbone, numbing it. He went forward, thrashing out his arms, stiff and bulbous in the heavy green blazer.

Arnold Jackson was three inches taller than he was.

Tom tried to stop those long arms poking their fists into his face. He grabbed them and pushed them down, trying to get a grip around his enemy. His arms were around Jackson's waist; he locked his fingers around his back and squeezed as tightly as he could – kicking out his feet to hook the other boy's ankles and topple him over.

Even though they were both the same age. Fifteen. Tom was Libra.

A fist stung his ear. His eyes smarted with salt and he dug his chin into Jackson's neck, trying to use its point as a spearhead. He stamped

159

on Tom's foot. Tom broke his grip and stumbled back. A wild, looping clout caught him on the shoulder and made him stumble even more precariously. Jackson came after him. Tom ducked, caught his knees – and heaved him into the air until he swung, suspended like a caber, and then he tossed him onto the ground.

The ground was muddy. Already there were three great shiny skids on his grey trousers. They stuck against his legs.

All around, there was a circle of excited faces: solid enough to keep the fight within sight, this circle would buckle and expand in any direction necessary for the struggle to be continued without interference. There were general shouts – no direct references – no one except the two fighters knew what it was all about.

Jackson fell flat on his back and Tom was on top of him before he could even twist over. He landed across his chest and hung on. Jackson bucked and kicked like a stallion. Tom got hold of his hands and tried to keep them still. Jackson's long legs swung over unexpectedly and almost pulled Tom backwards. He threw his body on to his opponent's face and smothered him. He could feel the mouth working against his blazer.

It was lunch-time. English in the afternoon. English with Mr Tate.

Tom had managed to force his knees on to Jackson's biceps. He leaned up from him. As soon as Jackson started to struggle – Tom bent down over him and covered his face again: this was repeated until Jackson gave up and lay quite still.

Tom's whole body was shuddering with effort. Then, for the first time since the fight had begun, he saw Jackson's face. Immediately, the same blood-thickened fury possessed him as had made him tear into the bigger boy in the first place. He wanted to kill him. He screwed his knees into his arms and bashed his forehead against Jackson's nose. He could see nothing. He thought that he was going to have one of his blackouts.

'Say it again!' he shouted. 'Say it again!'

Jackson turned his head to one side and said nothing. His nose was bleeding heavily and there was a small patch of ripped skin on his forehead.

'Say it again!' Tom dared.

Slowly, Jackson shook his head. For a second, Tom went completely weak with exhaustion. Feeling the loosened hold, Jackson bucked himself into a bow-curve. Tom immediately flattened him again and he gave up.

There was nothing else to be done. Carefully, Tom lifted himself away from his opponent and stood back a few yards, fists ready clenched in case of a counter-attack. Jackson got slowly to his feet. He stared at Tom for a moment and then turned away.

Immediately, Tom was surrounded by a gang of well-wishers; he bore with them only for as long as was absolutely necessary and then he went in one of the cubicles. It was no relief. He wanted to keep the blood-haze thick in his mind. He could not bear to hear Jackson's taunt – even from his own mind.

But it threatened, threatened like a snake at the back of his mind. He screwed up his eyes and pressed his forehead against the cold stones – trying desperately to hold it off.

Then it struck.

'Some of us know who our fathers are!'

That's what Jackson had said.

'Some of us know who our fathers are!'

It was not true. It was not true. And Tom would prove it was not true.

The hammer swung on to the anvil and Tom's hand was pincered blue. The car skidded, slid across the muddy road and bared its steaming snout at him before slamming against him and cutting him in half against a wall. Rat-tat-tat-tat-tat-tat-tat! Surrounded by broken buildings and shattered, flimsy glass, with machine-guns strafing him in all directions: bombers overhead; he looked through the smashed floorboards; the house had been skinned alive; only he was left – its nerve end. A bullet thudded into his shoulder and he spun around to come face-on to the slicing blade of an axe which swished silently towards his neck.

It was not true. It was not true.

Tom was in the English lesson and then he was on the road which would lead him home. He was at his door and, as usual, the door opened without effort because it was only locked after his father had come in from work. There was his grandfather. His mother and father were both still out at work: so he went to his bedroom to wait.

> *'Lives of great men*
> *All remind us.*
> *We can make*
> *Our lives sublime.'*

He read the notice over his bed, very carefully. He discovered that his right arm was still hooped through the strap of his satchel and so he crooked his elbow and let it slide down to the foot of his bed – and it was there that he worked. He sat down at it. Pasted in the top left-hand corner was his 'Ideal daily timetable' with each week-day evening neatly ruled off into special hours for this, special break-times, special 'cruising' times when he would read outside his subjects or revise. He was taking his 'O' levels in just eight months' time: everything had to be perfectly planned to bring him up to a peak. He had learned a lot from the training methods of England's 'middle-distance' runners.

Usually, he would take his books out of his satchel and pile them neatly on the bed beside him. This he had done without even thinking about it.

His mother and father would not be in for another hour or two. He decided to work – to keep those words out of his mind. Yet, somehow, they did not press against it. Nor could he feel their hidden force. He was calm. It might have been any other day.

But his work belied this. Tom's pattern of work usually fashioned itself into long periods of dreaming or wishful thinking and short, violent bursts of activity or ambitious planning. His inability to concentrate all the time shamed him – but, in a way, he accepted it as a necessary duality. Now, however, he forged through his set homework like a drill through softwood. Everything was clipped into place without the slightest pause or fuss. On no occasion did he tilt back his chair into a rocking position and ride into one of his mists or nightmares. He was soon finished his set tasks – and so he doubled up on these, and then he did what he could of the next night's work.

There was no exhilaration in all this. Nor was there panic or the forced movement which counters anxiety or fury. There was precision and speed: that was all.

The only omission to his evening ritual had been his reluctance to unstrap his watch and place it at the top right-hand corner of his desk. Somehow, it had seemed to be tempting fate too far; as if the absolute imitation of normality could result only in an impasse between his new and his old self. For he was changed: that he knew; even his actions were different – right through to his handwriting which leaned further over to the right than ever before, dangerously angled. Without the watch, he could enter into his working kingdom without hindrance, his difference symbolised in that one omission.

As a result, he took no account of the time. When he looked at his watch – it pointed to ten minutes past eight. He must have been in his room for four hours!

Refusing to consider the reasons why he had not been called for supper – he tidied away his books, neatly, marked down the number of hours he had worked in his notebook, went to the bathroom to wash his hands and comb his hair – and then walked downstairs with conscious firmness.

'Your mother's out.'

'Edward spoke from his armchair. He was cutting out some plans from a magazine. Tom's grandfather was sitting almost on top of the hearth, whittling a piece of wood into a ship; the shavings flaked slowly from his penknife and he chased them into the fire with soft breath. The table was laid for one.

'Why didn't you shout for me?'

Edward looked up, smiling.

163

'We did, many a time . . .'

'I didn't hear you!'

'I know.'

Tom persisted.

'How do you know?'

Edward warmed to a smug confidence: the episode he was about to relate had obviously moved him very deeply.

'You didn't even hear me?' he said, tantalisingly.

'You?'

'Yes.'

'When?'

His father smiled even more broadly.

'When I came up to see what you were doing.'

'You came upstairs?'

'Yes. *And* I opened your door. *And* I looked inside. You never even noticed me! By God! You stick at those books of yours all right! I'll give you that!'

Tom strained to remember any indication which might have informed him – however obliquely – that his father had actually been in his room while he was working. He could think of none.

'Are you sure you came up?'

'Yes. Oh yes!' Edward settled back in his chair and gazed at the wall in front of him as if he were looking at a screen. 'Now, let me see. You had your blazer on. I noticed that because you usually take it off. Your bag-satchel was on your bed-end pointing that way.' He squeezed his hands around an invisible concertina and aimed it at his father-in-law. 'Now then. There were three piles of books beside you. Now let me think – just a minute . . .'

'All right. I believe you.'

Tom had to stop his father from going on about it. He sniffed offensively, went across to the table and began to eat what was left out for him.

He spoke twice during his meal. Once to wish his grandfather 'good night' when the old man suddenly lifted to his feet and made for the staircase.

The second time, he spoke from no conscious intention but rather from some sudden impulse which quickened his tongue to blurt out:

'What's Mam out for on a night like this?'

His father shrugged his shoulders and attempted no explanation. Tom was again aware – as he had been increasingly frequently over the past few months – that his parents had something to say to each other which deliberately excluded him. The fact that the normal response – 'she likes walking' – was no longer brought out with demonstrative assurance revived and sharpened yet again the intimation of uneasiness which he had collected in so many fragmentary ways. If she was not walking, what was she doing?

He deliberately refrained from following his question up.

When he had finished eating, he washed up his dirty dishes. Then he cleared the table and put the soft green cloth back on it.

He sat down in his grandfather's chair and looked at his father. 'Some of us know who our fathers are.'

But he could feel nothing.

He bent down and tidied up some shavings which had fallen into the hearth. His fist crunched them into spiky powders and then he opened his hand and scattered them on the flames.

He took to his horse and galloped towards 'The Saddle'. The rain lashed, lashed at his face with its long, wet thongs, curling around his neck and lacerating his cheeks. He howled out, louder and louder he howled out, but the rain and the wind deafened his words into nothing. An enormous boulder tilted on its balanced point and then thundered down on him. He did not flinch but dug, kicked his bloody spurs into the horse's flanks and charged at it. The boulder came straight towards him – hailing a cloud of stones and scree above its head like a lasso. Tom bent his head and rode faster, faster, up the hill, into the stone.

'Mr Dalton sends his regards!'

The words came from nowhere.

Edward shrank away. He looked at Tom in terror: the scissors pointed across to the empty chair.

Again, Tom said:

'Mr Dalton sends his regards!'

Edward moved his mouth awkwardly, the magazine and scissors fell down on to his knees with his hands.

'When?'

Tom leaned forward and looked at his father as clearly as he could.

'When I saw him last Saturday – with Mam!'

Edward said nothing.

Tom leapt across the kitchen floor, grabbed the scissors and stabbed him in the face – again and again and again! His father never moved.

Tom's mind ached to say more – but it was desert-dry and he felt it crack open with black, jagged fissures, under the strain.

'When I saw him last Saturday – with Mam!'

'With Mam' 'With Mam' 'With Mam!!' The words echoed and re-echoed around the hollow of the room – whipping from wall to wall like a scorpion's tail, stinging Tom with their vicious point each time they struck into his ear.

Edward said nothing.

Tom began to shake: his whole body shuddered as if with extreme cold.

Quietly, his mother came in through the front door.

'Hello!'

Tom turned to her – winded with surprise – and then he jumped to his feet, spun around and darted over to the staircase. He glanced back once. His mother was gaping at him – astonished. His father had not moved: had not even turned.

'Some of us know who our fathers are.'

He locked himself in his bedroom.

CHAPTER FOURTEEN

Tom sat in the empty church as small as a pebble on a broad beach. Winter sun eked through the windows of the south wall, but its force was barely strong enough to take it into the nearest pews; the dark-grained December gloom of the church absorbed its light without showing any effect.

He was half-way down the nave, sitting beside the cross-topped rod of the churchwarden, calmed and rested by the great bare silence of the huge building. There were flowers on the altar – even at this time of year.

'Hello, Tom.'

He turned; stretching up into the air beside him was the Rev Pursur. His rest was over.

'Don't let me disturb you. I'm glad to see you using the church as your home.'

'I'd finished,' Tom replied.

The vicar sighed and smiled gently.

'Finished,' he echoed. 'Sometimes I wish *I* could use that word – and mean it. But we are never finished. Neither you, nor I, can let ourselves finish anything.'

Tom looked up at him. The vicar was so far away. If he put out his hand it would be like looking at it through the wrong end of a pair of binoculars. It would seem to stretch so far – but it would never touch its target.

The boy said nothing. He accepted the interruption as part of the risk he had taken by coming into the church.

Tom thought that the vicar was going to sit down beside him, and he leaned against the end of the pew to prevent it.

'Have you thought any more over the decision to become a server?'

Tom nodded.

'Thought in the direction I would like, I hope?'

Tom sat quite still.

Then the vicar began a long monologue. How disappointed he had been when Tom had failed – he would not say 'failed' – when Tom had decided against becoming a server. How doubly hard to bear this blow had been because of Tom's qualities: his enthusiasm, his dedication, his intelligence. Tom, he said, had been one of his 'brightest hopes'.

'And then I began to think,' the vicar continued, 'to wonder whether this disappointment I felt was not selfishness on my part. I wanted you for one of my servers. But was it right for you – at that time. Might not those whom He has most carefully chosen be those He tests most harshly? Might not your reconsideration be an act – not of weakness, but of strength?'

We did not always know what was planned for us. We did not always see what God perceived in us. Perhaps He had seen pride and decided to try it. That was unlikely. Perhaps, more likely, he had seen courage and so presented an opportunity for its display. That was his own interpretation – as Tom's vicar.

'I won't ask you now for a definite "yes" or "no". I'm not asking you anything. Call it "thinking ahead".'

Tom was quite unmoved by the compliments heaped on him, and acutely depressed by the vicar's hopeful words.

He stood up and, finding himself almost chest to chest with the vicar, pulled away sharply.

'I'm thinking it over,' he said.

'Good,' said the vicar. 'A decision long thought out is invariably that longest held to.'

'I'll make up my mind as soon as I can.'

'No rush. No hurry. No worry! As long as the thought is with you – within you.'

'It is,' said Tom. 'I've got to go.'

'But of course.' Although he was not blocking the way, the vicar stood to one side and swept the boy past him.

Outside, Tom walked out of the church square and away from the main street, making for the country towards Lowmoor road.

Lies! Everything he said was lies! He had not the slightest intention of becoming a server. The mere thought of it made him feel filthy with guilt. If he were honest, he would stop going to church altogether: he had no place there.

Lies! His parents had said nothing. That was a lie! He had asked them nothing – and, the first missed opportunity leading to the second and the third and the fourth and an endless, hollow procession of mocking silences and empty exchanges – he had never found the courage to ask. His lack of courage was a lie! If you did not admit to a truth, then you were living a lie. He could not bear his own body.

His father had not gone to work since that evening. Three days had passed since then. No one said anything about his father's absence. The doctor was not called. If his parents spoke to each other, they did not look at each other: and whenever they looked at each other, they said nothing.

All that Edward did was to sit in his chair. This pose matched that of Tom's grandfather. Like abandoned shapes of old clothes, they balanced the fireplace. The fire could go out between them without either of them noticing it. Edward's magazine and scissors were the sisters of old Tom's penknife and wood: sad tokens of a past activity.

The house was still with the portent of what had happened. And yet, the result of Tom's thrust was so carefully disregarded that its non-being sometimes persuaded against anything having changed at all. No one said a word in place.

Tom walked along the dour road. He was covered with crawling black lice which bit and sucked at his skin, drawing all blood away from him. His skin trembled with the passion which could not find a reason to explode and so broiled inside him with scaly heat. There was no reason for walking along the road: no reason for stopping: no reason for breathing in and out: no reason for the road itself.

As before, he felt himself sliding towards that double consciousness, double vision, double existence which, previously, only the nub of wonder had linked together. To awaken that nub to its real strength by shouts or by spasms of activity – that had been his method of joining himself together again.

But now he welcomed the rift. It released him from the weight of the imprinted secret which had swollen inside his mind like some poisonous bulb. He welcomed his own division. He would make no effort to rejoin himself.

He stumbled and meandered along the road as if he had been wounded.

The rain pressed down the grey slate of Thornton, watering it with so heavy a dowse of damp misery that the houses huddled together like the sheep in the folds of the surrounding fells, and shivered coldly with the banging of doors and the tightening of windows. The one or two darkly mackintoshed forms which scurried across the empty, shiny streets were no more than wet sparrows hopping along a rock. And then the evening came to thicken the blank greys of wall and pavement to black; and the street lights flickered weakly like dispirited candles; and candles were sought out in the houses of the old and careful in case of what might happen on such a night.

All who had business made it their business to transact it within walls. Those corners which were usually clotted with groups of men were now bare. On Dalton's farm, the rain hissed down like a warning against too much hope; no real work could be done until it eased. The tarn prickled and chopped unceasingly as the rain battered down on to it. The roof of Fell Cottage had already begun to crumble away and Tom sat in the corner of his old bedroom, watching the thin lines of water slide through their holes and splatter the bare boards. The walls glistened with damp and the thick, cream wallpaper was slowly sagging down to the skirting-board. Its dismal aspect comforted him.

He had had to climb in through an upstairs window. The doors were locked with new locks and all the windows tightly fastened: but he had always had his own way of getting in.

Already, he had waited for an hour for the rain to stop. He could not make up his mind. He vastly preferred the rain to the indoor damp. He gave himself five minutes. Three minutes, one minute, ten minutes. But he was stuck fast.

He might have been stiffened with the paralysis of wide-awake sleep. He was trapped in the same locked equilibrium which would fasten on him, sometimes, when he knew that he had to go to the lavatory; he could not decide not to go, nor could he go. His mouth was half-open under the double pressure of dry panic and expectant ecstasy. There was only one way out. He would have to wait for an unthinking moment and then lunge himself into a decision, pulling himself out of the dissipated fathomings or intense immobility, filling himself with life like a pail pulling out of the bottom of a well.

So, eventually, he jumped to his feet. He could not go outside all at once. First, he had to prowl around his old house – now so securely bolted by his uncle Henry. His grandfather's bedroom was tiny, and pitiful; untidy scraps of paper had assembled from nowhere; a wall crack had split open the paper in a great zig-zagging scar. Tom shut the door on it, quickly. The rain drummed on the roof: ten thousand fingers in a mile-wide drum.

He walked across the short landing to his mother's bedroom. He had already decided that he need not go downstairs; this second visit was a formality; the associations between his grandfather's bedroom and the old man himself had reminded him of his new home, tangibly; he had been out for a very long time – he had to get back.

He opened his mother's door and looked in. What he saw in front of him drew him right into the room. There was a mattress in the corner opposite the door with four khaki blankets neatly folded on top of it. The walls were not damp: he noticed the paraffin heater. There was a drum of paraffin beside it and a box of Captain

Webb matches beside the drum. That was all. The rest of the room was as bare as the rest of the house. Yet these few objects made Tom feel, immediately, that he was being pushed back by a great crowd which congregated on that spot every day of the week. He had intruded. He touched nothing and backed his way to the door, listening for any sound which would indicate that he was not alone. Sounds began to arrive from everywhere. The house was creaking with an orchestra of noises.

He slipped back into his own bedroom, through the window, along the slippery branch, and down on to the ground. It squelched rudely under his feet.

He tried to work out an explanation for the mattress as he walked back. The obvious ones came and went with dutiful speed. He hoped that it was the old tramp: deaf and dumb. It was no use searching for an extraordinary explanation; he was not sufficiently interested.

He enjoyed being plastered by the rain. It flattened his hair and soused his clothes until they lost all resistance to it and the water came right through on to his body. His feet were already soaked from the drop off the branch, and he plodded through every puddle that was in front of him. The rain splashed and splattered against his face like a well-aimed spray from a hosepipe. He welcomed it. Its steady force freshened him and by the time he arrived home – having passed no one on the streets – by now, almost pitch-black – he was steady, if not secure.

'Have you seen your father?'

His mother spun around from the fireplace. His grandfather slowly gazed at him. Tom suddenly felt a sharp jab of frantic hatred for his mother. He would not tell her anything.

'No,' he replied.

'Go and dry yourself!'

She turned her back on him. His grandfather continued to stare. Tom shut the kitchen door and stepped back into the little hat-box which served as hall, cloak-room and foot-scraping area – and there, he stripped off. He hung his clothes on the small laundry rail, set up a makeshift water-collecting arrangement with pans and paper and then ran upstairs to dry and change. His mother had not remarked on his being drenched; she was in a mood; she would say nothing about the mess in the entrance, or she would blow up; he did not care, either way.

He was back downstairs within a few minutes, rumpled and glowing from the change. The kitchen was stuffy with the heat from a high-banked fire, but within seconds, Tom was cool, wary. He was served his supper and ate it in silence. The table was cleared after one word: 'Finished?' He nodded.

His mother came back in and leaned her forearms against the low mantelpiece. Her body bent in towards the fire. Her hair was loose, coming right down on to her back.

Old Tom looked from mother to son and back again, several times, his head darting almost briskly, his eyes, when he looked at his grandson, resuming the tone of their former liveliness. He spoke clearly.

'Your father went oot after his tea. Just afore that rain. He hasn't cum back.'

The old man paused. The rain throbbed down, quieter now in the darkness, thudding against the streets and buildings with a sound like a tractor-engine. He looked at Anne – without response – and went on:

'Yer mother's been across to Blacklock's. Denis there said that he'd been in't 'Lion'; then he'd gone oot. Yer mother's been to one or two other places: he doesn't seem to be anywhere.'

'He's bound to be in one of them.'

His grandfather leaned back in his chair and shook his head.

'Now A'h wouldn't say that. He knows he can find drink here.'

And the old man sat bolt upright with his new intelligence: the achievement of arriving at a point at which an answer was demanded had excited him into the appearance of energy. Tom looked at his grandfather's fire-burning flushed and thin face, winced again at the fat blue veins and brown stains which spread

173

over his hands like the ribs of clothless gloves, and then he turned away and heaped his miseries on himself until he was stuck fast in a thick stupor.

The kitchen did not swell and contract as it sometimes did. Things were in their usual place. Tom felt the lack only of something to determine him as to what he should do. His father's absence had taken the substance away from the shadows of his nightmares. There was no foundation.

His father! The words popped a tiny explosion in the boy's mind: far away. He could not examine them. He was grateful for the silt which kept their impact so far away from him: he could not think about his father.

Again, time swept on leaving Tom stranded: unaware of its passage; but off from its new significance.

'Twenty-past ten! Twenty-past! If he'd been drinkin' he'd a bin in long since,' the old man said.

Tom agreed, uncomprehendingly; said nothing.

His mother swung around from the fireplace, went across to the hall and came back into the kitchen, pulling on her coat. Her face had been scorched by the fire, and the coolness of the hall had immediately softened the heat with moisture; she looked as if she had been crying. Her hair was dispirited and bedraggled on her forehead.

'I know where he is,' she said. She looked at her father as if she wanted him to discredit her certainty. He was bolt upright; his frame quivering its thin flesh with the anticipation of action; but he waited for her to instruct him.

'I should have guessed long ago. I did, but I wouldn't admit it.'

She seemed unwilling – even unable – to move. She spoke sadly and with such deep tiredness in her voice that Tom wanted to make her sit down and rest. But his curiosity was far stronger than his concern: he listened for further explanations.

'You know then, eh?' His grandfather's head on its dry turkey-neck jerked up and down like a bird's.

She replied without looking at either of them.

'He'll be at Norman's.'

The old man nodded vigorously. Any answer would have been the expected one. Tom contracted to one still point of icy cold.

'I'll get Henry to take me there in his car.'

Still she was reluctant to move.

Norman Dalton! An icicled shriek opened itself silently in Tom's heart and then bit its jaws together. Norman.

His mother stepped forward towards her father.

'You stay here and – look after him.'

She turned.

'Norman'll kill him.'

The open door let in the clean hissing sound of rain and then it banged to.

'He's a good fella, your father. A good fella. He puts up wid a lot. He's a good fella.'

Muttering to Tom, the old man trundled around the kitchen in search of his clothes. He had been so long without a regular succession of clothes that now he behaved as a tramp in front of a spilling wardrobe. He could neither decide what he needed to wear nor what would fit him.

Tom waited for him to be out. The old man had started his foraging the minute his daughter had left.

'Aah'll see that Norman. Aah'll give him Norman! Yer father's a good man.'

He stopped for a second, arms spread out in his half-donned raincoat.

'A good man!'

Tom closed his eyes and hoped that his grandfather would have disappeared when he opened them.

He was tugging at his boot-laces.

'Yer mother dissn't know what she's at! Yer mother's just as daft as everybody else . . . Aah'll give him Norman!'

The lace broke. The old man jumped to his feet in irritation. His arms flailed around in the windmill temper that had once been common with him. Now, however, it seemed that their efforts would disjoint him altogether.

'Damn the bloody boots!'

He took courage from his swearing as from drink. Impatience and indecision boiled on to his face, scattering out so many contradictory expressions that he looked tangled in a mesh of fast knots. Suddenly, he whirled around and shouted:

'Aah'll git them, the buggers, Aah'll git them!'

Tom held his breath. The door slapped against its frame three times before it closed properly. The boy sighed with relief.

Within a minute he was out of the back door and in the makeshift shed where he kept his bike. He tugged his cycle-cape out of his saddle-bag and burrowed inside it until he found the hole for his head.

The rain would be behind him all the way to Dalton's farm. Already it had flattened the cape against his back. He went out of his way and cycled towards his uncle Henry's house first. As he approached it, the car rose out through the gates, a great, roaring night-fighter, beaming out its headlights on to the enemy. Tom swung into the pavement and stopped; it twisted on to the road and shot away, the two wet red reflectors growing dimmer each second.

He went after them.

He concentrated solely on going as fast as he could.

He had to be there to see what happened.

The old man must have taken the path through the hills: Tom did not come across him.

The rain pelted against his back with one constant slap. So many rhythms, so many pellets of rain hitting against him so quickly that it was a single pressure.

This large, cold palm pushed him right up the great hill. He soared over its crest and pedalled furiously on the wet road. The dynamo rubbed so fiercely against his tyre that it almost dried it out. In front of him was the ray from his headlight: a stabbing cone, a lane of thick yellow light, piercing both darkness and rain, pointing its bearer to the Daltons' farm.

He was near the corner at the foot of the hill. Water ran across the road as across a window-pane. He would not slow down. His hands had been cupped underneath their grips to include the brakes in their holds; now he wrapped them tightly around the slippery rubber sheaths. His knees smacked against the sagging oilskin cape. His headlight flashed out its whiteness. He kept pedalling. He was water. He slowed the machine over to the right and swirled into the corner. He was almost on his side. The skin on his face was stretched back, aching back over his bones.

He was round! He swung the bike upright and flung his feet against the pedals, more keeping up with them than pushing them.

Then he free-wheeled to slow down. Still going too fast, he had to squeeze his brakes to slow down. His light picked out the bare gap of fence on his left; the farm was just around the next corner. He stopped, dismounted, unfastened his dynamo and walked along to Dalton's.

There was neither light nor sound. The rain had by now become a natural accompaniment to his thoughts. He was at the gate before he had had time to think about drawing back. There was a faded glow at one of the side-windows. That was all.

He was lost. His expectation had been so enormous that he could not face the emptiness of reality. He would wait for something to happen. Pushing his bike across the road, he hid it among some bushes, concealed himself beside it and refused to think of anything except the incident, the showdown he had come for.

He was as light as a flake of snow. The earth spun around smoothly and violently on its God-seen axis and Tom swooped gladly into its movement. He would wait.

His mind was blocked – save for its concentration of the necessary battle. If that were already over – then he would be all the more certain after some time spent waiting. Nothing, however, as far as he could see, had in the least disturbed the pattern of the night. He could not feel that anything had happened.

This was the first time that he had been outside Dalton's farm without thinking of Betty. She was another subject, locked away.

Everything was put behind bars. Everything else could wait. Except this.

He had to know this. He dare not let himself feel how much he had to know this. He would smash rocks against mountains if he unleashed himself on this.

His grandfather was already through the gate when he noticed him. He stood up, looking over the bushes for a better view. The old man disappeared around the corner to the back door.

Tom cursed out loud. He had not thought of looking around the back! The car could be drawn up there; they could all be in the house; he could have been at the window, listening.

Now he listened as hard as he could. But without time for anything important to have happened, his grandfather reappeared from behind the corner, with Mr Dalton. An outside light was switched on. Tom saw his grandfather gesticulating wildly, frail in every movement. The farmer seemed to be trying to persuade him to do something. He grabbed the old man's arm and began to march him over to his car. The old man struggled – Tom heard the far end of some shouts – and broke free; then he ran to the gate. Mr Dalton came after him – but Tom's grandfather was already on the road. Tom ducked back into the bushes. Then his grandfather's steps were cut short and Tom knew that he had crossed the stile and was on the path which led back to Thornton through the fields. Mr Dalton stood at the gate for a few moments. A raincoat hung around him, unfastened. Tom could not move. He just watched him.

Finally, the farmer seemed to come to a decision. He turned and marched back up the yard. Tom expected him to get into his car, but he went right around the corner.

The light went off.

Tom waited some more time.

But that was all that happened.

He took a long time to cycle back – heading right into the rain.

CHAPTER FIFTEEN

The house was a thoroughfare, everyone passed through to see what death would claim. The door was always open and the mud of the streets trailed through the kitchen – up the stairs like the brutal first scatterings of death – soon to patter down on to the coffin, then to thud, then to seal its new wood in the wet church-yard. Everyone came with relief that it was not them, and left with anxiety that it might be soon. The junketings of a barren festival filled out the last days of life; those closest to the sleeping body, jostled each other in companionless solitude.

At first, it was a decent drawn-out affair. The old man was strong, the doctor said, and though he was dying, he was not yet dead; not yet, not yet. Soon? Who knows? But the vicar was prepared – for he had worked in the churchyard until – never mind that now – for he had worked in the churchyard. The vicar's bustling, blousy robes filled out the small rooms like a tent in an attic, coloured. Never did his finery, embroidery, elaboration, liturgy, seem more out of place now. Now that old Tom Paislow was lying, a distant form under mounded sheets, staring with glistening eyes at the white ceiling; not wanting to die, not wanting to die. But the vicar was prepared – and, as the only one of them in that position – he was welcome to come and try to give meaning to the inexplicable – and welcome to go when he had done.

Tom made the acquaintance of many-a-years-lost relation who could not – in this case – claim suddenness as his excuse and who mounted a bus, now reconciled, happy in duty to witness the end of the seed of his seed. And came with a waistcoat or black dress – already – for none else was so fitting, so smart; and lifted the cloth-cap while mounting the stairs – 'mind them, Sarah'. She scrambled up, heavy, to bed. A different bed from the first; a bed thickly canopied with tributes from life.

So many who knew him. From this farm and that they rode in in their carts, in their cars, in their clean-washed fresh skins to look once again. And the face smiled its thin smile with water at lip-edges and water on worn cheeks and horror in the clenched, locked fist, stiffened-fingered fist, under the sheets.

He was dying slowly, silently.

Found in a field at four in the morning. Battened by rain and coated with mud. Unconscious. Found by no direct relation: Henry. Henry, who had been in the kitchen when Tom had come back – with Edward and Anne and the fractured atmosphere of a violent argument. They had not told him anything; nor had they asked him more than the one question.

'Where's your grandfather?'

Henry had gone out with Edward to look for him. His mother had sent him to bed. Nothing had been explained.

Tom had slept late into the next morning. He had come down-stairs to find the doctor in possession of the fireplace and his father, unshaven, wild-looking, eating his breakfast in his shirt sleeves – a thing that he never did.

His grandfather's illness had been briefly and finally explained. Double pneumonia. With scarcely a decent pause, the doctor had answered an unasked question. No chance.

The whirl of the last days had started up. Like a rude, incessant chant, it had beaten out its meaning inside Tom's head, day after day. Everything else became part of the illness. What was most important – and so most likely to be painful or disturbing – that was forgotten; what was trivial was cherished. The past was inverted and its great question mark was no more than a tiny stump at the bottom of a steep hill.

Tom felt the dance grow around him. He found himself joining in – being the messenger boy, the shopping-boy, the tea-maker.

All this preserved him from the sadness of that small room. His grandfather lay there with hardly a movement. He asked for nothing at all. He neither stared at people harshly to fix them with the terror of his situation, nor did he lean into their sympathies and mingle in their comfortings. If his eyes shone, then the tears came from some ageless source which took no account of his feelings: for he was patiently waiting to die.

When he did speak – it was to make some request that something be tidied up. He was anxious that Tom should have his workshop tools. His gun was to go to his eldest son, Arthur, a man Tom remembered seeing only once before. He asked that his clothes be given to the church for the next rummage sale, and finally he called for his 'desk'. This was a large tin box which only Anne knew where to find. He opened it with a key which was standing in the lock and took out a soft, dirty layer of banknotes which he laid on the bed in front of his daughter, nodding to her without a word. Tom cried without a sound. Then the old man took out some letters, a few coins, two medals, a small wooden box which he put to one side without examination and, finally, some photographs.

At this point, he called out for Tom. The boy went over and sat on the wooden chair which stood by the head of the bed. The smell of medicines and ointments lifted thickly into Tom's face – but he took one deep breath and then ignored them. They went through the photographs. There was one, hardly visible, brown and curly-edged, of the old man's parents: innocent and white-haired, piercing the fading brown with their steady eyes. There was a photograph of the old man himself when he had been at the mines: squashed in the middle of about forty black-faced and grimy men – all with stern faces, all with their arms around each other's shoulders. There was a photograph of Mr Paislow's wedding: bride and groom standing at attention with never a sympathetic touch or glance or line of movement between them.

Of his eight children, the old man had photographs of six. Anne

181

had been too young to have her photograph put in the box: Joseph had disappeared for good – without ever having had his photograph taken. For the rest, Tom was given short biographies with comments which were as the unalterable judgments made on a child as soon as he makes any definite move. When the photographs were all gone through, they were put back in the box and the box was put by the side of the bed.

He did not fight for life, but he came from a family and traditions which had so long fought for any life it had gained that his impulses held him alive in spite of his apparent surrender. His skin was so textured with the stripes of the earth that it seemed he would live for as long as the ground he walked on. And yet he had gone to bed to stay there, and Tom waited for the news almost with hope – quickly checked – for then he could release the feelings which at present had to be camouflaged by cheerfulness.

Those nine days muffled themselves into an age. Tom was considered old enough to know all the facts about his grandfather and so he found himself checking the pain he felt, with imitation of the newsy concern his elders seemed to show most of the time. This was another brake on him. And the feelings themselves – thus held back – were, in themselves, largely a protection against the question which had been diverted before it had been posed.

In the last two days, Tom's grandfather racked the house with his coughing. No one could sleep. The breath rattled out of him, shaking his body, battering him without pause. Anne was up and downstairs with dishes of hot water – laced with ointments, with clean, dry sheets and steaming hot water bottles, with the tiny portion of food which he would now eat.

Now, Tom was kept away from the room. He passed it as he came down for his breakfast; he re-passed it as he went into his bedroom after school, and again, late at night. There were always towels hanging on the bannister outside the room. Only his mother and the doctor rushed up and down the stairs now. The vicar still came every morning after the early service, with communion, but Tom was out by then and he did not see him.

There was no corner of the house which did not seem to be a corner of that one room. The tea-pot was always hot – ready for anyone who came in. Tess, now much fatter and grey, lay in the kitchen in front of the fire and whined to herself.

Tom finally enjoyed a long sleep. When he went downstairs the next morning the light was on, the blinds drawn.

His grandfather was dead.

CHAPTER SIXTEEN

'There's no earthly reason why I shouldn't, now.'

'What would you do?'

'I would find something.'

Anne flopped back in her chair, impatiently. The argument had been going on, picking up and relapsing again like the recurrent scratching at a sore, ever since she had come in from work. Edward had not gone back to the factory – first a letter, then his cards had been sent him: neither had been acknowledged. The death of his father-in-law had, however, changed him in one respect: he was now clean and tidy once more. But his clothes sat on him uncertainly, as they do on convalescents.

Tom had come downstairs from his homework as soon as he had heard the argument. He stayed to listen without any discouragement. They practically ignored him.

'Look,' Edward went on, 'there never has been anything for me in Thornton. You know that. I was too well known to make a fresh start. And that's just what I needed.'

Tom stared at him. Edward was fighting hard. He had been drinking, as usual, but he had carefully stopped while it was acting as an ally. He neither fidgeted nor mumbled. Tom could see fear in his eyes, sometimes, but that fear only seemed to drive him forward more purposefully. Anne had not been allowed to disrupt his line of attack by turning her temper on to him. He was determined to win. Tom could not help himself from being on Edward's side.

He went on—

'And I haven't said much about this – but it hasn't been easy with Henry doing so well. I wouldn't ask him for anything – but maybe it would be better if I had done. When you've a relative in his position, nobody else thinks they need to do anything for you.' He paused, but Anne said nothing. 'I mean, there've been at least three jobs – three promotions – that I should have got down at the factory – and I deserved them – but they never came. Not that I wanted Henry to do anybody else down because of me. But they seem to think that, if your own won't help you, then they needn't. I can see their point.'

'Henry didn't have to ask anybody for help.'

'No. But be fair, Anne. He had his father's business to go into. There again, he had a better war than I had. He was luckier there.'

'Luckier!'

'Luck has a lot to do with getting on. I've never had any. There again, though, I'm not setting myself up against Henry. I'm not the man he is – in some ways – and I admit it. But I know I'm a better man than I'll ever have a chance to be in this place – and I'm leaving it. I am, you know. I've had enough.'

'What if I say no?'

'I just hope you won't.'

Edward looked at her like a little boy waiting for his mother's permission to go out and play. This seemed to infuriate Anne more than anything he had said.

'You'll never do anything wherever you go! You live in a dream of your own! You haven't changed one bit since the first minute I set eyes on you. What makes you think you can work all these miracles by taking us all two or three hundred miles away?'

'I can try.'

Edward was red in the face – but his words were still steady, almost sharp.

'You tried before.'

'When?'

'When you went to London.'

'I was nothing but a lad then.'

185

'And you're nothing of a man now!'

Tom hated his mother.

'I'm going to try it. There's nothing for me here.'

'Well, there's nothing for me anywhere else. Do you think that I'm going to be dragged off on one of your stupid schemes just because . . .'

'Because what?'

This was the centre of it. Tom held his breath. His mother's face tightened and she proceeded to batter down both question and questioner.

'Edward, you've been giving me this "changing" business ever since the day you were demobbed. You've done not one thing since then that proves you can change anything except your mind. You can do that well enough. I've never known anybody as good as you are at doing that! And you've changed nothing else. All you've managed to do is get yourself involved with Carlin until you're running about after him like his little dog. And you've lost your job. Now then. Listen to me. If you think that I'm going to put myself in your hands in somewhere I don't know – *you* certainly won't know it – and scratch and scrape a house together, not knowing whether I'm going to know where next door is before his lordship decides that he needs another change – well, you can think again. I'm telling you. I've had enough of all this.'

'What if I decide to go anyway?'

'You do that! I certainly won't stop you. But don't expect me to come after you. I won't.'

Edward paused. Then he looked down at the carpet.

'I'm not staying here, you know. I've had enough of all this.'

'And I'm not leaving.'

Again, Anne seemed to check herself from jumping up in a rage. Edward's head dropped even further and he whispered his next sentence.

'If I go, then, I go on my own?'

'You do.'

The reply was shot back at him immediately. He lifted his head. Tom saw that he was crying.

186

'All right then, Anne,' he said. 'All right then. I will go. On my own. I'll go.'

The kitchen was as bare as a cell. Without people, without a fire, without noise, it was a strange place. Tom had not been able to sleep. His room was too well-known for him to forget everything. In the kitchen, a new room in its early morning emptiness, he could, perhaps, throw off the heavy, pointless shifting and swirling weight of thoughts which had pressed upon his mind ever since he had gone to bed.

There had been no alternative. His mother had gone out soon after Edward's final declaration that he would leave. Edward himself had been so miserable in his appearance that Tom had felt that he could not demand anything of him.

The boy sat down in his usual chair at the table. He tried to make himself think of his grandfather by looking at the old man's chair: but he could feel, and so, in his present state, think nothing.

He wanted to keep steady. He had been told nothing – and so while he could imagine, he could be sure of nothing. He was glad of this. It prevented him from facing the truth – which he feared. He made plans as to what he would do when that time would come – but they were no more than castles of matchsticks.

They had admitted to nothing. The unacknowledged secret bedded itself underneath their lives like rotten matter. Its smell pervaded each breath of their exchanges; its power contained their action with the promise of its effect.

The death of the old man had been an incident which could explain all the differences between them. They used it as their protection. And, meanwhile, the unexplained clamour of that night was less heard of than the echo of a dumb man.

Tom was so confused that he could see no way in which he could straighten himself out. It had gone past the stage of a straightforward innocent question, and yet the affair was far from being thought so harmless that it could finally be explained.

His father's decision had broken the spell. Tom had to do something. He had spent all the night considering what that should be.

He was cold, but he did not notice it. Outside, the sky was pulling up the morning behind a large awning of murky, grey clouds. The boy could hear the soft-boned moans of warm bodies as they rolled out of sleep and out on to the freezing floors. Everywhere, people were huddled in ones and twos, hugging themselves into themselves, happy in the bliss or chaos of their greatest privacy. Soon, they would be up against each other once again, forced to pass judgments, make decisions, reveal what the night had put a pause on, conceal what their dreams had revealed. They would walk around, hiding their secrets inside themselves throughout the whole day. They would never tell of the squalor and violence, nor of the grandeur and charity, which was in each of them to hope for. All would be unexplained. All but that miniature representation of themselves which smoothed them through three meals and a job. They would not shout out; they would not clean the past and start again. But neither would they break with the revelation of their helplessness; neither would they give up out of knowledge of their sadness; they would not abandon their lives, nor would they destroy them. They would withhold their secrets and live another day. They would tread on the decay and look up to the tent of dreams, but they would walk on. They would not crack.

Tom felt the burden lift away from him. He had slipped again into that division of himself. He was no more than a cold body, one more accumulation of matter in the middle of several others. His mouth opened to scream – but he could not disturb his mother and father. Father! Father! The word chopped between his mind and his body like a sharp little axe. Father! Father!

He could not bear the secret. He had to know. He held his breath, fighting to find the central point of detached observation which would enable him to come back to himself. He had to shout! He had to break!

He would see Norman Dalton.

The long hammer swung an arc in the air and landed plumb on the new post with a soft, wet thud. Dalton drew it off its target without breaking his rhythm and leaned back to allow the hammer to swing up again. For a split second, it hung in the air, black against the slate sky, and then it accelerated down on to the post.

The fence was nearly complete. Three sides of the field were barricaded by thick, bushy hedges. The other side of the fence provided its exact counterpart. Mr Dalton believed in smaller fields for grazing. Betty had told Tom that most of the farm was being changed. Her father had trebled its profit since taking it over. He had bought a tractor, built a new Dutch barn, put electric light into the byres.

Tom had walked all the way. Cycling would have reminded him too much of the last occasion on which he had come out to the farm. Dalton had his back to him. The boy watched the broad, moving back of the man, and squared his own shoulders in response to an urge to be like him. All the way through the morning-wet and soggy fields, he had tried to remember exactly what Mr Dalton looked like. As soon as the picture became clear, it slipped away. All that was left was a shape which Tom would once again try to fill in.

There he was. Tom stopped, feeling the heavy drone of a night's sleeplessness lift and drift away. He wanted to rush up to his father and hug him. The hammer rose and fell: the wire which had already been hooked, shivered off some more of its rain with each blow. It was still early morning.

He walked up to him.

Mr Dalton turned, noticed him and kept on hammering.

Edward could not ever have lifted that hammer.

Mr Dalton's shirt was wide open at the neck.

Tom undid the top button of his shirt.

The post shuddered less and less violently. Finally, it was steady.

'Good morning!'

Dalton spoke brusquely.

'Morning.'

A pair of pigeons, having waited for the hammering to stop, now lifted out of the stubble and soared up into the sky. Grey on grey.

189

Both man and boy watched them, and used the time to draw in the disparate movements of the morning around them and make a cocoon in which their talk could be heard and understood.

'Your grandfather would've been runnin' for his gun!'

'Yes.'

'Grand old lad. Before he had his accident, you know, when he worked in Flimby pit, they used to say there wasn't a 'ewer like him.'

'	'ewer?'

'Digger. A 'ewer's man that gits it out – wid his hands if he has to.' The farmer spoke slowly.

Dalton looked at his own large hands tenderly, and smiled down at the boy. Tom wished that he, too, could show some physical power which would put him among those men.

'You're like him,' Mr Dalton said. 'Same build. A bit thinner. But – same shoulders.'

Tom looked away quickly.

'Are you putting this fence up on your own?'

Mr Dalton laughed – so loudly that Tom had to join in to hide his ignorance.

'*I* can't have other folk running about after me, you know,' he said. 'Not yet anyway. Not 'til I can farm – all the land you can see around you.'

Tom looked up at the hills, at the great fellside fields which the tracking walls of uncemented stone patterned into this and that man's property.

'When will that be?'

'When God and cash decide I'm due for a rise!'

He laughed again and put his hand on to his hip-pocket to pull out a small cigarette case – Tom liked his laugh. It smelled of hedges and corn; it had nothing to do with poky kitchens and jokes: it rang round the open land freely, belonging there. Tom wanted Mr Dalton for his father.

'You work all this yourself?'

The older man nodded and buried his face into a match. Edward

190

would never swagger like this! No one Tom had known would have
dared hold himself like Mr Dalton. Tom would bet that he could
have fought anyone in Thornton.

'How many sheep do you have?'

'Two hundred. Fag money.'

'What else?'

'Friesians. Milk. That's where it really is.'

'Yes.'

Tom found it easy to talk to him. He had not known what might
happen – but all his conjectures had ended in a great melodra-
matic cry – either of recognition or of denial. At one point, Tom
had strangled Mr Dalton to his last breath until, just in time, he
had admitted:

'It's true. I am your father.'

But they talked as if nothing had happened.

'Can I give you a hand?'

Dalton looked at him for some time before replying. Then he
shook his head and spoke quietly.

'No. No, lad, there's no need for that.'

Tom waited for the judgment.

'Come on. I'll walk back to the road with you.'

The farmer took his jacket from one of the posts, swung it over
his shoulder, and set off. Tom settled into step with him.

'What are you doing out on a morning like this, anyway?'

'Came for a walk.'

He looked at Mr Dalton, trying to make him understand. But
the older man was looking straight ahead.

'You'll have beaten your mother this morning.'

'Yes.'

Dalton was hurrying. Tom had to shorten his step to move
quickly enough to keep up with him.

'Everybody all right at home?'

'Yes.'

They were nearly at the road. Tom tried to slow them both
down. He lagged behind – and had to run to catch up.

191

'I'm responsible for part of this road, you know. I've got to keep it up for a hundred yards either side of that gate.'

Tom nodded. Nothing had been said.

They were at the stile. Dalton swung over it and dropped on to the grass verge, his coat flapping out behind him like a short cloak. Tom climbed the stile and came down beside him.

The farmer was looking away. Tom stared up at his face, but his eyes found no expression to reassure them that his question could be asked.

'Edward all right?'

'Yes.'

Dalton was now speaking very sharply.

'It's a long way back.'

'Not very far.'

'Got your bike?'

'No.'

Dalton looked displeased. Tom tried to make up.

'I like walking.'

'More than I do!'

Tom waited.

Dalton shuffled, almost stamped the ground, impatient to be off, impatient to say something conclusive.

'It'd be better if you didn't come round here any more.'

Tom flinched, as if he had been whipped.

'Your mother'll tell you why.'

Tom kept as quiet as he could, willing Mr Dalton to say more.

'All right?'

Again he looked straight into the boy's face.

'Yes.'

His hand came across to the boy's shoulder. It gripped it gently for a moment and then released itself.

'You're a good lad.'

And then he had turned away, and, before Tom could do anything about it, he was turning into the farm.

* * *

192

The waters had closed over and left no trace. Tom's clue had broken the surface for a moment only: by the time he had opened his eyes to look deeper, he saw nothing but the shallow reflection of what was going on around him. He had not taken the opportunity – and now it was gone. The matter was closed.

But closed on such a lonely anti-climax; closed with so little regard for what had been opened up; closed so tightly and finally that he felt shut out from everything. Everything had lost meaning except his father's – Edward's – dash and his mother's attempt to cut him off. Suddenly, Tom had been given a calendar of importance: nothing before had so decisively shown him the division between what was important and what was not. It was essential to confirm his knowledge. He had tried, and failed: he had not even been able to fight; he had been snuffed out like a minute spark before he had even begun to flicker.

He went into his bedroom and ripped down all the flowering display of verses and pictures and diagrams; he tidied his desk and his drawers until not one loose end of disorder remained; and then he lay on his bed, staring at the grey ceiling, wishing his double-mindedness, his madness, on himself. He would scream and rage in a lunatic asylum; gibber, spit froth into the faces of his warders, lacerate his hands on the iron grill, and turn his back on Edward and Anne and Mr Dalton when they crept to see him.

It was Easter once again, and the church bells rang out a past so innocent and uncomplicated that he hated their reminder. The streets dried out and people began to pause on their doorsteps for a word or two before going in to supper. The young mothers were first out; in their cotton frocks, still creased from packing, pushing their prams boldly up the street, holding them like great black guns. Motor-bikes swished through the slow-setting, light evening air like boulders loosed from the fells and roaring randily towards their mate on another hill. The grass sprang up and wetted the iron-handed winter with lush dew. Snowdrops, daffodils, crocuses. Branches stretched out their fingers, and buds popped out at their tips. The town filled with sounds and the auctions lasted throughout the whole day: drinking went on later into the night; cricket-nets went up beside goal posts; the cinema manager started his long run of horror films to keep them coming in; girls in new dresses, girls in new stockings, girls in new calf-shaped, foot-arched legs clipped and nylon-rasped down the wide-open streets like young foals given the run of a meadow for the first time. The dawn chorus sweetened the drilling wwhhrrr of the alarm clocks. All the town, all the hills, all the county and country and island lifted up its head from a deep ostrich winter and sniffed loudly and deeply at the sea and hills and trees around and about it.

And Tom fattened in his own grease of confusion. He could not move without his heaviness weighing him down. Every action worked its way through a great heap of glue. There was no centre to him; and the parts of him drifted away like so many planks of an exploded ship. And he could not care – because he could not know why he should care.

Things happened to him – not as in dreams, for there, action was swift and decisive – but as in an ever stickier, ever-widening web. One event would follow another, but they would seem to concern different parts of him and he would never be wholly affected. He did not know that he was not mad.

In a biology lesson, a particle of a nerve – magnified hundreds of times – swirled and squirmed in the same confusion. He watched it for the whole forty minutes of the lesson.

He was working hard at school. His report said that he was top of his class with an average of 74 per cent in the eight subjects he was to take in his Ordinary Level examinations, and so, certain to be able to stay on into the sixth form – if his parents were willing.

His father had not gone. Something about Mr Waters – his uncle Henry's partner. Something about some money which Edward's mother had lent to Henry's father and everyone had thought totally lost; only to discover – only recently, Mr Waters had stressed – that this had not been quite true; that, in fact, Henry's present position in the town had been built up – not largely, but to a certain extent – on the money which Mrs Graham (as Mrs Falcon) would surely have intended to be divided between the two boys equally. Edward had treated his good fortune as a curse – for a few days – but he had not objected and now he was set up as a fully paid up partner in the firm of Smallwood and, now, Graham – auctioneers and estate agents.

His mother had decided against moving house. But all the rooms had been newly papered. And she could have given up her job: now she did it out of enjoyment and not necessity.

He did not go back to Dalton's farm.

One night he met Betty. She was deep brown with a gaudy pink dress swinging down from her shoulders to her knees – her brown, newly-nyloned burning knees – in great, soft, cotton folds. Her hair was blacker than his mother's hair. Her face was the rich, petalled softness of a flower. Tom unbuttoned her dress and set her on his knee. She said nothing. He tried to will his groin into the action which had given him that feeling. But it would not come. He slapped her face. His hand was bloody when he took it away. Then he took off all her clothes and made her lie on the wet grass. Arms up, arms down, all ways. Her father was with him. They had talked about farming. Tom stared at her back; a narrow, ridged tapering of firm, soft skin. He bent down to turn her over. He could not lift her. His fingers sunk right into her skin. She was too heavy. He began to beat her, to flail her back with his fists . . .

Only in such dreams could he find relief.

PART FIVE

PART FIVE

CHAPTER SEVENTEEN

'There it is then. Man is distinguished from animal because of his power of communication. Not only in the sense of direct communication – Graham had pointed out that even pigs can snort at one another! (tired, general giggle) –, but also in the sense that man can digest centuries of communicated information and use it to enrich the present by giving it an open road to the past. And this road has many – I won't say turnings – but many "lanes" – if you like – many lines of traffic going backwards and forwards along it. One of them is, of course, memory – as Graham said, swallows, even those taken away from their parents almost at birth, still fly those enormous distances into unknown lands – another is the *oral* tradition, another, the *written* tradition, another, the *solid* – what I call "solid" – tradition of buildings, churches and – suchlike. And, we also agreed that the more open this road – or these lanes – is, or are, kept, the more "traffic" – of one sort or another – goes along them – the more complicated the inter-change between the old and the new becomes, then the more civilised our society becomes. What we mean by civilised we can discuss next time. Any questions? Time for one last question.'

Mr Tate looked straight at Tom with the favourite look of a favourite master to a favoured pupil. Tom stared at his table (they did not have desks in the sixth form). He was tired of contradicting Mr Tate – especially in these 'General Classes'. It was like playing tennis with an old man: in the end, the effort of playing a game within a game cancelled out the main reason for the encounter and the whole thing became a hopeless duty. Mr Tate switched off his Expectant Reprisal look and cut to the quick flash of Wondering Apprehension which, had Tom been looking, might have tempted him to feel sorry for the teacher and so reply. This being unseen and unsuccessful, however, Mr Tate pondered with a sigh of silence, as if to impress the whole class (of seven; the Ordinary Level results, Tom's apart, had not been very good) with the solemnity of learning; and then, after listening to the school bell ringing for the end of the day, he flicked to Cheerful and Businesslike and said:

'Right. No questions. No questions – no answers. No answers – no information. And then we shan't be much better off than some of Graham's more delicate examples. (Quick, book-hustling giggle.) Read the first part of the Politics before next time. Good Afternoon.'

'Good afternoon.' (Seven-fold.)

Tom had lifted his head to watch Philip White. Philip, the doctor's son, had somehow lost his brilliance at the prime age of fourteen, and, instead of sailing through his exams and into Six-Science, he had stumbled through them over two years and landed rather bumpily in Six-Arts. There had even been talk of sending him away to St Hive's – a nearby public school.

Philip was stuffing all his books into his shiny, new-creased brief-case, bending their backs, crumpling their pages. Tom watched this with disgust. Of all those he had come to ignore, at school, Philip was the one he could least trust himself to take notice of. His insensitive, false-faced, simpering, modulated carping, cadging ways disgusted him. And Tom knew that he was on his way to meet Betty.

He had just found out about it. He would stop him.

His own books had been packed before the lesson started.

He pushed back his chair and waited for Philip to move first. He would follow him. Philip bustled up – like an old woman, grabbing a bottle of ink on his way and throwing it into his case.

'Graham!'

200

Mr Tate used his most carefully rehearsed voice. Confidential without being Familiar: Particular without showing Favouritism.

Tom turned on him.

'Yes!'

'Could you stay behind for a moment?'

Philip was at the door.

'What for?'

Mr Tate registered Disapproval. He had been too lenient.

'I've something particular to – discuss with you.'

Tom stopped in his tracks and waited for everyone else to clear out. As usual, plump Miss Babs Little flickered, fat-mothlike – around the tallowed form of Mr Tate. In the end – with a grand peroration of scarf-flying, glove-embracing, finger to forehead – last-minute considering – and general pooing and paahing – even *she* managed to begin her long walk to the door; and then she was gone.

Realising, perhaps, that Tom would never move towards him, Mr Tate moved towards the boy.

'In a hurry, Tom, are you?'

The Christian name was produced like a password.

'Yes!'

'Well, what I've got to say needn't take long.'

He twinkled his eyes at the boy. They were the same height.

'Sit down.'

'No, thank you.'

Mr Tate rose up on to his toes. His BA gown fluttered out behind him like the ragged lining of a pair of wings.

'Well now. You're in a hurry. I can see that all right, Tom. Now then – let me get on with it.'

Philip was feeble on a bike. Tom could give him at least five minutes start. Mr Tate cleared his clear throat.

'You've been working extremely well since you came into the sixth.'

His brow furrowed with seriousness.

'You've only been in it a year and a half – and yet – let me tell

201

you this – if you took your "A" levels now, you would probably do better than anyone else at this place has ever done.'

Tom relaxed slightly. Flattery can soothe anyone. Philip would never get near Betty, however long Mr Tate gabbed on.

That was certain.

'Now, Tom, the point is this. There is, at one of the Oxford Colleges, what they call a closed scholarship. Closed, that is, to Grammar schools in this part of England. It can be taken in any subject – and, so, in a sense, it's more open than an open scholarship! The Wheelright Scholarship. Heard of it?'

Tom nodded. He hadn't – but it would speed things up.

'Well now. This comes up in a month's time. No: I'm wrong: in five weeks . . . yes, five weeks. Anyway, about three months before you take your "A" levels. I want you to take it: to go in for it – and to win it! But I know you. I know your ways! I don't want you to over-strain yourself. But, again,' and here Mr Tate chuckled conspiratorially, 'there's always the point that if you get the Wheelright, you needn't bother to take "A" levels: in fact, you'd have the summer free and be at University a year earlier into the bargain!'

He paused.

'What do you say?'

'Fine,' said Tom. 'I'll do it.'

Mr Tate frowned. He pulled himself out of his Friendly pose and almost took a step backwards in the process. He wanted the matter to be sniffed at and nibbled, and tasted with fear and surprise and only then – under his own Confident Assistance – finally absorbed. Tom gobbled it down like a carrot.

'You realise what you're taking on of course?'

Tom did not give a damn about that.

'Yes.'

'Hm.' Mr Tate paused again, as if to reconsider the matter in the light of new and important evidence.

Since the death of his grandfather, Tom had worked at his school-work like a slave. Doing it, he could forget everything. He would set himself all kinds of the most complicated tests and lash himself into them night after night. He worked towards no other end than bed-time. In the work, he found pleasures which he would never have thought it possible to enjoy: the overwhelming pleasures of new knowledge. But it was the action of forcing himself so hard that gave his work its real attraction. He could fight and tussle with himself for hours on end. He could reject whole areas of his own personality. He could pretend that nothing of him existed except what would be cast in the mould he was forging and that would have no long-reaching and spidery black roots pushing down into parts of himself and the past best forgotten. For they were ignored by Edward and Anne: and when he remembered them, he felt that the communication of this memory would have been like trying to convince his parents of an eclipse they had neither seen nor heard of. Almost as a by-product of this activity, he became the star of the school.

Schoolwork did not occupy all this time. He found that the more he did, the more he could do. He went to dances two or three times a week – setting off, through the week, at about eleven, after his homework. He played for the rugby team in winter and ran himself into the ground in the summer. Other things. He had stopped going to church altogether.

'You are sure about all this?'

'Yes.'

Mr Tate gave Tom a pulverised smile.

'OK then,' he said, slowly, trying to impose some of his expected drama into the situation. 'OK,' he repeated, casually.

'Sorry,' Tom said. 'I really have to go.'

Mr Tate nodded.

Tom packed up his satchel and almost ran to the door. Mr Tate watched him, almost disconsolately.

It was too late to risk chasing Philip on his bike. He went back home for his motor-bike.

Mr Tate was a drip. Tom normally withheld judgment on anyone – for fear of being judged or examined himself. But he could not refrain from laughing at his teacher's dry pomposity. To think that such encouragement as Mr Tate gave would be counted by him as being responsible for Tom's energy! Its calculated and business-like air would have put off anyone not driven on by some force of their own.

He reached his house and went into the backyard where his motor-bike was kept. It released him to think that he could call Mr Tate a 'drip'. But he deliberately refrained from going further. There, at least, was a world which he could control. It was not to be thrown away for an easy jibe.

He mounted the great machine like a stallion. Its body was solid and powerful between his legs. He eased himself out into the street.

Speed was his nirvana. The concentration it demanded locked his mind and kept out all other thoughts, while its physical exhilaration opened up every pore of his body to the wild gush of the streaking wind. He shouted silent cries and jammed his knees tightly against the round body of the machine. The throttle opened easily to a great wide roar which sucked up all other sound and threw it out again into the air, tossed it above the hedges and trees and into the sky, blasted it into the puffy, dithering, slack bellies of grey evening clouds, like so much shot out of an old gun. Tom's bare head bulletted into the tightly pressed air; his feet rested so lightly on their rests that he could have stood up and tap-danced on them; the clutch was as big as a large basin in his hand.

He swept up the hill, hung on its crest for a moment, saw Philip, a disappearing dot below him, and dived down after him.

Philip grew bigger: like a clouded face in a nightmare, he moved steadly forward, his image sharpening every second. Tom's eyes stretched out wide: he could feel the soft edge of his pupils smart against the wind. He wanted to turn up his speed and crash right into the back of Philip.

He opened the throttle. The bike almost left the ground, bouncing off tiny humps as if they had been ski-jumps. Philip's back wheel buckled into a figure eight and the motor-bike crashed over his body, imprinting it with clearly-cut tyre marks. Spokes burst out of the frame and sprouted into a spindly thicket of quivering wire.

Philip turned off the main road. Tom turned down his throttle. The lane led to the tarn. To the same field that Tom himself had once been in with Betty.

When he turned into the lane, Philip was only a few yards in front of him. Tom went past him, positioned his bike across the track, and stopped.

The silence settled slowly; and then it was still enough for him to hear the small sounds which were sniffling on its surface. Philip swung his bike to the right and tried to dodge past the motor-bike. Tom pushed it back and it nudged the front tyre heavily enough to change its direction and point it to the ditch. Philip fell off.

When he stood up, Tom was waiting for him. They faced each other without a word. Philip ignored what had happened and carefully applied himself to recovering his bicycle. The two boys sized up the situation without a word being spoken. Perhaps Philip had heard of the treatment Tom had given others who had tried to 'go steady' with Betty. Tom respected his intelligence in accepting what was going on so quickly. This only made him more determined, however, not to let him through. He was afraid of the control Philip might come to have over Betty; and afraid of the discovery which might result from it.

They were in complete contrast. Tom was like a sunburnt strip of leather; his black, uncreamed hair fell over his forehead in a thick curve. He was not still for a second. The ride had battered his clothes — but they always looked ragged; slung on him; impediments. Philip was all neat collars, straight ties and properly adjusted bicycle clips; and yet, with all this flat precision, there was a confidence about him, even in the stiff, formal manner of his movements, a style about the settled tidiness of his brushed hair, assurance in the way his head was withdrawn from his neck at an angle — as if it would see all without actually taking part in one thing. Those imagined qualities with which Tom had once endowed him had now coarsened by becoming so easily discernible, such tangible distinctions which found their expression only in the meaner forms of difference – such as dress or mannerism – and yet, even in this debased form, they had the exclusive – if temporary, effect of a row of medals or a well-pipped and striped uniform.

Philip had years of training in being told to keep silent and obeying. Tom spoke first.

'I'm not letting you past, you know.'

He tried to speak quietly; the other's code, stamped on him in indelible hauteur, influencing the tone of his attack.

Philip smiled and held his bicycle beside him as if posing for an ancient photograph. Holding it thus, he seemed to proclaim its superiority over the stumpy power of the motor-bike. His hands almost fondled the slim handlebars and the tall bicycle peered down at its base successor with the indifference that amounts to insult.

Tom was sulky. Fundamentally, he knew that he would not let Philip past, but he did not know how to deal with this social counter-attack which still retained some of the dignity which Christian teaching had once given to its formation.

'You can stand there as long you damn well like.' He sat on his motor-bike, both legs out in front of him. 'I can stay here all night.'

Again Philip withheld a reply. Tom stared at the ground. The track was still muddy. Early spring was beginning to soften the earth, but there was not yet enough strength in the sun to dry it out. That sullen lethargy which Tom would pull down on to himself, deliberately, now muddied his vision and he looked through a weary tangle of intertwined, unexplained and unexplored feelings. He was like some animal retreating into the darkest corner of its den to nurse its wounds and allow necessity to grow around it so that action would be forced on it.

Philip edged his bicycle forward. Tom's arm shot out and he grasped the slim tyre. Philip pushed harder. Tom stood up and lifted the front of the bicycle into the air.

'Have you no respect for people's property?'

Philip just managed to stop himself shouting.

Tom held the front wheel high in the air.

'Put it down!'

'Put it down,' Tom lisped.

Philip let go of his machine altogether in disgust. Tom immediately banged it into the ground on which it bounded up and down, unsupported, for a few seconds, before toppling on to its side.

'I suppose you think that that's funny?' said Philip.

'Hilarious.'

'God! You're a thug.'

'Pardon?'

Tom arched his body as he arched his voice. He was bone dry and tense in a bow curve. He liked the feeling. Here he was fighting not only Philip, but his aunt Catherine with her sideways looks and impregnable judgments, the settled respectability of Philip's father compared with Edward – or Mr Dalton – both of them guilty – all the cleanly presented life of the town which condemned the foulness of his own position every day by its insistence upon rules and habits which made it clear that, if known about, he would not be tolerated.

Philip stared at the ground.

'Pardon?'

Tom repeated:

'You heard.'

'I'm afraid I did.'

So cocky now, so tightly in control of the situation, Tom eased his loathing of the reasons which supported his attitude by playing the act as hard as he could. Again, there were two parts of him: one, the silted base which would fester forever and never rest: the other, the act of an action, strung between his mind and his body like a tightrope over a swamp. He bounded on the wire and felt its thin-edged strength.

'I'm glad that you seem to have forgotten what it was. Glad for you!'

Philip looked at him as if he were measuring him for a bargain. Then he seemed to abandon whatever notion that particular

207

expression indicated, and he hissed out his words with unornamented, rude viciousness.

'You really think you're Somebody, Graham! You can't stop me seeing her any more than you can stop her not seeing you.'

'Oh yes I can!'

Philip kept to words.

'Who do you think you are? You can't stop everybody seeing her.'

'I can stop you.'

'Why?'

'I have my reasons.'

Philip had been denied for too long. He grew red in the face and started to shuffle up and down with rage. Doing it, he looked about forty.

'What have I done to you? What has she done to you? Why won't you let me past?'

'Because I won't.'

The hollowness of Tom's replies was such that Philip's questions rained on him like hailstones on a drum. He did not know what it was that he was defending.

'Now – piss off!' Tom shouted.

Philip swung back on his heels and then came up to attention like a soldier on a rubber ball.

'I have as much right here as you have.'

Tom glared at him. He sat as though caged. The thickened silt of his mind jumped and swelled into a rage which he could not find an excuse to expel. He kicked at his motor-bike viciously with the back of his foot. Philip had to make some sort of a move.

For a while, Philip stood stiff at attention. Tom's anger rushed across to him, almost invisible in its hateful force. The two boys were bound together, noting nothing of the hedges and fields around them, the clouds shifting into a tighter formation for rain, the labourer a few score yards away walking from a car, the stray dog barking on the fellside and sending the black-faced sheep scurrying like a quick rush of scree, the boat pulling into the side of the tarn, lifting slightly on top of the wind working under the surface to break up the water so that the new supplies could the more easily pour in.

Philip suddenly came forward. Tom jumped up to meet him, his strength racing down to his knuckles which swung, expectantly, by his sides. Philip flinched, and for a couple of seconds he wavered, undecided. Then he bent down and pulled his bicycle towards him, refusing to come close to Tom and pick it up by the handlebars.

Tom stamped his foot on the front wheel.

'Damn you!'

Philip screeched the two words in falsetto fury. Tom was stopped by them. He stood in the same position, but he could not have laid a finger on Philip even if he had been attacked by him.

For Tom knew that he was damned. Knew that this desire he still felt for someone who was his sister was an unnatural thing. He was afraid of discovery – that was true. But he was much, much more afraid of his own jealousy. And Philip's anger of being obstructed reminded him of it, forced him in fact to feel it – so that he was almost sick. His whole body went slack.

'I don't know who you think you are!' Philip screamed, dragging his bicycle towards him. 'You stand there as if you owned the place! You can't be there all the time! This is the last time you'll stop me seeing her!'

Tom removed his foot. Philip was almost sobbing now. He turned the bike around and put one foot on the pedal. But his reserve had broken completely. Words poured out of his mouth, now whining, now screaming, now painlessly malevolent.

'I've been with her, you know. Oh yes! And you weren't there! You can't know what happened then, can you? You can't know everything. Graham, Teacher's Pet, Swot, clever little boy he is, isn't he? Isn't he Mr Tate's little pet, isn't he? And I'll see her again. You can't be here all the time! She wants to see me. More than can be said for you! Nobody wants anything to do with you! Nobody likes you. You realise that! Nobody likes you at all.'

Tom waited for him to go. Philip was unconsciously playing for a rejoinder which would give him a reason for staying. But Tom was going to say nothing.

'OK. Listen to me. I'm going. Look!' He rang his bell. 'You've won! Doesn't that make you feel good? Doesn't that make you feel a big man?' He pushed on his pedal and swung over on to his seat. Even then, he could not stop. Even as he went away down the lane, he turned to shout:

'You know what's wrong with you, Graham? You're bigheaded – that's what's wrong with you. And crackers; mad! That's what's wrong with you!'

Tom watched him until he turned the corner on to the main road. Then he sat down on his pillion, put his head between his hands, and stared at the muddy path. Large drops of rain fell down on to it, one by one, as if someone were throwing water darts, one by one.

Tom decided against going home. He need not do any work – and he wanted to soak himself into stillness through the even, comfortable recognition of a pub.

He turned towards Bothel. Bothel was eight miles from Thornton – and across a ridge of fells which had served almost as a frontier for generations. He had to be careful; he was still a year short of the licensed drinking-age.

Mrs Stanton was the landlady. A woman as old as her oldest customer; silent as a toad, opening her mouth only to gulp in an order; otherwise posed in bent expectancy on a little stool behind the bar with only her frizzle-haired head showing above its edge.

'Evening!'

Tom blew away some of the dust, but the cleared passage only served to show up the dark walls and floors and concerns of the rest of the room.

Mrs Stanton nodded, and, with effort, displaced her bulk into a more upright position.

'Half bitter please!'

Her mouth opened wide. This was occasioned by no natural movement: her bottom jaw simply fell down, like a drawbridge.

'Half bitter?' she repeated.

'Yes. And two packets of crisps.'

For a moment she was uncertain. Then, deciding that she had better do one thing at a time, she moved her right hand to a tray of glasses, watched it select one of those furthest away from her, drew it back into her lap and jutted it underneath one of the three frothy-nosed taps. Her left hand clasped the pump like a lever. She hauled it towards her face, slowly. The beer spurted out, hitting the bottom of the glass with a fresh, fizzing smack that livened up all the limp particles of air around it, so that they danced in their reflection like sun dots around the sun. One long pull and the glass was brim-full. Wiping its bottom with a dry, glassy palm, she planted it straight in front of her on the counter.

'Did you say two packets o' crisps?'

Her mouth opened and then closed again: closed primly, as if pulled in tight by purse strings.

'Yes please.'

Two packets were eventually extracted from a shiny grey tin. Money was offered, accepted and then slid into a wax-smooth box.

Tom took his purchases over into a corner. Mrs Stanton returned to her stool. The room was so dark that it might have been the gutted hollow inside the base and roots of an ancient oak tree.

Tom relaxed then. He enjoyed the smack of the cool beer on his palate and half-closed his eyes as it ran down his body. For a few seconds, the cool drink held out against his warmth, and then it allowed itself into the embrace and the boy glowed from his toes to his face. He ripped open the crisp packets with a rude, almost metal-tearing sound and crunched the baked wafers between his teeth. He was set for the evening.

He felt ashamed of himself for his treatment of Philip – but he would not allow himself to explore any explanations of the action. He had not allowed himself to continue, or even begin, properly, pestering his parents for further explanations about Mr Dalton. He had even slipped back into calling Edward, 'Father'. He had not allowed himself to think over what he was doing in the light of what he meant to do. Every twinge of guilt, each crack of weakness, or warning of a discovery that might lead to an examination of what was happening – all this was tumbled into the pile at the bottom of his mind; a pile which smouldered always, giving urgency to the tightly-outlined new world constructed out of schoolwork, pressing against it like gas bubbles against a cork.

Tom believed that he could exist only so long as he ignored all that had gone before. But by making such a definite distinction between what he would and what he would not acknowledge, by insisting on living his life only with those resources he could most decidedly command, by deliberately closing his ears to what most preoccupied his mind – he opened the way to panic, hysteria and blackout depression.

This was what he had feared after his encounter with Philip. One of Philip's jibes had pierced the tightly-stretched armour of his new-settled life, and his old nightmare had begun to hiss through. He had come to the pub to settle himself.

When he looked up, the bar was already as full as it would ever be. On the table in front of him, his glass was empty and two empty crisp-packets made the whole corner look scruffy and untidy. He had missed two or three hours. Such blackouts used to worry him; now he was glad of them if, afterwards, he felt that he had escaped.

The parlour was a sanctuary. Here, he could imagine the customers to be the shades of his own fear. They moved around in the dusky room almost frighteningly: what made them acceptable to Tom was their own ease in their situation. And with them, he, too, felt at ease. By illustrating something of his nightmare, by being even the faintest echo of the cries which bubbled and poison- ously spurted inside him, they allowed him to see into his own repressed deposits of experience, without the terror which usually seized on him when he did so.

He went to the bar for another drink. The two sisters raised their glasses in greeting and made sure that the effort was not wasted by continuing the upward movement until the beer met their teeth. Tom nodded back to them. And, while he was waiting for Mrs Stanton to perform the operation of pulling the half-pint, he nodded and 'Good eveninged' his way into accord with everyone. The greetings stimulated everyone, making a break in the pattern which was yet sufficiently part of it to put no one in any danger of being forced into surprise. Tom loved this simple and complete acceptance. Everyone – so it seemed to him – came into the pub bodyless: only what happened inside the four walls – or it might have been five, it was too dark to be certain – was relevant to the group. They might have been in Limbo. They might, at any time, have turned on each other and seen faces run into black water, melt and disappear, leaving only the skeleton head. The group was – so it sometimes seemed to Tom – no more than a country in which they could live out their forgotten lives. This was their smouldering pile of ignored life: but they accepted it and, in a company, made it yield them some comfort – and so, in their way, they drew out some of its force into their daily pattern of habits. And it was as a group – for all its silences – that they chose to live their evenings. Tom felt as if he had been tucked up in bed during an illness on a cold night.

The postman, Mr Wiggins, was the centre of what conversation there was. He was an emaciated man of about sixty or seventy: his skin was like loose-hanging crepe; even his hands looked as though they had been pushed inside over-sized gloves made out of dried-out skin. He always wore his uniform and his wellingtons, summer and winter. His cap was set square on his head, giving the impression of having been jammed on so tightly one day that it had stuck there ever since. The only prominent thing about him was his nose, which stretched out as far as the peak of his cap, thus demonstrating, it might seem, that he was well up to his situation. He always arrived after everyone else, shuffling in inside his skin and swinging his nose around like a rifle, picking off his friends like so many plastic ducks.

Tom was re-seated when he came in. The nose barrel rat-tat-tatted around the room while he stood with his back to the bar. Mrs Stanton poured out his pint without, as yet, their having exchanged one word to each other. One second after it had been plonked on the counter, he swung around, picked it up in one hand, held it up to the light – thus causing his skin to slip down to his wrist like a ruffle – squinted solemnly for a moment, brought it to his mouth carefully, took a huge gulp and then said:

'Still charging elevenpence?'

Mrs Stanton on cue for her one joke of the evening, replied:

'Still want to pay me in stamps?'

The famous incident having been referred to, to the delight of both concerned and the breathless amusement of the rest of the party, elevenpence was counted out on to the counter in a succession of chinking half and whole pennies – each of which might easily be imagined to have come from the lining of some forgotten jacket.

Mr Wiggins then orchestrated and conducted a conversation on the subject of 'the big farmer'.

Tom was too shy to join in. And, indeed, he greatly preferred to watch, outside the particular references but contained in the general atmosphere. He was well liked in the pub; some reports of his abilities at school had seeped through and he was thought of as being clever: his silence confirmed this good opinion of him. It was also to his favour that, on the few occasions he had been referred to on points of fact, he had given the correct answer modestly and in a considered manner.

The affection was balm. At school, though a great number of people admired or envied him, he had decided that everyone hated him – and that was that. This had been initiated after his fight with Arnold Jackson: for, after that, Tom had been terrified that any communication with his fellow-pupils might lead to a similar incident. It seemed magical that no one else had referred to his father since then, while Arnold Jackson seemed to have been convinced of the doubtful veracity of his accusation by the fight which Tom had put up, and he, too, had never again repeated it. But Tom took no chances. And at home, of course, he refused to recognise any feelings: the claims of affection between himself and Anne and

214

Edward had been bound so tightly by the silence which had followed his grandfather's death, that all breath had gone out of them, and, while Tom felt an overwhelming passion to speak, to confess, to love his mother on many occasions, there was no means of communication. The roots of his feelings dangled above the earth, swollen by some inner nourishment, but unable to tap their true source. Here, in the pub, he was well liked; and he relaxed.

'Saw your mother today,' said Mr Wiggin.

Tom smiled. Mr Wiggin, having discovered that Tom was his mother's son very soon after his first visit to the 'Bell', made a point of referring to it every time they met, almost as a confidence.

'Grand on a bike, his mother. Should be a biking champion.'

Everyone took Mr Wiggin's word for it.

'Now then, Else,' said the postman to one of the sisters, 'how would you like to be up on a bike, eh?'

This was accompanied by a graphic 'illustration' of bicycle-riding, further enlivened by bell-ringing, brake-pulling, accident-avoiding and, finally, dismounting – first the 'gentle-man's way' – with one leg swung around in a arc, and then, with a loudly smirked 'beg pardon!', the 'ladies' way' – knee and ankle delicately drawn through an open frame. Elsie's beer shivered in its glass as she giggled with embarrassment.

Mr Wiggin shrugged his skin back into its normal position and took up his glass for another pull. He had set off the company well enough for it to continue in various groups without him. He himself glared earnestly at the spirit bottles neatly ordered above the bar, as if looking for some real conversation.

Tom felt sorry for him. He did his enlivening act almost as a theatrical turn, and his face was now weary. The whole thing had become part of the pub's furniture, and as hard-surfaced and darkly-smoked as the old counter itself. What had begun as rest-less spontaneity and fun had quickly collapsed into a steadily demanded routine.

Wrenching his eyes away from the whisky bottle as though afraid of tempting himself too much, Mr Wiggin lolled back on the bar and turned to a large man on his right. This man – Tom had never discovered his name – had come in, ordered his beer, planted his right foot on the bar rest and his palms flat on the bar edge, and gazed unblinkingly ahead of him ever since; like a wooden mast-head on some Viking ship.

'How's Kenton these days?'

The man swung his head to one side, very slowly.

'Aw reet!'

Mr Wiggin continued, rather desperately.

'Ah yes and by Christ 'e should be! Eh?' Everyone looked at him. Even Mrs Stanton focused her eyes on the particular area of his face. 'Eh?' he repeated. No one said anything. 'He should be! Aa know what I'd du wid them as stopped here an med a packet in a war. Eh?' His voice rose. 'It's not right, you know. Not right that he should mek a profit and set hissel up like some Marmaduke when iverybody else is fighten. Eh? What do you say?'

The large man grunted – but quietly. He was not to be caught out.

'Aa says it's aw wrong! They tell us to work and one thing and another. They talked about "labour hath its own reward". And then they let Kenton git away wid murder!'

But Mr Wiggin was on his own. His excitement was too quick for general approval. He looked around, embarrassed, as if he had been caught out telling a lie. Tom wanted to help him – but again, as so often, he felt that he would break a shell which must remain whole. He had to take all from the pub: he could give nothing.

As if to reassure both of them, the two sisters finished their drinks and rose to go to the bar and re-order. This broke up the company, and kicked some of its embers into life. Four old men on the table next to Tom saw it as their cue for a game of dominoes, and the board was produced from behind a chair. Mrs Stanton, after completing her business over the two mild halves, passed over a tin box marked Oxo, and the black and white liquorice dominoes spilled out on to the shiny board. The man whom Mr Wiggin had been addressing, finished his beer and left. Mr Wiggin assumed the

216

same post – only he looked more like a gargoyle than a warrior's mast-head.

Tom finished his drink and decided to go. It was strange how satisfied he felt, even though he had eaten nothing since the school-lunch. He was still wearing the school-blazer. He imagined Mr Tate's affronted disappointment should it have been pointed out to him that one of his pupils was known to frequent the 'Bell'. For some reason, this thought was a bonus to Tom's enjoyment of the evening.

He stood up and moved to the door. Everyone, including Mrs Stanton, wished him 'good night'. Outside, it was fresh, but not cold. The first signs of summer overlaid the last traces of winter.

He hauled his motor-bike from the wall.

He felt the black air pour into his lungs and thanked God that he had pulled himself together. His bike was wet with heavy, moist dew. He bent over to wipe it.

When he looked up, he was surprised to see Mr Wiggin. The postman stood at the door, uncertainly. Then, perhaps, seeing nothing in Tom's expression to deter him, he closed the door and walked over to the boy. His voice, when he spoke, and even his stance, was shy.

'Ga 'en home, lad?' he asked, eventually.

'Yes.'

Tom's voice slipped into broad dialect unconsciously. The very feeling of the words made him feel warmer.

'Ay well!' said Mr Wiggin. 'Let me tell thee summat, lad, eh?'

'Ay.'

Mr Wiggin cleared his throat; skin ran up and down his neck like ripples on a lake.

'If Aah was thee – an' Aa 'ed thy chances, yen way an' another – Aa would keep oot o' spots like this. Ther ne gud for folk like thee. The can du thee nowt but 'arm.'

'Aa don't know.'

'Well. Tek my tip. Aa *do* know. Thou just keep away fra that sort o' stuff.'

Tom was too thankful for this interest and advice to do anything but nod, silently. Mr Wiggin stood quite still for a few seconds and then he pulled at the peak of his cap, wished Tom 'good night', and returned to the bar.

Tom busied about and got his own supper. His mother was more and more inclined to let him do this – and Tom preferred it. He could do it neatly enough – and he enjoyed the uninterrupted flow: he wanted his supper, made it, and ate it – without any of the irritations caused by other people's mistimings. His own rhythm was always the best. He liked to think that he lived alone.

But his mother would not let him alone. She had waived her responsibilities but clung on to her rights. She waited until his fork was in the piled plate before she began. And, as often now, she attacked Tom through Edward.

'Aren't you going to ask him where he's been?'

Edward twitched up from his newspaper. He had started to spread – the effect, partly, of so much drink – and he blinked open like a podgy mole caught by a beam of torchlight.

'What's that?'

'Where he's been? I can smell his breath if you can't!' She glared at her husband – but not at him, directly, through him rather: although Tom was sideways on to her, he felt her look.

'What's he been doing?'

'I don't suppose he'll tell you if you don't ask him! Good God! Can't you smell his breath?'

Edward looked at his lap guiltily. Nowadays he tried to evade his wife by plunging into silence. Usually she did not take sufficient notice of him to force him to that. Now, however, she demanded his allegiance. It was almost as if she was afraid to turn her own power on Tom right away and wanted Edward to go out as the advance unit.

'Well, ask him!' she shouted.

Edward refused to budge. Tom's throat tightened on the mouthful he was about to swallow. He could not bear his mother to humiliate Edward.

'I've been to t' "Bell",' he said to her. 'And you damned well know it.'

Edward's left hand flapped up like a broken wing in sign of protest against the bad language. But he said nothing. Still, Anne refused to look at Tom.

'Hear that? He's only seventeen you know. I suppose it doesn't matter to you that he's under age. Apart from the fact, of course, that he's going the right way to end up as you all have.'

'I had one pint of bitter.'

'And he's still on his feet! He *is* a big boy, isn't he?'

Tom banged his knife and fork on to the plate. The food had become dry and stringy.

'Like I said, you know where I've been.'

Anne swung around on him. She had not changed one bit since Tom had first seen her as a woman. Her hair was still jet black and long – down to her shoulders; her face was clear, white and red running delicately into one another: black eyes, full, but a tremblingly perfect figure: her legs pushed out of her skirt in deep brown nylons which she made look like satin; she was a beautiful woman.

'Does it make it any better that I know?'

'It makes it unnecessary for you to keep on at *him*.'

'Do I have to tell you things all the time?' she demanded.

'You do, whether you have to or not.'

'Tom,' she warned, 'I'll have none of your cheek.'

'And I'll have none of your bullying.' Tom was perfectly cool. He even enjoyed the argument. It was better than the usual simmering in infected silence.

'Don't you speak to me like that!'

'Don't you speak to him like that then!'

The two of them were almost hissing at each other. Tom was completely wrapped up in the fight. All that he could think of apart from that was the coarseness of his mother's voice. It was so harsh that it should have disfigured her in some way. But she sat in her striking beauty, almost detached from it, unspoilt. And gradually, as they went on, Tom's own voice seemed to loosen itself from

219

him as it had done when he had read the lesson in church, until the two lines of words grappled and entangled with each other in mid-air: the two bodies locked in possessed silence.

'You're going to trip up one of these days, my son; you are, you know.'

'Not to please you.'

'I wouldn't expect you to do that.'

'You wouldn't deserve that.'

'What did you say?'

'Come on! You don't care what I do, where I go, what I say – anything that concerns me doesn't interest you one bit.'

'Do you expect me to be interested in everything a boy like you gets up to?'

'I don't expect anything from you.'

But she carried through this point.

'Wait 'til you grow up. Wait 'til you really do something. Then I might be interested.'

'If you're not interested in anything I do – why should I take any notice of you!'

'It might just occur to you that I'm your mother.'

Tom laughed – the dry-squeezed laugh of an old man:

'Claiming all traditional rights now?'

'What d'you mean?'

'I mean that I've you to thank for being born and growing up without rickets – for which, many thanks. But there is no reason at all that I can think of for my carrying on in strict obedience to your wishes – even if you have any with regard to me – which you haven't – because whatever you want, you want it for yourself, not for me. I don't mind that. I prefer it. I'd sooner act on my own. But if I have any debt to you – then I'll pay it off to my children, if I ever have any. At least I would know that I'm doing good.'

'You're hard.'

'A chip off the old block!'

Here, Anne stiffened, and Tom tensed himself as for a blow. But she stayed where she was.

'You needn't be any relation of mine for all the respect I get. You aren't even a lodger – you don't pay anything. You treat this place as a boarding-house and me as a servant.'

'Throw me out if you want.'

'I couldn't be bothered.'

And Tom stopped. He knew that she had spoken the truth. She had given him birth as a cat delivers kittens, stood over him until he could wash his own face – and this out of some instinct too strong even for her to break – and then gone her own way and left him to go his. Yet, even in this, she had not been just. For animals do not return to fondle their offspring once they have abandoned them. But she had kept him in the house – and, on the occasions of an overflow of goodwill, had nursed his feelings as mother to child. Even now, there were isolated times at which they were together, sharing the warmth of provider and suckled. And these reminders kept alive in Tom the old memories of those times when he had always expected – for he had sometimes received – help and comfort. So she had held him in reserve, neither giving nor leaving; but using him. He had started to fight back, however, after his discovery; to reject any advances she made towards him, at first out of fear and of almost physical revulsion, and then, as he saw her more clearly, out of disgust for the cloying vanity which saw him as a prop for infrequent twings of maternalism.

Tom knew, however, that she 'could not be bothered' – this was a truth which silenced him. For, although he was proud in his solitude, he did not like to be reminded that he was totally alone. While being convinced that he was separate from his mother, he still unconsciously retained his mythical belief in the solidity of their union – and even in its most deeply embedded form, it could provide a reassurance which her words broke.

'I'm going to bed,' he answered.

He got up and made for the door.

'Dishes?' she snapped, curtly.

Tom turned. His few dishes rose from the corner of the table and spread their indictment of his position across the whole room.

His head clouded with sickness. He pressed his hands tightly against his things to stop himself going across to the table and throwing them through the window, breaking the window, breaking the chairs, the table, the whole house.

He blundered into the door which opened on to the staircase. 'Do them yourself,' he said thickly.

Only in bed could he relax in some way. The past two years had been a terrific strain. Never to refer to Norman Dalton. Never to call Edward, 'Father' – that had broken down, but he could not allow himself to think of him as Father. Never to say anything which might lead to the whole question being brought up again. Never to ask any more questions himself. Never to see Betty again. Never to see Betty.

He had seen her. He had spied on her. He had seen her grow as wild and solitary as he was himself. Dark, as he was; brown; quick in her movements but restraining them as if afraid of the consequences. Slim but firm breasted, and her skin as sweet-looking as wet grass.

All the other girls he had been with had been more or less useless substitutes. Only here, in his bed, could he think of Betty. He knew that he would never love anyone else.

Sometimes, thinking about her, he found her image overlaid by that of his mother – and then he twisted in agony. For he could not bear to think of his mother.

He saw her clearly now. He saw his mother for what she had always been – and he wanted to keep far away from her. She was completely for herself – she was everything to herself – she was isolated but in command – and he did not want to understand her. He feared their similarity. Edward, she ignored, except, occasionally to despise him: Tom, too, ignored him, except to feel sorry for him. She was as ruthless as he was in working out the little organised world she had made for herself in Thornton: that hers was a post-round and his a school curriculum made no difference; both of them forced their way through with masochistic pleasure, seeking no other reward than their own satisfaction or sense of strain. For the rest, she, as he, retreated to some unrevealed abyss, to squander life, to brood, to sin, to be reckless, to be mad – it did not matter. They fell back into silence, both.

But Tom feared his silence. He feared its power, its sapping demands, its strangeness. Anne seemed to welcome hers. She came out of a dream, or back from one of her walks elated – then only, brimming with life. And suffused with a power so strong that Tom almost suffocated in its radiance.

Tom did not know where she went. He did not dare follow her – afraid of what he might discover. Certain attitudes, certain signs had led him to believe things about her which he could not admit. For to know anything more would shatter him.

He was just able to manage as he was. Locked between his work and his feelings, he felt that he could keep on. He had no ambition. He did not even think about the vague new worlds of universities, degrees and new opportunities of which Mr Tate spoke: it was all that he could do to hold the two parts of himself together as he was now.

In two years, he had succeeded only in battening himself to the ground. Sometimes he felt completely trapped. He sensed that between the swamp and the tightrope, there might be another way of life which would throw off the perils of both those he now led. He sensed, too, that this would only be shown him if he made an effort to discover it – and that meant new dangers. His instinct knew that it was his mother who could tell him what he had to know. It was in her secret that his own would be released. And her secret was too overwhelming for him to begin to discover.

Again, by suppressing his curiosity for the truth about himself – the stated, acknowledged truth, he had come to accept all actions only as more or less successful – 'good' and 'bad' had gone. This, too, he regretted in his bed. He could not tell whether or not his opposition to Philip, his failure to help Mr Wiggin, his rudeness towards his mother, was or was not as it should have been. All that mattered was that he be allowed to continue, locked against himself.

Yet, sometimes, he would dream of a freedom. Thornton would

be shrugged off like an old and wasted skin, he would stand in new cities, new countries, with lightness in his step and lightness in his heart – all burdens lifted off him – free to go wherever he wanted, do as he liked, say what he wanted to say. He would no longer be a memoriser – nor would he be the guard against his own feelings: he would bounce like his motorbike down the hill, fly over all grounds towards everything.

Just before he went to sleep – exhausted, as usual, by the physical spasms which accompanied the settling down of his mind – he saw the name 'Norman Dalton' long and slim as a silver spear, racing towards him out of the black distance. His tongue curled back into his mouth as he waited for it to strike. It slit the slippery muscles which held his tongue to his mouth, with the soft sting of a razor. It slit all his finger-joints in two, it cut through his eyeballs; it sliced the softened billowing of his white lungs.

He could not cry out. His mind was withered up and empty.

CHAPTER EIGHTEEN

It was no good his peering through the door. His father's office was in the back; as shut off from the street as he himself was from its business. Mr Smallwood made the estate agency what it was. And it was an unflurried small-town concern, successful by unhurried small-town standards. There it was on the door 'Smallwood & Graham' – and below the names – 'Auctioneers, Valuers and Estate Agents'. Mr Smallwood's previous partner had been the auctioneer and valuer: Tom's father, it might have been imagined, would have trained himself to take his place. But he had disappeared in his own plans of action, hauled out to some sort of responsibility only as Mr Smallwood's stamp licker.

The sudden chance which had brought Edward into the job in the first place was part of the time which Tom refused to acknowledge. It was a strange coincidence that his uncle Henry should only then – when Edward was about to leave – discover that some money or trusts had been left him by his mother and only at that particular time able to be given him. It was even more strange when it was almost admitted by Mr Waters that these funds – or their security – had been Henry's corner-stone of early development: funds which, had they been left for both brothers – should surely have been divided between them immediately after their parents' death. Strangest of all was that Edward had made no complaint: he had been grateful as for a kindness. And the transaction was accepted by him as charity.

Tom went in. Mr Smallwood carried his pen to the end of a sentence before looking up.

'Is he in?'

'Your father,' said Mr Smallwood, very precisely, 'has been out with a client since lunch-time. He has not yet arrived back.'

His smell was the office smell of faded polish and old, dusty lino. His voice and manner were of the same character; tidy, shell-bound, well-acquainted with camphor and costs, stifling. He was an old medicine chest in which, among a great number of some-how-arranged empty bottles, there could eventually be found a remedy for the advance warnings of pain and ailments.

'Could I wait in his office?'

'You could.'

Mr Smallwood bent his head to his papers. Tom shared in the invulnerable inconsequence of his 'father'.

Edward's room was smaller, more sparse, colder, less client-comforting – and a palace yard to his partner's padded pigeonhole. Tom sprawled on the battered leather armchair which faced the desk, at an angle – clients would have to screw their necks around to look Edward in the face – and he waited.

As he waited the room found its own size and mood. No longer a relieving contrast to the front office, its bleakness and dirty grey, wall-facing windows made it dejected. But not intolerable – not to Tom whose mood could so often have found its image there. Yet, for that very reason, it was rather frightening – like the confirmation of some awful misfortune.

He was glad when Edward arrived. He jerked in, pulling himself out of the all-spreading and sodden thickets of drink and irrespon-sible work. He greeted Tom – but without breaking his advance towards the desk – trying, for a few moments, to convey his adult business and purpose by the action. Plumping wheezily into his seat, he faced Tom with the shot-worn state of someone in position for no other reason than the time of day. Already, he felt as he knew Tom saw him. Tom looked away.

'Busy day?' he asked.

'Fairly,' Edward replied carefully.

'Who was it?'

'A schoolmaster. A Mr Williams. Welsh.'

'Our school?'

'No. The Catholic.'

'I thought they only had nuns.'

'He's going to give them music.'

'Ah.'

Tom continued. His hypocrisy was of no account in staving off – if not obliterating, it was too late for that – the knowledge which their first full look at each other had given them.

'What's he like?'

'Pleasant enough. Wants to settle here!' Edward snorted with professional knowingness.

Tom blushed.

'Did you sell him anything?'

Edward leaned back in his chair; his right hand pushed away imaginary cigar-smoke.

'Can't say really. Maybe he'll buy. Maybe he won't. I explained things to him. But it's his choice. He knows that as well as I do.' His hand flapped around, almost excitedly. 'I always tell them at the start that it's their decision – and not mine. I can't sell anything – I can only help them to buy!'

'But do you think he'll buy?'

'Maybe will. Maybe won't. He's bringing his wife, that's a good sign. But she doesn't want to come. That's bad. The price was too high – that's normal. But he agreed with everything we said, about the house – that isn't.'

He laughed – a dirty, after-dinner laugh on an empty belly. Tom could go no further. And without his help, Edward was immediately as helpless as before.

'Isn't there anything I can do to help?' said Tom, almost desperately. Edward jerked his head towards Smallwood's office, as if afraid of being overheard.

'What could you do?' he whispered.

227

'Oh – I don't know.' Tom suddenly felt gangling and restless, useless, constricted and thirsty for the taste of action. 'I could leave school and come in here as your clerk – or whatever you want to call me. I could build up the valuing side of the business. I could pass some of those silly little auctioneering certificates!'

Edward's head went forward. Tom saw that if his arms had not already been propped on the table, his forehead would have slumped against the desk. Tom went on.

'I'm doing nothing at that place. All I do is useless. I sit at a desk and listen to things and argue and learn things. I would be far better off helping you. I would like to, anyway. We could make this old place into something really worth it.'

But his last sentence was as bleak as the grey wall outside. He had committed the unforgivable sin; he had totally dismissed Edward's importance, his efforts, his life-work. And even such as it was, it could not be dismissed without causing pain. Even if the intention was kindly – it was a cruel thing to do. Tom realised this and slumped back in his seat, crying dry tears.

It was here, however, that Edward showed that courage and goodness which made Tom value him above everyone else. A failure to himself, a wiped slate to his wife, a cripple to his son, he yet could raise himself to a dignity which swept all pity away from Tom and touched the boy's feelings with love. Then, he wanted to break down – to tell him that he knew that Mr Dalton was his real father but that he did not care. Did not care. Did not care. Did not care.

'No, Tom,' said Edward. 'Nothing that you do now can be useless. Nothing that *you* do will ever be useless – you're not the sort for it. But here – you could do nothing that somebody else couldn't do just as well. Maybe not me, but somebody. You have a chance, at that school, to get to a position where you can do something really worth it; something that nobody but you could do. You mustn't leave. You mustn't even think of leaving! You have the chance there to make yourself independent. To make yourself free of everybody's bossing – no matter who they are or where they come from. And you've got to take that chance. You've got to be independent to be anything at all. I'm not. A lot of people aren't. There you are. But it's those that are, those that don't owe a thing to anybody else, don't care what other people think, don't have to worry about what other people think of them – they're the people who really are worth something. They're independent of everything. You have a chance to be one of them: you take it. You take it.'

The two of them were silent. Tom wanted to move towards Edward in some way, to show him the feeling he had for him – but he could not. In spite of all that had been said, the barrier was still up: he must not explore. He could not go back.

'Coming back home?' he asked.

Edward shuffled his hands into his pockets and brought out a packet of cigarettes.

'No,' he said. 'No. I've just something to find here.' He jabbed a match at its box; the match snapped in two. 'You tell your mother I'll be home later. Tell her I'm busy.' He looked up – his eyes once more impregnated with the shadow world of business. 'Tell her something, anyway.' He winked, dirtily.

Tom felt sick. But he made one more feeble effort.

'I can wait.'

'No. No. Don't bother.' The cigarette had been lit. His face. was surrounded by smoke. 'I'll be in soon enough. Don't bother.'

Tom nodded and went to the door. Edward tugged open a drawer and bent down to scrabble inside it.

Mr Smallwood was patting his long row of ledgers. His back was to Tom and the boy slipped out without a word.

He sucked in the fresh air as if he had been underground for a week. His father had destroyed his own dignity as soon as he had raised it up.

Whatever impression of that dignity remained with Tom himself, it would have to wait for some entirely different circumstances to be brought properly to mind. All he could feel at the moment was relief. Edward's clutches were the shallows of the despair which waited to suck him in. He had to despise him. He felt that he was being unjust in doing so – but that did not matter.

Once he allowed himself to be drawn into Edward's life, then he would do something terrible: he would confess his knowledge and his ignorance and ask for explanation. He would be forced back to the illumination he had so deliberately blotted out. He would be broken in two.

He found an empty shop doorway and stood inside it to collect himself. He had to put Edward back into the closed black layer of his mind . . .

Lena worked in the shop across the road. He was waiting for the shop to close and her to come out. The convenience of Edward's office had been Tom's sole reason for visiting it. He had been scheming to see her again since the dance two nights ago.

So his 'I can wait' had been a lie. He could answer to Edward's need with a hand already held out for someone else. This was no respect. He could neither respect him nor think about him. Except to feel sorry for him.

Lena came out of the shop.

She had only to walk across the street and his desire rose like spring through the ground; at first seeping tenderly through the surface which had repressed it and kept it dark, and then lifting high with its newly freed power.

He could not look at her lath-thin, brown legs without feeling his hands creep out to stroke them, from tense calf to soft white inside of her thigh. Her slip dangled below her tight skirt like a seventh veil. Her breasts were thin, but he knew their fresh firmness; as sweet and piercingly sensual as the most intoxicated dream. Her hair was wild, straggly, dishevelled and long over her shoulders – but whereas Betty's hair was luxuriant in dark, almost nun-like mystery, this was bangled with wildest incitements and promises. Promises which flickered out from her eyes like flashes from a black ruby each time she looked at him.

He was celibate. He had ached for Betty: he had dreamt of her, spied on her, drawn out her body with the fingers of his hope, wanted her. But he had not taken her. Other girls, when he went with them, were merely the plastic and fake reminders of what he had to avoid.

Lena had met with him as he might have met with an accident. A few weeks previously, at a dance, with the hall rowdy with stamps and shouts and drumming music and barging, bellicose crowds and he – as usual – the icicle in the jungle – he had danced with her, felt her bare arms link around his neck, pressed himself against her, taken her outside, and ravaged her clothed body with his blind, painful hands.

He had not yet made love to her. That was to happen tonight. He was certain.

His excuse when – as usual – he had retraced the day in his bed on that night – had been that Lena was absolutely nothing to do with anything else. What he felt for her was isolated from the rest of his life because she had no place in it; no place in his work, no place in his past – and so he was safe. And – so it seemed at present – this was true. He rarely thought of her except when he was on his way to meet her, or was with her, or was thinking over a day of which she had been a part. And although he could no more think of leaving her than he could think of hacking off a leg with a knife, he comforted himself by the belief that she was not essential, not a necessity.

But he had not yet made love to her. That might break the barrier between his passion for her and his own life. So he willed himself towards it with hope and terror. He wanted her to be part of him so that she could guide him through the locked roots of what had gone before; but, at the same time, he was afraid. It was to happen tonight. He was certain.

He let her walk towards him without moving. As she came closer he heard her nylons rustling against each other, swishing their sensual friction under her skirt, like an axe slicing through the air, swinging backwards and forwards in front of his face. His throat, his hands, his whole body, was caked with dryness. She stopped and looked him in the face.

'Been waiting long?'

Her voice woke him up. It was cocky, almost sparrow-cheerful, the merest flutter on the top of her beauty.

'Just come.'

She nodded and glanced up and down the street, peckingly. She was never still for a second.

'Made up your mind?'

He looked at her stonily, dreading the answer, either way.

'I should go home,' she replied.

'It's up to you.'

'They'll be expecting me.'

Tom took a deep breath.

'Will they miss you? That's the point.'

She laughed. Her teeth burst through her brown skin, white-petalled and happy.

'Of course! They always miss me.'

Tom joined in her laugh. But behind the laugh, he was waiting.

'How do we get there?'

'I've got the bike.'

Again, she looked quickly up and down the street.

'Where is it?'

'Round the corner.'

She moved off.

'Come on.'

They mounted the bike in silence. She hitched her skirt right over her knees so that her thighs spread out creamy brown, shimmering. But he rejected all superficial urges to muss her clothes and kiss her. It was important that they get away from the town. He drove slowly through its streets and out on to the road that led to the path alongside 'The Saddle' and beyond it to the cottage in which he had once lived.

On the open road, he speeded up. She loved the danger of speed as much as he did. Her arms were around his chest and she bent her head on to his shoulder. His hair flattened back on to his head. The speedometer showed 60 mph. He opened the throttle wider and the great machine thrust forward between the hedges. The wind that rushed up against him was the merest puff of spring air compared with the storm which flowed and leapt out of him.

Lena was from The Sands. She was tarty. Tom could smell it – and he loved the smell. She was dirty. And he revelled in her dirt. She was coarse and direct and flashy and splendid. And he would make love to her! That was certain!

They shook and bumped along 'The Saddle' path, bouncing like rocks flinging themselves down a mountain. She screamed out with pleasure and he yelled war cries of excitement.

The cottage was derelict now. Even the Brinns would think twice before squatting there. But it was still properly locked. Tom swung up the tree and into his bedroom. Lena followed him, lithe and quick. They went into what had been his parents' bedroom. The mattress and blankets were still there. So was the paraffin heater and the drum of paraffin. Only the matches had gone: they had been replaced by a candle stuck in a bottle.

Tom had brought matches of his own. He lit the candle and went to the window with one of the blankets. It was unnecessary – but he wanted darkness. There were nails already fitted on each side of the window, and he fitted up the blanket in a matter of seconds.

Lena was standing beside the mattress. In the shadows, she was more desirable than she had ever been. Tom could not speak. He sighed deeply and felt his legs shake from its power as he went over to her. She opened her arms and he leaned forward to suck and press at her mouth. Her lips melted on his and they swayed together like a young birch in the wind.

Lying down, surrounded by the dishevelled, half-torn clothes which had been tossed all about them, he crooked her head and shoulders in his arms and looked at her naked body. It swirled with lapping shadows and her own breathing rhythm. The breasts were posed almost humbly on her chest: Tom wanted to dive at them with his mouth. Her waist nipped in to a neatness which could be stared at for minutes on end, in wonder. And her long legs, slightly curved in a half-conscious attitude, lightly touched together, brown, smooth, drew him down her body like a river. His hand touched her skin with tense tenderness, like a glove trailing across fur.

They had clung to each other; he had swept over her body like water over a stone – his hands two oceans of surging currents, feeling for new lands. And then she had turned on him. Dumbed with surprise, with shock, with wonder, he had felt and watched her small hands lap and then press against his body. They had discovered each other and yet they waited to make love.

Gently, Tom put his hand between her thighs and worked her legs open. She spread out on the bare mattress. He looked at her face. Her eyes were closed, their lids heavy with expectation. He took his arm from under her neck. She spread out her arms in a great V. He eased his whole body on top of hers and felt her breasts crush softly against his chest. She moaned, quietly, mournfully. Carefully, gently, he placed himself inside her.

His legs, his back, his arms shuddered spasms of white fire and silent lightning. His hands stretched out to mate with hers and they clasped and twisted together in sweat. Sweat lifted out of his body and settled on his skin like oil. Lena's moans rose higher and she began to yelp and then to scream. Tom triumphed in his act: he thrust himself towards her with all the power he had. She twisted her hips. He felt the cold ecstasy of her legs, drawing together around his back. His hands left hers and searched for her breasts. And then he stiffened, arched in pain, and shuddered down on her in long collapse.

They lay, exhausted, for a long time.

Afterwards, they rested, staring at the black flickering ceiling – Lena smoked a cigarette and blew out the smoke in a long grey cone. Tom let the power run up and down his body. Occasionally, he stretched himself full in complete satisfaction. So they lay for some time.

Tom knew that if now he could keep Lena at the front of his mind for the rest of the night – then something new would really have happened. But already, that thought brought in the self-consciousness which would destroy its wishes. Already he was thinking of their love as something separate from the rest of his life. Already he felt the depression deep inside him rousing itself from what had been a pretended sleep.

It was no good his trying to fight it off by repeating what he had just done with her. That itself was diminished by its lack of real effect.

He had not been able to give himself wholly. Even then, even in a room isolated from the whole world, alone with Lena who could satisfy the physical needs of two years, he had kept himself coldly to himself. Not only petrified, but preserved, for ever. She had released him – but she had not absolved him. There had been communion but no confession. He was still as he had been. And always would be. Always would be.

He twisted on to his side in a torment of despair and jumped to his feet. His arm caught the bottle; the candle fell on to the floor and went out.

Tom had done enough work. The school was empty save for himself. Mr Tate had given him permission to work in the library in the evenings during these last few weeks before his exams.

He was alone and he enjoyed it. The black, empty corridors drew away outside the door to tiny twisting staircases and small rooms, full of desks and chairs. The school had once been a large town-house. It was a restful, lulling emptiness. There was none of the irritation of space and time being wasted, none of the resentful exhaustion of a large factory or an office-block. The school building had been taught to function between nine and four – and then only as a larger drawing-room or kitchen: now it rested, calmly and contentedly. He felt himself burrowing against its free-wheeling carefreeness – and he enjoyed it.

But it was nine o'clock and he had done enough work. He had brought sandwiches to school with him so that he need not go home for tea – but even so, he was hungry. Moreover, since his affair with Lena, he had been disinclined to push himself towards a breaking point over his work. Not, however, because of the affair alone – though that was the easiest marker of his change of mood. For the imposition of the Wheelwright Scholarship had given him an end to which his work ought to be directed: but it was an end he neither respected nor cared about. More than that, it was an end which made of what he did a stamped and branded sub-section of a system about whose standards and characteristics he was largely ignorant and totally indifferent. His own personal sting – that of a lowering queen bee, dark and instinctive – was removed from that swollen part of his mind which had filled itself with work – and in its place was put the tiny prick of scholastic success. He could test himself more now by seeing how long he could stay inside Lena without exploding. Yet his reaction, though basic in its effect, was slight in its immediate consequences. For he had straddled too much in his gathering and spinning of new knowledge to withdraw himself completely and immediately. Therefore he worked on – but the personal demon alternated with the clanking action of automation, and the imbalance caused him at first to daydream and then to stop.

Still, he surveyed the spread of books and papers on the long library table with the nostalgia of a gourmet for good dishes now spent. There was more in the books than the muscle-tightening exercise and blind lash for which Tom had largely used them. The curiosity and imagination of great men rose up from their disarranged display like the organ music and song which beds itself into the pillars of a church and plays only for those who go in to listen in silence and waiting solitude. There was the calm authority of men who had held to one purpose; the wonder of explorers, the sweet passion of fine scholars. He was attracted both by the worlds made by men and those described by them. And yet, as the ravisher, the robber, the rapist, he knew himself to be alien from their world. Their acts were completed and understandable. Even their bad thoughts and evilness were based on some constant idea, which the good among them bowed to a clear, unmuddled, uncompromising purity which he envied with all his heart.

He had no part in them. He had come to them not to learn but to be distracted; his eyes were not to be opened, but closed; his senses were not to be moved, but dulled. And he knew nothing of their 'good' or 'bad'. He had once known – through the church – but even then, 'good' and 'bad' had co-mingled with so many amoral responses in him, whirled around so many incalculably subtle ranges of his mind which could not discern, even less apply, those distinctions either to acts conceived or to actions completed – that, in the end, he had been left only with what he did not want to know and what he did want to know; what he could acknowledge and what he could not acknowledge: his past and his present.

These books were neither past nor present. From them he had lifted a sheltering tent of comfort woven of the fibres which were part of their tapestry – but, in doing this, he had despoiled their own beauty and pattern. For himself, that was, for the books themselves remained, ever open to all with the opportunity to reach them and the ability to read them – and both these he had. But now he had to put them aside. There was not time to unwind the skein and re-weave his own tapestry. He had made of them a temporary shelter against the cold; they were not absorbed into him as part of his past – nor were they more to his present than the nearest substitute for courage. He was alien to them.

Even so, however, he could see what they might one day offer him. The tent had not been so tightly woven that it did not have air-holes leading to the sky. He could see what he might become through them.

But not yet. Now he had to get on with what most preoccupied him. He packed up the books, taking care that the pages did not slide in on themselves and crease, returned them to the shelves, arranged his own things and went out.

The air was still fresh – but its scents were those of spring. A large quince stood just to one side of the main door of the school – and wistaria looped along its walls like so many plumed flags. He breathed deeply in the night air and observed once again how much more he was of the night than the day. He picked the way down to the school gates with far more assurance than he would ever have done in the day-time. There were chestnuts along the drive: if he stopped, he could hear the thousand-leaved murmuring of their inter-rustling leaves, scudding on top of the night like spits of foam on a calm, deep sea. He stopped every so often, just to listen – to bid up the sounds of the night – as if to reassure himself of the littleness of his own constant, dark activity. But he could not stop for long. He was compelled to go home.

The urge was primitive and inexplicable, for he had neither business, pleasure nor interest there; nothing but a bed – and that he could have had without paying for it by exposing himself to the company of Edward and his mother – which was what he intended to do. His despair needed to gnaw at itself – as a fox in a trap will gnaw at its own leg – to bite through it and release himself from one death even at the risk of another.

For the unexplained had now become a despair. As he withdrew from his work, seeing it in the light of an imposed aim – so he was withdrawing from his forbidden attitude towards his past – seeing its end in Edward. Edward was the result of secrecy, lies and desperate ignorance. Tom sickened with pity and nausea whenever he thought of the position Edward had come to. His own potency with Lena had clarified the shame which Edward's impotent position must bring him. He had become no more than the over-fat gristle on a fat and moulting dog.

He could not become like Edward! He must not and he would not be trapped in that spread-eagled sluggishness of non-feeling which split slowly over all actions of the will like poisonous wax over the opening pores of a soft cheek. For although Edward could show no feeling – no feeling, that was, other than a pathetic representation of what was least irritating to others for him to display – Tom knew that the deadly juices of guilt and shame hissed and pressed into him all the time. All had been turned in on himself. And, this Tom knew because he himself had something of the same feelings. Until now, however, because of youth, because of resilience, because of a will to dominate something outside of himself, they had not spread their tendrils like fanged nerve endings

238

throughout and to every part of his body. But they might. He was frightened: he could not become like Edward. He would go mad.

So he went home. To find whatever there was there for him to find. To sit and say nothing; if necessary, for weeks. But to try, in some way, to re-create such a balance between the three of them as would allow the past to be spoken of with truth – and so be made harmless.

Why he had this faith in explanation he neither knew nor cared. If it was superstition, then it was a superstition that had become a living creed. If it was an aspect of an abandoned religion, then it was an aspect closest to some magic of instinct – for though he might think in terms of 'absolution' and 'redemption', what he was seeking was destruction. Destruction of the past through its own truth. Freedom to break the image which stained the bottom of his mind like the bloody reflection of a terrible, warped gargoyle. He had to ignore his mother's silences and Edward's blankness – ignore them for what they were, but see them as part of the pile smouldering in his mind – symbols, even, of its unreflecting, iced silence and its heaving, poisoned unrest. If he could challenge them, he could challenge himself.

He stood for a while in the street in front of his house and looked at its innocent dab of light behind the cream curtains. They were not properly drawn and the bare light of the electric bulb framed the soft light of the curtain, braiding its edges with unabsorbed glare. He looked up the twisting street and felt, with a certainty which followed frequent irritation, its smallness, its unnecessary windings when there was nothing new around each corner. Once he had been so overawed by it that he had been able to creep in and out of it only at one end – like a man who will see and take only one path up a mountain – and no other. Now it was too small. He could walk through its length without noticing it. And when he reached one end, from the other, he knew that he had walked across a good part of the town. A few more steps and he would be on the fells. He wanted it to enclose him – and it would not.

He went in. His eyes screwed up in the light and this enabled him to disguise the surprise he felt at what he saw. Mr Tate was sitting in Edward's chair – or rather on the edge of it, his knees so far forward that his behind merely grazed its seat – and opposite him, in the same misbalanced position, was Anne. Edward was not in. In that second of silence which follows a sudden and unwelcome interruption, Tom noticed many things. He saw his mother look at Mr Tate with apology and then at himself with an impatient tolerance which showed at once regret and, more important, the high spirits which could make tolerable even such an obviously unfortunate intrusion. He saw Mr Tate shrink back into his seat with a very proper cough intended at once to show his innocence and to exhibit his guilt. He saw himself breaking down in front of them, pleading for the denial of what he suspected and knew. He saw his mother tarted up to go out for the night; Mr Tate prowling across the schoolroom to peer over his shoulder; Norman Dalton hammering in a stake; Edward scrabbling in his desk; himself with Lena, again in the house, again on the mattress. And, seeing all this, he rejected it all, allowed it no access either to his expression or to his words – but nodded curtly and moved over towards the table.

His mother – not moving from her position, arched her breasts and put one hand behind her neck to gather up her hair around its nape. She spoke with mock jocosity.

'I thought you were staying at school all night.'

'No,' said Tom, shortly. 'Only until I'd had enough.'

'You give up rather easily these days.'

'You don't know anything about the way I work and you're not interested in it.' He said this calmly – calculating his tone to provoke her to the utmost. But she just laughed and shrugged her shoulders.

Mr Tate had his back to Tom. He twisted his neck to speak to him and, whether it was as a result of that act or of something else, Tom found himself looking into the bottled and flushed face of a man drunk on his first night out of jail. The controlled, schoolmaster expressions were just a haggard shadow under his prickly skin.

'How did it go, Tom?'

240

Tom held back his spit.

'OK.'

'Find Plumb useful?'

'Hm!' He nodded.

'Very good, isn't he?' Mr Tate persisted. 'Did you check that quotation of Melanchthalon's?'

'No.' He hissed the word out. He had checked it.

'I'll do it for you when I get home tonight.'

He waited for encouragement like a monkey for a banana. Tom glared to one side of him and said nothing. Anne stood up with great patting of her skirt and shaking of her leg as a reaction against pins and needles: Tom knew that she never had them. She filled the kitchen with her womanly pleasure. Tom's only defence was complete control.

'Anyone for a cup of tea?' she asked, gaily.

Tom waited for Mr Tate to speak, and as soon as the older man began to emit his words, he shouted 'No, thank you!' very loudly, drowning what he was sure would be Mr Tate's acceptance. Anne was put off her balance for a moment. Tom followed up quickly.

'I think I'll wait until my father comes in. He should be in soon, shouldn't he – Mam?'

She first smiled and then began to laugh at him. He kept on.

'I think it would be better if we waited. Don't you, Mr Tate? It would be better if we all had tea together. Besides, I don't like to think of my mother making two pots at this time of night. She has to be up early, you know, for her job.'

Anne laughed out loud. Mr Tate twisted his mottled face around to see if Tom would give him the clue which would enable him to join in. But Tom continued, blank-faced and monotonous.

'Of course, she needn't do the post-round now – with the job my father has. But she likes the exercise. Keeps her slim. That's what you say, isn't it, Mam?'

Anne had never said any such thing.

'Yes,' she replied, still laughing.

'Besides,' Tom continued, his voice pitching towards more and

241

more polite tones with each sentence, 'you will certainly want to see my *father*, won't you? I imagine that your visit will concern him as much – if not more – than anyone else in this house. That is, of course, if my guess is correct and your visit has something to do with myself.'

Anne's laughter must have been a valve for more than a humorous association, for she was now quite weak from it, and slumped on the arm of the chair she had just abandoned, for support.

'Of course, I may be wrong,' Tom concluded, loudly, glaring at his teacher.

Mr Tate first turned his head yet again to see Tom, then he swivelled it around so that it pointed to Anne – and then, completely unnerved, he bounced out of the chair and on to his feet.

'I came to see your mother about the Wheelwright,' he announced, over-loudly, standing in a jangling, hop-footed pose with hands digging for gold in his pockets.

'Oh!' said Tom, flatly.

'Yes. I thought I should.' Suddenly, he blushed violently. 'I was telling your mother' – he nodded in her general direction without taking his gaze from Tom's face, around which his eyes scampered like little wasps, looking for some place to settle – 'talking to her about not letting you work too hard. Mustn't let you work too hard. "All work . . ." But – er – seriously, I was just telling her that – I've told you yourself, of course – that you – mustn't work *too* hard. Hard but not *too* hard. Push, but don't shove!' He paused. Tom fixed him with a basilisk stare. 'Yes. Well. That was all, really. Your – mother's the one to keep you away from it.' He swung his whole body around to Anne, as if to be sure to address her formally. 'He's been looking very tired lately. That won't do for anybody! Tests are tests of how you feel at the moment as much as anything else. We can't have him all stuffed with information but fast asleep on the day!'

Anne shook her head in agreement. Her face had set in a controlled flush which showed off her skin to its greatest advantage. But she could not trust herself to say anything.

Tom took up the pause.

'I'm sure that my *father* would be better able to help on that. Are you certain that you can't manage to stay for tea? He should be back any minute now.'

'No,' replied Mr Tate with a flapping fin wave of his hand, 'I must get back home.' He looked at the clock. 'Goodness, how late it is! I really must get back.'

'You're very welcome!' said Tom, loudly.

'No! Thank you very much – and thank you very much, Mrs Graham, for being so, taking so much interest in what I – suggested. We have to look after him, don't we?' He looked at Tom with his favourite look.

There was no attempt at a reply from anyone to this. With a hoppity mixture of shuffle and apology, thanksgiving and regret, he eventually shifted himself to the door and was gone.

Anne sank into the chair with a soundless laugh; only the memory of the tension which had led to its protraction remained with her.

'Poor little man,' she said.

'Yes,' Tom replied.

'He just sat there. Didn't know what to do with himself.'

'No.'

'You shouldn't have been so cruel.' She pulled herself to her feet: the joke was over. There were other things to be done. 'He's quite pleasant, really.'

'I wouldn't like him for my father!'

She went towards the staircase. Tom called after her.

Anne turned, quickly.

'Well, you haven't got him – so that's one problem solved, isn't it?' And she went upstairs.

Tom found that he was trembling. His fury had been packed away like a wound forgotten in the heat of fighting. Now it spat up inside him like a fire blown up by a wind. The scene he had encountered on coming into the room jumped up in front of his knees. Mr Tate – old 'taty-balls' – shuffling and cringing up to his mother like a pet little puppy on a leash. And his mother; pulling him into her throbbing, startling womanliness – just for the hell of it. For the relief in her laugh had been a relief for Tom also; she did not really care for Mr Bloody Tate. Tom hated him. Despised him from his smudgy suede shoes to his silly, shining, stiff white collar. Hated his accent, his manner, his teaching and his intentions, for Tom's future. Despised his slug-like exit.

But his mother had been purring. Shrugging in her skin like a fine cat stretching slowly in front of a warm fire. Encouraging him.

Upstairs, she was moving around the rooms and humming to herself. Tom could hear her quite clearly. Humming – so that some of the excitement must still be in her. Tom banged the table with his fist. The humming continued. He banged it again. Still the humming. And yet again. The humming grew louder: her movement stopped, but the humming grew louder. He banged on the table with all his force; once, twice, three, four, five, six times. And after he stopped, the humming still came down to him like a perverse variant of the water-torture. It was tuneless, wild, but deliberate, endless.

He could not stand it. He jumped to his feet and crashed both his fists down on to the table. And again and again he did it – shaking the kitchen fit to smash the whole house. He did not pause to listen for the humming but glared at the table and watched his stiffened arms batter, batter, batter down on to its surface. He was locked in the rhythm of his own actions. His fists shuddered into the air and then crashed down on to the bare table. He could feel nothing.

Then, he stopped to listen. The humming had stopped also. He heard only his breath sucking through his mouth. He looked down at the table and at his fists – now red and sore.

Quietly, his mother opened the staircase door. Tom looked at her, pleading with her to explain – or not to explain – to do whatever she wanted, but to give him something to cling on to; something to hate or to love; something to know.

'What do you think you achieved by all that?' she asked.

* * *

244

The next few weeks whirled around Tom as if he had been a spinning top and everything with which he came into contact no more than a blurred morse of shapes and feelings. As yet, however, he spun in a straight line. But he wanted to find his own way. He feared the lash of his secret for the power it had over him: it would lock him into a dried and rotting knot. He wanted to cling on to it no longer. The restlessness which he had discounted as being part of what he had to suppress, now thrilled him with a liberating intention too strong to be resisted. But the habits of years can rarely be thrown off in days – especially if their context is unaltered. And it needed courage.

He tried to find it first in the straining and changing of such routine as he had. Although his examinations were just a few weeks away, he would force himself not to work for two or three nights in succession. Then, if he was not going out with Lena, he would walk around Thornton until its last drinker was finally off the streets. He confined himself to the town deliberately. But for no clear reason. He wanted to impose himself on it – or to be imposed on, to break the shell in which he had wrapped himself for so long.

In these solitary pacings – for soon the town became no bigger than his bedroom – he would seek for clues which would lead him to nostalgia. The town was not at the roots of his life, but he wanted it to be. There was nothing at the cottage: Lena now occupied all that remained there. So, in an old man's way, he sniffed along alleyways in which he had played king-can and cops and robbers; roved around the auctions to which his grandfather had taken him; walked around the streets where he had first walked in amazement at their size and business. But little of the wonder came back to him. Shutting off his childhood, he had stopped up his sense of glamour and surprise. He could feel only tinges of what he regretted not having happened.

He had read and seen enough to know some of the standard English pictures of 'happy childhood'. Always – though sometimes with a few compromises – he had accepted his own childhood's pattern as one of those pictures. He was rarely read to, never in charades, never taken to the zoo; he had not founded a Kingdom on a lost river island, made a house in a tree or written pages of poetry to black knights on horseback; nor had he been surrounded by a jolly gallery of warm-hearted, though eccentric, aunts and uncles. But there were other things. And he had assumed, until now, that their traces could be found whenever he wished; he had almost enshrined that part of his very early childhood, storing it, even, as a useful memory for some later time; but nothing remained except the dry web of facts: all feeling had gone out of that part of his life – everything had been spent on keeping himself screwed to his purpose.

Even the people he had known gave him no feeling of association, of security. The vicar was as he had been when he had dropped out of Tom's life: the frail, rather embarrassing representative of a faith which had been cut off from Tom as soon as it had entangled him. The days in the choir seemed not sweet, but uncomfortable, shifty. Mr Carlin was no longer an omen, poised somewhere between joke and gangster – but a shuffling fat man. Nothing remained of his time with Catherine in the garden – and the whole of that respectable half of the Graham or Falcon family had removed themselves from his feelings to such an extent that they were now newcomers in any situation. His uncle Henry had nothing to say to him: Tom even suspected that he avoided him. Old Sall still squatted around the town on empty benches and in isolated porches – but he passed her by with only the knowledge of their encounter between them; no memory at all of its effect on him.

He had fed on himself alone for so long that he could taste the air and understanding of hardly anyone else. There was nothing from the far past which he would resurrect as an aim. All that remained was the grey shadow – and his own regret at missing the wonder of it all.

At other times, he would shut himself in his bedroom immediately after tea and work right through the night – or until he fell asleep at his table. He would force himself to the most rigid tests of memory, trying constantly to trip himself up; set time-limits on all he did – the nearer the impossible, the better – and flog himself through a timetable which he liked to overload completely and then extend it, the closer he came to the end. He would never allow himself to underline and reach the conclusion of his work. With one week to go before his trip to Oxford, he worked through three successive nights and then – totally exhausted and numbed and whisperingly wild in a painful, sodden dream – he decided that he would do no more work. He would spend the rest of the time with Lena.

As his first meeting with her had been an accident, so each subsequent meeting had the freshness of an accidental encounter. She fitted into no pattern of routine – and so his reactions to her were not pressed into a habit. Nor did he declare himself towards her in any way. He felt at times a tender gratitude, at other times an almost total obsession. Neither of these attitudes were attached to anything other than the spur of the moment. She was his free spinning wheel; and he clung to her – to go wherever their mood should take them.

Sometimes it took them back to the cottage; sometimes not as far as that, into fields nearer the town. They went swimming, naked together, in the cold tarn. They danced. He took her to the 'Bell' once – but that was a mistake: he never returned again. Neither of them was inclined to push the affair into the imitation marital position – with mutual exchanges with parents and relations – which distinguished the affairs of nearly all their acquaintances. Tom felt that they would stay together only as long as their legs were fresh and their love-making wild. He rarely thought of their drifting away from each other. Yet Lena's reputation stood as little for constancy as it did for chastity.

Everything bemused him – as if he were very tired, exhausted and shocked at the end or at the beginning of a day. He went down to The Sands to meet Lena. The brick-hostility and tight ugliness which had made him avoid it was now nothing more than a small huddle of jerry-built cottages which flouted the almost wistful air of past usefulness. All the flavour had gone. He had sucked himself

247

to the point at which he could bear it no longer: he was sickening from a self-regard which, for whatever motives, had become a kind of narcissistic suicide. And yet – nothing else had taste.

Except Lena. The taste of her wet body against his.

But even there – there was something inside him which was cool and withdrawn. The secret had become a fixation which could not be prised loose – nor shaken off by any amount of physical abandonment. The taste was never allowed to dominate.

Yet this was not surprising. He had decided to go forward – but he had not yet decided to go back.

Everywhere he looked he saw nothing but shiftlessness and weakness in his own attitudes. He had held after no purpose except that of keeping himself from his real difficulties. To his mother, he had played his mother's game; to Mr Tate, he had played Mr Tate's game. He had gone with the vicar and then left off when the going had grown rough. He had shut out Norman Dalton – but only to suit his own purpose. Betty was not pursued – but protected – from himself as from everyone else. Philip White was far firmer of purpose.

He had none. His purpose had been to evade – and now it was no more than to evade the evasion. He had no centre. He had destroyed it. A new spring could be found if he dared to lift open the trap-door: but it had been closed for so long that he had not the strength.

He could go mad with this emptiness eating on emptiness. There was another thing: he felt no real inclination to do anything about his position; he was, in a way, content to drift in shallows.

It was the day before he was due to go to Oxford. Mr Tate fussed instructions in his ear – but his ears had been closed to Mr Tate since that night. The world around him was no more than the fine spray of incidents and people: brushing against him with no other effect than that of bringing out a reaction – automatic. Yet it was by these automatic responses that he existed. There was nothing else to live by.

He would go to the exam and sweat at it – just for the hell of it. For nothing else. And Edward was excited about it: that was important;

or he wanted to think that Edward's attitude influenced him enough to respond with a feeling of dutiful, affectionate concurrence.

He went out with Lena. Into the churchyard. The grass was damp but they were well-hidden between two grey, rectangular tombstones. He could not have said that he 'loved' her. It would have been impossible for his throat to have allowed an exit to the words. Yet it was not crude, what he felt for her.

He 'screwed' her. That word summarised all his feelings. He thought about Edward as he did it. How could he make him happy? He screwed her. What did it matter?

CHAPTER NINETEEN

When the last paper and the interview were over, Tom decided to stay on in Oxford for a few days. He sent a postcard to his mother including the information. He was homesick and had nothing to do – but he enjoyed the idea of being alone in a strange place. He wanted to let it take hold of him.

He had given reasons for the rise of the novel in the nineteenth century and described the significance of Rochester in *Jane Eyre*; he had discovered weighty differences between two pieces of poetry on the subject 'Rain'; he had danced around Chaucer's *Prologue* and translated from Voltaire. He had made a mess of the interview. The chief questioner had reminded him of the vicar. Now he would stay on and learn something.

The first thing he learnt about was speed. Speed which was noisy and impatient. Cars were driven past in a procession that might easily have been mistaken for a funeral cortege moving in top gear on an open road. Shop windows succeeded each other like an endless line of brightly-wrapped sweets: he either stopped in front of each one successively – and felt that he had walked a mile in a hundred yards, or he went past them quickly and felt that he swept past a hundred shops in one yard. Pavements might just as well have been barred off from the road: they were escape routes. Not only were there no lazy dogs asleep in the street – those dogs that were, were toy-like and condensed. There was never a minute without someone blowing a horn, pulling brakes, accelerating. The noise was exciting – but it was exciting in a way which led straight to exhaustion.

He stayed in a boarding-house for the outrageous sum of nineteen and six a night, bed and breakfast. Mrs Cranberry, the landlady, looked at him with deepest suspicion every time he was late, noisy, quiet or early and smiled only when he ate. She told him that she would 'ask no questions' about his staying on after exams.

With that assurance behind him, he stepped out on his first morning of freedom. He went to the colleges, but the colleges were too heavy: the heat touched on them lightly, yet they had not the freshness to throw it off. St Mary's was hollow, clinking with the scattered tapping of well-heeled shoes: pennies dropping occasionally into the poor box. The streets were busy on the roads and sluggish on the pavements. The heat pressed everyone into a sticky tide – a congealed mess of clammy bodies, forever swaying forward.

Tom went into the parks. He lay down in the long grass beside the Cherwell and looked at the river. The grass was not sweet and sap-filled but somehow sickly, limp. The world was becoming his imagination: he was inventing a reality instead of looking for what was real. The figures in the punts, the punts themselves, the silken-glass river, the trees dumbly self-regarding, the toy curved bridge – all were a miniature enamel reproduction of a Watteau who had strayed out of his century. There was movement without purpose, prettiness without meaning. Or there was a park with a jaundiced eye on it! More than jaundiced – filmed, covered, swathed in a skin of non-recognition.

For he would not recognise that the different parts of himself had to mingle if he were to live. He would not allow himself to digest what he read, nor to read what might stimulate him to activity, nor to be active in any direction other than that which pointed directly inwards towards himself. He was sick of himself – but it was a sickness which had grown over such a long time that it had become a comfort, a hub to his life, a sort of happiness.

He walked on, following the tiny river to the pub which was full front-skirted by punts, and had beer and sandwiches for dinner.

He was surrounded by sunburned chatter, the flushing of animated gestures, the long, public stretching out in weariness on the lawn, tinkling noises of plates and glasses. It was all as distant as thunder to the deaf. He had no existence as part of the crowd. Nor had he existence away from it.

The heat was intolerable. He was wearing the suit he had travelled and been examined in. The beer lay in his stomach as a separate part of it; as if he had swallowed the glass with its contents. He walked on upriver. The fields coarsened; fewer trees poured over their reflections.

Suddenly he was under the by-pass and in the middle of a scruffy caravan settlement. The caravans had little gardens in front of them, fenced off. They were neither flashy nor gossipy; a miserly huddle, rather, squatting antagonistically under the baking sun. He walked through them and up the bank on to the road. Cars whizzed past with not even a particular smell to mark their passage. There was only the general smell of tarmac and hot petrol. He crossed to the other side and went back into the fields.

The fields were empty – of animals, people and all feelings of fertility. Food could have been grown there – but the produce would have been no more than the tired reflection of an outdated purpose. There was a fatigue in the very curve of their easy slopes which made all vigour vanish like a whisper in a wind. He walked heavily. Finally he came to a rickety bridge beside a farm; crossing it, he found that he faced a long avenue of chestnuts. He lay down under one of them and took off his jacket. Still hot, he stripped off his shirt, his shoes and socks, and then, seeing that no one was about, his trousers – and lay in his shorts.

It was painful for him to think over his position – but he tried. He had eaten away his own guts in an attempt to preserve he knew not what. For he had no aim. He could ride on whatever impulse or circumstance presented itself: he could bury himself in his work, he could make of Lena an obsession, he could go and help Edward – but he would do all this in no other capacity than that of a man who clings to activity to hide his own stagnation from himself and others. The world was a husk – and he had eaten its kernel.

Yet there were movements of ideas, which stirred him. When he thought of the injustice of a world which would give one man seventeen houses, five wives, incredible luxuries, power, success and ease – and another so little food or protection that he died of disease and starvation – then he was appalled at his own soft rottenness. When he understood the death and battle which had been fed into the nation which had given him a free rein to educate and exercise himself as he wished – then he was contemptuous of his pampered self-regard. Men had lived who had blasted great valleys through mountains of ignorance; they had discovered the whole world and brought it to the possibilities of understanding; they had discovered worlds within their own world and given themselves the potentialities of destruction. And he swung, tightly bound, in a hammock of self-pity.

Yet he was there. He was what had made him alone. However much he castigated himself, he could not make essential to him anything which did not directly relate to him.

But he wanted to. He wanted to dam up, to forget, to heal his own wound and move out into a world in which he could work for others, think about others, play and live for others, as well as for himself. He did not want to be everything to himself. He was already dried up – a stump of what he might be. No one cared whether or not he found the acknowledgment of who his father was – no one except himself. But that was enough to hold him locked.

He had to find the truth so that he could throw off everything that had held him back; and then he might go forward to discover some idea which could use him – or even be used by him. He would not fester in his own obsession.

The shade had spread out from under his tree and now it lay over the avenue with a light coating of dark dew. He stood up and stretched out into an enormous yawn. For no reason at all he felt cheerful. He put on his clothes and set off for the town.

* * *

253

By the third day he was broke and fed up with Mrs Cranberry. Her peculiarities – which included an instruction that no one should go to the lavatory after ten on account of the noise – the cistern was subtitled 'The Original Burlington' – coupled with a horror of finding anything improper in that proper place, assisted by the fact that she rose at six and went on a pilgrimage to that place of sanitation at precisely one minute past that hour – those had finally disabused Tom of the feeling that he could find endless opportunities for laughter in her tyranny. For he had been late one night, so brim-full that discharge was imperative; compelled by the sellotape-stuck notice not to pull the chain, however, he had obeyed its instruction and found himself faced by a bitterly outraged Mrs Cranberry at breakfast time. He argued with her but it was useless. He had broken the letter, the spirit and the meaning of the law and he was outlawed. He paid the bill and left.

With twelve and eight-pence halfpenny in his pocket, he walked up the Banbury road, his case, Edward's brown, leather-bare relic of his London interlude, thwacking against his thigh. He had bought some books in Blackwells and the case had to be given the regular support of his leg to assure both object and bearer of its withholding abilities. He passed endless houses, the like of any one of which would have been an ornament to the domestic architecture of Thornton. Their very number, however, reduced their attraction – while, at the same time, drastically diminishing the importance of, say, Dr White's new bungalow on the west road. Eventually, he reached a roundabout.

The difficulty was to work out whether it was a better tactic to remain on this side of the roundabout and wait for a truck, or to circumnavigate the island and stand on the other side. It depended on the hypothetical driver's psychology: would he be the sort of man who preferred to take advantage of the necessary act of having to slow down and so decide that a short stop at such a point was no great loss? Or would he be less philosophical – though, perhaps, more logical – and decide that it would be better to take the roundabout first and then, that completed, and his speed necessarily reduced, find it no irritation to pause, as it were, in that dead point before picking up speed? Tom had hitch-hiked only rarely – not at a roundabout – and he had not worked out the problem in any way. It all depended, of course, on the willingness of a driver to stop in the first place. That granted, it next depended on Tom's basic assumption that speed was the central obsession of a driver's life. Yet this had been contradicted in many lay-bys, roadside cafés and kerb-crawlings. There were so many alternatives that his final decision could be no more than a majority view; there was no way in which a proper solution could be found. It was a problem.

When he looked up to move on – for he had finally put himself in a driver's place and decided that he would stop after the roundabout – he discovered that by some instinctive traveller's sixth sense, he had stopped by a bus-stop – though without noticing it. He was at the head of a sizeable queue. As he moved off, the bus drew in.

On the other side of the roundabout he encountered a line of servicemen. Spaced out at twenty-yard intervals right up the road. He walked past them to take his place. The procedure was straight-forward. The one nearest the roundabout got into the first vehicle which stopped; then all moved forward twenty yards. Tom was sixth in line. He looked around him.

It was a grey, English day, with a swish of fresh wind, a crowded, but not a heavy squadron of clouds; scent of rain to come. An ideal day to be out-of-doors. Yet, beside the wide road – with its four lanes of traffic, it was impossible not to feel on a half-way point between two cities. No matter if the next city of any consequence was twenty miles away, this place on the road was a main street between the two. The road thwacked its way across the country, and the flat fields on either side were its flanks; they had the air of waste land, ready to be churned up, packed with cement and rubble, levelled into yet another route for the incessant driving traffic. They were out of place as fields.

He moved his twenty paces forward. Eventually he came to the front position. His thumb worked like a flipper indicator and a lorry slowed down and stopped. The driver took bolts from Slough to Widnes.

'You'll catch me 'ere every other morning,' he said.

They drove on.

'I can put you on t' A4. Just a hop after that.'

They stopped at a café for some dinner.

'I always stop here. It's clean.' (The place looked filthy.) 'Quick.' (They joined the long line heading to the small counter.) 'and friendly.' (A juke-box blared out tinned cheerfulness in loud mouthfuls.) 'And they know how to make a sandwich,' the driver added. This knowledge, Tom found, consisted in the art of putting two fat sausages and a hard-fried egg between three, thick slices of bread. 'Get yourself a double-decker. And some tea.' The tea was entrusted to a chipped white mug which held about a pint of the hot brew.

They went to a small table, swept its scraps on to the floor and faced each other, hiding behind the enormous sandwiches. After the tea had been gulped down, cigarettes were brought out, to freshen the stale tobacco smoke which hung around the room as if someone had let a cloud in.

Tom enjoyed it. Before leaving, they went to the cement-cracked, wet-walled lavatory which stank with urine so strongly that the only reaction possible was to spit, scratch on the walls and belch loudly. Shaking their flies, they went back into the high cabin and swung on to the road.

Tom discovered that the driver's name was Arthur. That he had been working this route for three years – before which time, he had been in the navy. 'In the hell-hole. Engineer.' His wife was a 'bloody nag' but he would not leave her, 'unless I really felt like it – you know what I mean?' The lorry he was driving was 'dragged back from a rubbish heap when nobody was looking'. His job suited him fine, 'but I'm keeping an eye open'. He was addicted to long silences interrupted usually to comment on some woman. He knew what he would do to all of them. That was what they all wanted. They went around looking for it. And he was the right feller to give it to them. He even discovered sex encased in a police-woman's uniform at Lichfield.

Tom dozed and chatted until he was dumped on the A4. Arthur left him at a strategic point. Within ten minutes he had been picked up by a truck which was taking planks to Penrith. The driver was intent on reaching his objective in the shortest possible time. The truck hurtled through Lancaster, Carnforth, Kendal. Tom wondered why he had bothered to stop.

'I like company,' the driver said. And apart from one or two grunts, that was all he said.

Penrith at eight-thirty on a summer evening just on the edge of the holiday season was neither a bumbling market-town nor a quickly-moving resort. Trippers moved in groups, for protection or warmth, and their chromium, streamlined coaches stood empty, the driver in position, ready for a quick getaway. The eyes and ears of the town itself – on the street corners – were wary. They were not yet outnumbered.

Tom went to buy some fish and chips. When he came out of the shop, the street lights were on. Night had been declared by the town council. He walked along the road which would take him to Thornton.

There was little traffic and no one seemed inclined to stop. He waited for over an hour.

Then a large Zephyr drew up.

'Hop in.' The voice was as smooth and new as the leather on the car seat.

He got in.

'Going far?'

'Thornton.'

'Oh!'

The driver sounded disappointed.

'I can take you to within three miles of it.'

'Thanks. I'll walk from there.'

'With your suitcase?'

'Yes.'

The man spoke admiringly.

'You chaps get around.'

Tom nodded. The seat was so comfortable that it made him realise how uncomfortable all his other seats had been. He wanted to sleep for these last few miles.

His benefactor was a chubby man, balding, thickly spectacled, tightly collared, his neck filling out of the white noose like a soft pumpkin. He drove quickly.

'Where've you been?'

'You mean, today?'

'Yes. Where've you come from this morning?'

'Oxford.'

'Oxford, eh? At college there?'

'No.'

'Playing cricket?'

'No.'

'Work there?'

'No.'

'I know,' the man said, completely unperturbed, 'you're in the forces.'

'No.'

Tom hoped that that was an end of it.

'What then?' The man asked.

Tom blurred his reply.

'Taking exams.'

'What was that?'

The man leaned sideways and the car swung to the left. Tom decided that he had better speak up.

'I was taking exams!'

'What for?'

'A scholarship.'

'But what for?'

'To get into University.'

'I see. That's nice. To do what?'

And so it went on – non-stop. Tom was asked his religion, his

258

ambitions, his hobbies, his habits, his aims, his ideas, his ideals, his pet hates, his pet loves, his opinion on world affairs, his opinion of local affairs, his sports, his system of work and, finally, as he got out – only fifteen or sixteen miles on, his name. He paid without much protest – just as long as the car was going forward.

'I hope I see you again sometime,' the driver said. 'Good luck at old Oxford!' And he drew away, leaving Tom thankful to be within walking distance of Thornton.

He set off. Approaching from this direction, he would have to pass by Dalton's farm. It was late. No one would see him. He did not really mind if they did. He could not believe in any real relationship between Dalton and himself. Coming back, he saw, as he thought, clearly, that the passive acceptance of the situation had not all been on his side. Why had Dalton not done something? Or at least said something explicit? What exactly had he said on that occasion on which Tom had gone and sought him out? He remembered the conversation through constant rehearsal. It had always seemed conclusive. Now he was not so sure. After all, Mr Dalton had never admitted anything.

He would start at the beginning – with his mother, and work it all out from there. He walked on quite briskly, the suitcase swinging from one hand to the other every so often. No great weight.

Thornton was shut up for the night by the time he reached it. There had been rain and the streets were still wet. No traffic passed him on his way through the town.

He turned into Church Street and walked down to his house. The whole thing had become a paper problem, to be presented, worked at and then solved. He would do it.

He went in. His mother was alone. Edward's jacket over the back of a chair indicated that he had already gone to bed. Tom blinked at the hard electric light.

'I thought you were never coming back,' said his mother. There was something almost like satisfaction in her voice.

'Living in hope, were you?'

Quite suddenly, Tom was furious.

'That's right,' she replied, calmly.

'Sorry to disappoint you,' he jeered.

'I'm used to it now.'

'Yes. You've suffered terribly.'

'And less of your cheek. Didn't you pick any manners up where you've been?'

'Yes. But I know they wouldn't fit in here.'

'Well, don't strain yourself.'

She was perfectly calm. Rocking, slightly, in her chair. Not even looking at him. Tom felt a pain in the back of his neck and his head seemed to swirl around as if he had been hit by something. He could have killed her.

'Don't you want to know about it?' he shouted.

'Not particularly.'

She stood up and stretched herself out, turning to face him as she did so.

'Can you make yourself some supper?' she asked.

He nodded. Just as long as she would go away.

'All right,' she said. 'I'm off to bed.'

And she left him.

PART SIX

PART SIX

CHAPTER TWENTY

He slept late the next day, got up to find the house empty, made himself something to eat and sat down to read. He was not going to go to school. For want of interest in the book, he put on the wireless. It was difficult to find a steady out-pouring of music during the day-time. He did not want any advice, information or argument. When his mother came in from her post-round, he went upstairs. He needed money. Usually, Edward gave him pocket money each week. He accepted it ungraciously, embarrassed and torn: but there was no way out. His work at school had been necessary.

Now, however, he felt that he could never again take anything from Edward. He had not seen him since his return from Oxford. Nor did he want to. He had some money in the Post Office. He went round to draw it out.

He was so restless that he could neither keep still nor move defi-nitely in one direction. Thornton was full of smells, shop openings, people, loitering points, distraction – but empty of temptation: outside and round it were the fells, but their loneliness could, in this mood, intensify his dissatisfaction to the point of desperation. He did not want to see Lena. There was a dance that night. He would be able to find her there.

He walked up to the church. When he got there, he saw the vanguard of those coming out of school, already walking down the street. He went into the church to avoid meeting anyone.

It irritated him. It was over-large and pompous, organised only to perpetuate its organisation, as empty of meaning for him as it was of people. It was an obstruction to truth. By proclaiming past miracles and future pleasures, by threatening, patronising and consoling, it forced itself upon a present which had to learn to cope without it. Tom walked around it. It was clean and tidy; neat and dead. He had to check, consciously, the instinct to bow to the altar, the instinct to think in whispers, the ceaselessly stamped and by now habitual assumption that he was to see and wonder, to look with closed eyes, to praise with closed mouth, to hear nothing of the noise of the world but only of the silence of God. He could not accept the certainty of his own act of faith. He sat in a pew and tried to think of something else. Tried to understand what exactly he wanted to do. His mind was as full of useless lumber as was the church of empty pews.

He went into the churchyard. There was his grandfather's grave. His grandfather had died and he had been too preoccupied really to notice it. He never cried these days. He smiled – but rarely laughed. He looked for relief to pretty constructions – his essays, his notes – which had neither root nor sun. He could be excited but not exalted. Wonder had gone, even glamour had peeled off; there was only a changing pattern, to be shuffled into a new, instant, ephemeral sensation. He had guarded himself against feeling and now his feelings, defended him from almost all responses. There it was: in stone. The dates and names of his grandfather. He weighed nothing in the earth he had dug and worked.

Tom went for his motor-bike and took it to Mason's garage to fill up with petrol. Then he drove out of the town quietly and pottered around, looking for a quiet pub. He was too well known in the 'Bell and Anchor'. He had time to look around.

He drank much more than he usually did, and he drank slowly. He was soon in a light-headed stupor which resolved everything into an easy series of decisions, unnecessary to be taken just then because it was more comfortable to save them for a less delightful occasion. A gentle snowstorm began in his head: feathers swaying down towards a nest and falling into perfect place. The whole pub,

the whole world, was no more than his fingers and thumb around the stout body of a creaming, brown pint of beer. The froth had spun white-bubbled spider patterns on the inside. The pads of his fingers were magnified through the glass and he peered at the unique markings of his own prints. Although his hand was sweaty, the glass was quite firm in his grasp. Without a tremor or squiggle of discomfort, he could raise it from the darkly-varnished table top, aim its blunt edge at his lips, find them, rest the weight of the glass on his bottom jaw and swallow the warm beer perfectly steadily. The room was quite calm: nothing darted or spun: in fact, everyone seemed to have been stricken by a strange, fatiguing disease which made of their every movement a slow, graceful ballet step. They rarely bothered to move. Tom's moves were the only clear ones. Glass to mouth, lips to beer, beer to stomach, glass to table. He held the glass, whether drinking from it or just looking at it. Its regular disappearance inside him and its diminishing level inside itself gave him all his pleasure. He slid down the inside and splashed the top of the beer into more froth.

It was only nine o'clock but it was time to go. He had been there since five-thirty – and so if you looked at it that way, he had been drinking solidly for three and a half hours. On an empty stomach. And he hadn't really had a proper dinner because he was up too late. One way and another, he had not done too badly. He prepared carefully for the move and then tip-toed out of the bar with exquisite and graceful steps. Two people bumped into him – and he apologised correctly – even though it was not his fault.

The cool air contracted his bladder and he went to relieve himself.

Slowly, he went away from the pub. On the open road, he had a strong temptation to test his bike for a new speed record – but he restrained himself and, instead, he tried to keep the needle exactly on the 60 mark, whether he was going uphill, on the flat, or cornering. He floated along, a few inches above the machine, and, like an expert, he let it do all the work for him.

The dance was at the village of Welton. Or, rather, in the parish hall which had been erected in one corner of a large field to mark

the centre of the village. The hall was isolated. The nearest buildings were some abandoned cowsheds two or three hundred yards
away. At this time of night, with a dance on, it was burning with
lights like a runaway double-decker, and cars spread away from it
in every direction. Tom went right up to the door and drew up
sharply, in front of it.

He paid for his ticket and had his hand stamped.

Inside, the noise was of accordion and the scraping shuffle of
feet on the newly powdered floorboards. The lights were low –
that is, three-quarters of them were off – and the band was playing
a modern waltz; there was a solid circle around the dancers as if
the whole affair were a nocturnal spectator sport. Tom walked
around until he found a space and then he, too, stood and stared
at what was going on.

Lena was like a fierce, bright stab of paint on a greying wall. She
was wearing a tight pink dress which caught what light there was
and flashed it out all around her. The lace-looping hem of a black
underskirt was showing at the bottom of her dress. Her arms were
bare, but they were as brown as her legs which were swept in nylon.
Her hair was loose, shaken right down over her shoulders.

Tom was winded. She had her arms folded around the neck of
her partner, her face pillowed on his shoulders, her body pressed
against his so tightly that they moved like one heap of flesh. The
boy – more a man – was one of a crowd. His gang was standing
near Tom. When, eventually, he passed them, they shouted and
bellowed with excitement: he did not relax his position for a
second, but winked, made a V-sign behind Lena's back and grinned
through his chewing-gummed teeth. Lena did not look up.

He was mesmerised. He took in the man's sign, his gang, Lena's
grip on him, himself as one who should take some action. He knew
that there had been nothing between Lena and himself which
excluded this. He saw that it gave him a good opportunity to release
himself from the whole affair: he realised that this was what he
wanted. That, to be free, he must cut himself off from everything
which in any way held him. He was better off without her.

The singer put down his saxophone and came to the mike. Another light went off. The faces of the watchers'-circle glazed to glumness.

> *'All at once I saw your smile*
> *And then I knew . . .*
> *All at once I heard you voice*
> *And it was true . . .'*

Lena was rooted in nothing but a desire which was itself a false screen against his facing the truth. He had slept with her without loving her. Used her. Now he felt crazy because someone else was doing the same thing.

> *'Then I saw that we were made to be alone*
> *Just you and me . . .*
> *Me-e and you . . .'*

Maybe old Chewing-gum *was* in love with her. He had more right to be with her than Tom. Tom was ashamed, bewildered at his casual callousness. There was Lena; collapsed against his shoulder.

> *'You – and me . . . Mee . . . and you . . .'*

The singer began to hit the beat very strongly. The whole dancing surge now trudged heavily with one rhythm

> *'All at once I saw my life begin again*
> *Right then and there'*

He could feel nothing for anyone. He was an abstract of carefully conditioned reflexes.

> *'I knew that the God who gave us Life and Hope*
> *Would hear our Prayer . . .'*

267

He wanted to apologise. To be forgiven by Lena. To force her to convince him that it had never happened.

'Then I saw that we were made to be alone'

He could go across

'Just you and me'

He began to push his way forward.

'Mee and yoouu'

He had to reach her. He had fouled her.

'It was truuee'

Everyone hugged tightly together for the last few bars.

'Meeeeee an' Yooouuu'

Tom was caught up in the last whirls and shuffling. The lights came on. Lena was in a corner, still pressed to her partner. A patter of soft-palmed applause took Tom over to them.

Lena jerked her head up and grinned when she saw him.

'Hello!' She perked her greeting and they could have been in the middle of a street.

'Lena. I've got to speak to you. It's very important.'

Tom heard his own words come out in a quick, slurred, drawl. He tightened his shoulders and tried to show his earnestness in his pose. Inside, he was crumbling into a roaring chasm.

'Who's this?'

Lena got in quickly.

'Tom – this is Frank. Frank – Tom.' She giggled.

Frank swung away from her – as if he were opening a gate; but his right arm, the hinge, still fastened tightly around her shoulders. He stood very straight – taller than Tom. He stared down at him and chewed his gum slowly.

'It won't take a minute.'

Lena looked at Frank. He did not respond. Neither did he relax his grip.

'What is it? Anything you can't say here?'

The band started playing. This time – a quickstep.

'Look. Could I have this dance? I'll tell you then.'

Again Lena looked up to her partner. He did not move.

'It's booked,' she said. 'Sorry.'

Tom was finding it difficult to hold to a persistent line of argument. Frank's jaws, champing regularly on the gum, drew his eyes to them compulsively, and his head began to spin, heavily, in the same rhythm.

The three of them stood there.

'Did you have a good time at Oxford?'

'Eh?'

'Did you have a good time?'

'Yes. Can I say something to her? It'll only take a minute.'

He addressed Frank. No reply.

'What is it?' Lena was interested.

Tom knew that he had to get it out now – or he never would.

'It's about me. I'm sorry.' He was speaking terribly slowly. The jaws kept moving. The dancers jogged out the quickstep behind him.

'I mean – I didn't feel anything. I like it, that's true. I liked it. But I shouldn't have done it. Not when I wasn't feeling what I should have felt. Perhaps he feels,' looking at Frank, 'for all I know, what I didn't – you were just an excuse – not an excuse, what do I mean?' Lena stared at him, amazed. '– an escape. I shouldn't have done it. It was an insult.'

'He's been drinking.' Frank to Lena.

'An insult,' Tom mumbled.

Lena pressed out her words very quickly.

269

'I don't for the life of me know what you're talking about. I can't understand a word you say.'

Tom pressed his hands against his thighs very tightly in order to stop his body from drifting away into the air.

'I insulted you!'

He shouted.

'When?'

Tom gasped for enough air to make her understand.

'All – the – time!!'

'We gonna?' Frank jerked his head towards the dancing.

'I want to find out how he insulted me.'

Lena slipped out of Frank's hold and came right up to Tom.

'Now then,' she said. 'What are you on about?'

It was too late. There was too wide a gap between Tom's mind and his tongue.

'I used you for anything,' he mumbled.

Frank clomped him on the shoulder.

'Hey!' He shook him. 'Hey! Lightning! Tell her you're sorry and push off!'

'I am sorry. That's just exactly what I am.'

'I want to know,' Lena began.

'He's said he's sorry. Come on.'

Frank took her by the arm and half lifted her on to the dance floor. Then he encircled her with both arms, made himself comfortable, and held her as before while trudging slowly across the hall.

Tom's forehead was cool and dry. His hands prickled – but there was no sweat on them. His throat opened as if for a yawn.

He sat down. He would not be sick. He put his head between his knees and noticed the feet of a small group which must have gathered around him. He would not be sick. He steadied himself.

He had done it! This realisation forced its way through his dissipated thoughts. He had decided what he should do – and he had done it. He had begun to act.

He stayed with his head between his knees for about ten minutes. When he sat up, he felt weak – but in control. Lena and

Frank were on the other side of the room. She was in the middle of Frank's gang.

Tom walked out of the hall. He had made a start.

He felt terrible the next morning. His stomach was frying without fat. His headache needled every thought that even attempted to grow in his mind, and his impulses were all a sodden dissonance. He sprawled in lazy half-awakedness for an hour or so. The house was perfectly quiet. He enjoyed being alone there. He could surround himself with whatever he wanted from it – and forget that anything else existed. It was warm.

Downstairs.

Turned on the wireless. While he boiled the kettle, kept one eye on the toast and another on the bacon, organ music played in an ancient giant's abandoned dance-hall. It sounded just like all the chromium-plating and tinsel in the world melted into a three-note tune: which it was. It was as harmless as a river – but, in the end, not as pleasant.

He spread the checked tablecloth and set out his place neatly. A mat for the tea-pot; another under his plate. Everything tidy.

The organ music accompanied his eating of the bacon. The crunching of his toast was an obligato.

'Music while you work, this morning, is played by the band of the Royal Artillery under their conductor, Captain R. C. Johnson.'

And the pace quickened.

Tom finished his breakfast to the 'Trumpet Voluntary'. A brass rendering of 'a medley of Strauss Waltzes' floated him into the back-kitchen for washing-up. He sat down next to the unlit fire in a good humour and began to read *For Whom the Bell Tolls*. He would take another day off school.

In the empty security of his own house, he saw how straitened his feelings and attitudes were. He knew that many things affected and moved him which he could not acknowledge, for fear of their consequences. He wanted nothing to be dependent on that which he could not control.

Besides this, he moved in an arena which took ideas for somebody else's business. Its behaviour perpetuated the habits and superstitions – only recently outdated – of a sullen countryside creed whose main tenet was to hold into yourself what you had. There were few people in and around Thornton who treated an advance in prosperity as anything other than evidence of chance, while misfortune was always inevitable. People were locked in themselves – just as some old women in the town were locked in their houses; very proud of the fact that they had never crossed the doorstep for five, ten, twenty years. Gossip was the lubricant. But even that was no more than keyhole whispering between locked doors. The very avidity of those who sought and imparted it was, in a way, proof of the walls and silences which surrounded almost all of them. Only a crisis or a carnival brought people out into the streets. And Tom found it easy to accept those indications inside himself that there was more to life than Thornton, that there were more and greater problems than his own, things to be done and enjoyed of which he had, as yet, only the faintest intimation – to accept these as nothing more than his own eccentricity – no part of the men who went out into the fields and factories and worked all day in isolated silence.

Yet, he was drifting from this position. His past had become less important as, with Lena and his exams, the present had become more powerful. Now the exams were over – and Lena had finished with him. He was unhappy about that. He knew that he had done the right thing by himself – but he was already longing to take Lena out again. Or he wanted to think that it was Lena he thought about. Someone else would do as well. But someone else – and something else there had to be if he was to prevent himself from slipping back.

So he dreamed and brooded while he read the book.

His mother came in so quietly that he hardly noticed her. She came right up to him and stood beside his chair. When he turned, his eye went up her dishevelled navy-blue uniform. His mother's face was cream-skinned, flushed, happy.

'I thought I'd give it to you myself,' she said.

She handed him a telegram.

It was the first he had received. He examined its imperative yellow, curiously. Read his own name about a dozen times. He held it as if it had been the frailest tissue paper.

'Aren't you going to . . .'

'Open it?'

Tom looked up at her and laughed. Both of them shared in the excitement of the event. Tom wanted to hold the telegram unopened and let this new communion build into a wide bridge between them. The kitchen hummed with their curiosity.

He ripped open the envelope.

He read to himself:

'Congratulations stop. Awarded Wheelwright Scholarship stop.'

It was signed by the man who had been his chief inquisitor.

He read it aloud.

'Congratulations stop. Awarded Wheelwright Scholarship stop – that was the fella who asked me all the questions I couldn't answer.'

'What was he like?'

'A bit like Pursur – the Reverend.'

'Oh.' Anne lost interest.

This point cleared, she remembered her enthusiasm.

'Well,' she said. 'I didn't expect that . . . I expect you'll be pleased.'

'I expect I will.'

'When will you go?'

Tom looked at her, sharply. But she was not being malicious.

'Starts in October, I think.'

'Do you have to go to school 'til then?'

'I hope not.'

'You don't look as though you want to.'

'I don't . . . I might go for something to do.'

Anne came up and put an arm around him.

'It's grand, isn't it? Well done, lad.'

Tom felt his mother's cheek against his own. Everything was fine. The past was receding rapidly, diminishing, drying.

'I'll get you some tea.'

She went into the kitchenette. Tom re-read the telegram several score times. Anne came in, flapping the table-cloth.

'Wait 'til I tell everybody,' she said.

Tom laughed. It would be nice.

'Who will you tell first?' he asked.

'Oh,' she waved a hand in the air. 'It doesn't really matter, does it? I'll just tell everybody I come across. After all, there's nothing else I can talk about for the next month at least.'

Anne giggled.

'There's quite a few I'll be very glad to tell!'

'Oh?'

'Well, just about all your reactions to start with. And everybody at the Post Office, they all think I'm half-mad – or stuck-up – or both – for letting you stay on at school, you know.'

She had the air of one who had quietly but consistently championed her protégé through torment and misunderstanding, from every side. Tom's eyes fastened on her face like limpets.

'It means I get a grant,' he said. 'I'll be independent.'

Anne was back in the kitchenette.

The good feeling went on through tea. Suddenly, every day except this one had neither meaning nor relevance. Although Tom watched his mother closely for the slightest sign of hypocrisy or spite, there was none.

'Are you going to tell Mr Tate tonight?'

'No. He'll probably find out anyway.'

'You should.'

'I can tell him tomorrow!'

Edward came in. Tom was shy and almost buried himself in his book while Anne told him what had happened and showed him the telegram. Edward came over – almost quivering with pleasure, his face switching from delight to apprehension about what he ought to say, to determination to say something, to pride which needed no words. He just stood in front of Tom and beamed.

Tom stood up; he felt that he would melt if he did not move.

Edward held out his hand. Tom took it and his own hand was immediately covered by Edward's other hand.

'Congratulations,' he said. 'You've really done well. It's marvellous,' he turned round, still holding Tom's hand, 'isn't it marvellous, Anne?'

She nodded.

'Let's have another look at that telegram.'

Anne scurried over to examine it in the window-light.

They re-started tea.

The three of them were released and happy together. The tea was spun out for about two hours. Edward told stories about his adventures in London. Anne said little – but she neither sneered at him nor did she contradict him.

Edward was so pleased that Tom felt that he had paid off any debt he might have had. Then he was ashamed of thinking such a thing. Edward was kind and a good man. It was all childish nonsense about finding out who his father was. It was Edward: his only debt was affection.

'I'll tell you what,' Edward said, 'Let's all go out for a drink. Together!'

He pulled out his wallet and looked around. By some common instinct, Tom and his mother had gone upstairs to change after tea. Edward was still suited from the office – and his spry air lent his clothes a spruce manner which made their disorder seem casual and amiable.

Anne looked at Tom.

'Both of us know you drink,' said Edward. 'Known since he started, haven't we?'

Anne turned away.

'Let's see,' Edward went on. 'How far can we go?' He scrambled at his wallet, took out one pound and two ten shilling notes, and leaned back in his seat to work out exactly how many drinks each of them could have out of the money.

'We can have a good time on this,' he said. The small rectangles of paper were crumpled and small in his hands. Then he screwed

275

up his face in a mockery of the embarrassed affection which made him say 'I'll give you something for yourself, Tom. I'll go to the bank tomorrow. I'll get something out then.'

Tom was very quiet. He did not want to break the spell which bound him to his father. He wanted to draw in his goodness.

'Right-o, then,' Edward bounded to his feet. 'Coats on – no, we don't need them, this weather – and let's away.'

Tom got up. Anne remained in her chair. The two men looked at her. She stared hard at them for a few seconds, and then she thrust herself into the most enormous yawn.

'You two go out on your own,' she said. 'I don't fancy a drink in one of those pubs.'

Edward's face fell into a little boy's disappointment. He tried to jolly her along.

'You're just feeling lazy. You'll feel better when you've had some air. Come on!'

Anne did not reply.

'It isn't often we go out together. And it isn't every day your son passes a scholarship! Come on.' He waved his notes. 'I don't mind spending all of this.'

Already, he was pleading. Tom's stomach tightened with resentment against his mother.

'I think I'd prefer to go for a walk . . .'

'We could go for a walk – all of us could go for a walk . . .'

'By myself.'

She said the two words gently, but there was finality blaring out from them. Edward did not, or chose not to see it.

'Look,' he said, frailly-briskly, 'we could all go for a walk – we never do, do we? – we could all go for a walk, somewhere, together – not too far because we want to be able to get back before they – before we have time to have our side of the bargain – because, after the walk, we could all go for a drink. So we would have both!'

He opened his hands, spreadeagled by the reasonableness of his explanation. Tom stared at his mother: she was irritated.

'I've said I'm not coming . . .'

'But Anne . . .'

'And that's that!' She stood up, turned her back on them, and began to peer into the mirror. Edward looked at Tom confusedly. He took one or two steps towards his wife.

'Just this once?' he asked, humbly.

She did not reply. Tom saw her face contort to hatred in the mirror. Immediately, he hated her for what she was doing.

Edward was now crawling.

'I know a very quiet place. We'll be the only ones there. We can have a quiet drink. Just one. And then we can come back.'

He touched her shoulder. She froze – and his fingers jumped away.

'We should celebrate when our son does something like this,' he mumbled. 'We should do something about it. After all . . .' He petered out.

Anne spoke without turning round.

'Take him out yourself! Maybe you'll teach him something in a pub: it's the one place he could learn something from you.'

Edward winced. By now, Tom was taut with fury. Women were treacherous and vicious.

'He is your son.' This was Edward's last attempt: he made it barely audibly, but firmly.

Anne replied into the mirror. She tried to wind the matter up with a joke, but her eternal contempt for Edward made it into a sneer.

'I'm only half-responsible, after all. Aren't I? You take the son out!'

Tom was looking at Edward and he saw him wilt.

'Why can't you come out for once instead of always creeping off on your own?'

Tom was shivering with anger.

Anne turned on him.

'I don't want to come – and I won't be forced! And I don't "creep off"!'

'What is it then? Have you got some sort of wall-duty?'

277

'What?'

'Never mind. You wouldn't understand!'

'Don't you be cheeky with me!'

'Why have you got to wreck everything? Why can't you just come out like everybody else? Why have you always got to go out on your own?'

'Because of the company?'

'Are we that bad?'

'Oh! You don't understand! Do you think I want to spend my nights drinking like some old nanny in a tuppenny halfpenny public house?'

'I don't know what you want.'

'Well I do. And it isn't that!'

Tom was already finished. She would never, never, never, budge. She would never let herself become part of anybody else. She would never allow anyone to share what she wanted for herself – even if it concerned them critically.

Tom cried out.

'Why does everything have to end in an argument here? Why does everything always have to end in an argument? Eh? That's all I want to know. Why?'

Anne came towards him. Tom thought she was going to hit him. He held himself rigid so that he would not strike back at her. They hated each other. She passed him – with a great, furious surge of silence, and grabbed the brass door-handle.

'I'll tell you why,' she said. 'Because this house is full of kids! Kids and fools! For all your books and your papers. Fools!'

Tom and Edward listened as she marched away down the street. Edward was still crumbled in a pathetic pose. Tom almost screamed at him to do something. He was pathetic, standing there. But he – Tom – was rotten for even coming near to sneering at Edward. It was his mother who was pathetic! Pathetic! But the word had not enough force. He wanted to run after her and drag her back by the hair and force her to shout out apologies to both of them! He hated, hated, hated her!

Edward looked up. His face was dull and empty. His clothes hung on him like old sacks.

'Well?' he said, tonelessly. 'Do we still go, or don't we?'

Tom shook his head. He had to get out. He tried to tell Edward that he wanted to spare pain rather than add to it by doing this, but his throat was too burnt to allow the passage of any words.

He went out. He walked in the opposite direction to his mother. She went her way, he his.

He had to conquer her. He had to find out about himself in her. Otherwise she would always crush him by her strength. Otherwise she would always swell out her knowledge to make him ignorant.

The secret was there and that was all there was now. No present. Only past.

He walked right out into the country until it was dark.

'Do you believe in God?' she asked, the lisp newly off her lips.

'No,' said Tom.

The corn was thick-smelling and thicketed around them. The sky reached into blue forevermore. Her patterned cotton summer dress was already creased with the clammy ruffling of his hands. And still she talked.

'Why not?'

'Why not?' he replied, and rolled her over on the soft bending stalks, his hand leaping up to her silk knickers.

That was one.

Another was after a dance. Teetering in like a dying wasp looking for somewhere to settle, Tom had eventually, drunkenly, blindly, battened in to a shape, a form, and then a face of a woman. Much older than he was; in the WRNS. All uniformed and drill-collared.

'Would je like this danche?'

'You don't need a partner. You need a prop.'

'I need a danche.'

She supported him for a short circuit. Her body, pressed against his own, sobered him considerably.

It was another of those mid-field village dances with no resting places but the back seats of cars – already occupied, if large enough, by the owners and their friends; those unoccupied were locked. She was disappointed that he had no car.

'I've got a motor-boke,' he said.

'That's no bloody use to anybody.'

So they walked up the road – past the inevitable cow-byres – also locked – until they came to a church.

'I haven't been to church since I got married,' she said.

'Me neither,' replied Tom, and they went in.

It was dark – and when they found the lights, they did not dare put them on.

'Creepy,' said the girl.

'Police,' Tom replied.

He guided her into a high-bunked, narrow-seated pew: specifically made for flat-bottomed army men; the least uncomfortable position was to sit straight up. They soon abandoned this pose. The difficulty about lying down was that they kept slipping off. It was doubly awkward because the 'Wren' wore corsets. She was very helpful but rather unacrobatic.

'Let's go into the nave.'

'The what?'

'The middle.'

Tom had to wait while she looked for her handbag. It was black and difficult to find. There was the faintest pat of moonlight which made a weak halo around the windows. A touch of light caught the cross. Tom was brim-full of beer, was nicely worked up. He began to sing.

> *'Rock of Ages cleft for me*
> *Let me hide myself in Thee.'*

It was only a whisper. But the whisper filled out the church with echoes of Liturgical melancholy. The walls were charged with endless songs to heaven which had stopped right there; they warmed the solo voice into a rich harmony.

'Shut up!' she hissed, loudly.

Tom paused, and then continued in his normal voice.

> *'Let the Water and the Blood*
> *From Thy riven side which flow'd.'*

'Come and help me to find this bloody handbag!'

Tom increased his volume. The words rolled out.

> *'Be of sin the double cure,*
> *Cleanse me from its guilt and power.'*

He could not remember the second verse. He began the first again.

'Are you mad?'

He hardly heard her. All that was in his ears was the music: he mesmerised himself. Great scarlet processions – with purple and gold, tall candles and white surplices moved around the small church like so many phantom crusaders.

'I'll go if you don't keep quiet!'

This – in his ear. The handbag must have been recovered because she was now next to him. Without interrupting his singing he let his hand drop down behind him to reassure itself that the skirt had not been re-assumed. It had not. And the corsets were doubled down, bent ready, like a sprinter waiting to be off. He was content.

Time to say the verse through just once more.

> *'Rock of Ages cleft for me.'*

'Have I got to stand here all night?'

But – his tactile senses being temporarily satisfied – he was away on his own slide of coherent, confused, Scottish paradise. She was ignored. Her words reached him from across a deep ravine.

'I'll go back, you know.'

He knew only the singing.

Sounds of a struggle behind him.

'Somebody'll hear . . . there's something wrong with you, you know.'

The struggle completed. Never mind. What can be pulled on can be pulled off. A quicker, high-stepping rustle indicated that the second stockade was being put in position; more serious, but hardly dangerous. He sang on.

'I'm off!' she announced. Her regulation low-heels marched down the nave.

He could always catch her up. He would just sing the verse again. Beautiful words. Lovely tune. The door banged – a prison bang. He sang on. It was too moving to leave.

That was another.

There was a brief encounter at a Congregational pea-and-pie supper into which he strolled accidentally before setting out for serious business. But her mother was there – and he did not enjoy playing 'spin-the-plate' – so one way and another, that came to nothing.

Through the day, he went to school, late – but welcome.

'Welcome, Tom,' said Mr Tate, in solemn mockery. He led a little round of applause. All spontaneous good wishes were damped. 'I want to say, Tom that you've deserved it. No matter how hard I worked to get you to work – if you see what I mean – your work did the trick.' He paced across the room, holding out his hand. 'Congratulations! The headmaster wants to see you.'

The headmaster was a little man who lived in a small room at the end of a cul-de-sac. He took prayers, watched over Religious Instruction for the sixth form – but was otherwise unseen. He had been there for many years.

'Come in.'

For fully a minute, the headmaster gazed at Tom without saying a word. Then,

'What do you want?' he asked, rather sharply.

'Mr Tate said that you wanted to see me.'

The old man propped his spectacles on his large nose.

'Oh! Graham! Yes.'

And he relapsed into silence which grew, in time, to the soft murmur of 'well-dones', 'honours board', 'proud of school', 'remember Cumberland' – ending with another, even longer silence.

'Thank you,' said Tom.

And he went out.

Proper confirmation of the result came through in a letter addressed to Mr Tate. He would not let Tom read it – but he told him, roughly, what its contents were.

'Perhaps you'll let my father read it,' said Tom, sweetly, 'or my mother.'

Mr Tate pushed it into his hands. Among other things, it contained a reading list. He copied it out.

He avoided Edward. He was so little at home that he hardly saw his mother.

He was summoned to his uncle Henry's office. When he got there, he found his uncle flanked by his aunt Catherine. She beamed at him, still, somehow, looking down at him even though he was taller than she. They had grown so far away from him. Like everybody else. But there was something particularly uncomfortable in the sudden intimacy of three people, relations, neighbours, who had ignored each other for years – even though for the best reasons. The whole scene had a fake formality which underlined its lack of being anything other than an obligation.

Yet his uncle Henry, at least, seemed to be conscious of nothing except a feeling of pride in Tom. He need not have said anything – but he did: told Tom how much he admired him, how he deserved what he had won, how he ought to let nothing hold him back. Tom listened to the advice with conviction. His uncle, known, but unfamiliar, was in just the right position to be listened to. Catherine stared out in front of her with a lightly-painted smile stiff across her lightly-powdered face.

'And we would like you to have this,' said Henry. He passed Tom an envelope.

After that, Catherine left to do some shopping and Tom stayed to talk with Henry. They chatted easily. Both of them were sorry when they parted.

There was a cheque for twenty pounds in the envelope.

The next day was a Saturday. Tom went to Carlisle and spent the lot. He stayed there until the evening and went to a dance. It was crowded and unfriendly. He had a brush with someone over a girl. It almost led to a fight. He drank very little. He raced himself back to Thornton on his motor-bike . . .

So the week after his receipt of the telegram passed away. There were mornings when he woke up knowing that he had to do something. But he drowned the knowledge in activity. He did not want to bind himself again. If he could ignore it, perhaps he could forget it. It did not matter whether or not he knew the truth. All that mattered was enjoyment. He could enjoy himself. The rest would be forgotten.

CHAPTER TWENTY-ONE

On the Monday, he decided that he would leave school. He did this during the milk-break. At home, he decided that he would go somewhere on his bike.

It was a still, hot summer day. After lunch in a pub he went on towards Fell Cottage and turned up the path which led to the top of 'The Saddle'. When it became too steep, he left the bike behind him and walked to the top.

Spread out underneath him were Fell Cottage, Thornton, the town, another village, Allhallows, which was two miles from Thornton. And at his eye level, all around, were the fells which hid town and lakes from him and shut in the hollow of people he knew.

He had been up 'The Saddle' many times since his move into Thornton. He had swum in the tarn, he had raced around the town on foot and on his bike, he had spent afternoons in the fields playing rugby or running or just lying, he had wandered around that tiny plot of houses at his feet for hours on end. Yet he could feel nothing. In the attempt to keep his knowledge from harm – or in the attempt to do now he knew not exactly what – he had curled himself around a centreless kernel and become a husk. He could savour nothing. He was now seventeen and he was tired of what he was doing, tired of not being able to do what he might have been doing, tired of looking into the past, tired at the prospect of the future: in his mind and in his body, he was heavy with a constantly pincering nothingness. He could enjoy nothing. He could not remember the time when he had felt certain and secure; there had been no innocence, only ignorance; and ignorance had been replaced not by curiosity but by a certainty which stifled him. He could support nothing. He had discovered his secret, his dynamo, to be no more than a plug; once pulled out, he was helpless. And nothing remained.

Lena, the dances, his grandfather – there were times there when he had felt near to the recklessness he now longed for. He had preserved himself to sterility. Nothing mattered: nothing was important: nothing existed outside his own obsession with his own emptiness.

He did not want to live like this. He wanted to laugh without being aware of its brevity, to talk without being afraid of the discoveries which might disturb him – to release himself from this egotistical strait-jacket which now supported nothing but the rust of what it had been fed on.

There was sky and heat. It was soft and sentimental to relapse into such a helpless attempt at stimulation. But at least it was something outside himself.

He had long passed the stage of blaming others; or himself. His mother was as she was: he neither knew nor enquired what that might be. She cared for him as a cat might care for a kitten. That was all right. Edward – his father, or whoever the hell he was – Edward was all right as well. But he demanded so much sympathy that Tom's meagre stock was exhausted after five or ten minutes. Betty was no more than a charm – a taboo: he thought of her only because there was a gap to be filled.

And he had made love to Lena without knowing what he had done. It had come and then gone like – anything else: more exciting, more dangerous, more exhausting. Different because it was a different activity: but not different because it showed a new way to live. If he stayed in Thornton much longer, he would become a tramp. He would bang against people with no cause and no effect. He would be dead.

He had to stop holding into himself. First he conserved, then he held on for life, then he found that he had crushed what he had.

He wanted to leave. To throw himself into something. To forget reasons and consequences.

He free-wheeled down the fellside and looked over at what had once been his home. There was a car beside it. He decided to go over and see what was going on. From some impulse, he got off his motor-bike once more and walked.

As he drew nearer the cracked and shoddy little cottage, the garden so overgrown that it looked like a toy jungle, the peeled doors and smashed windows, he was surprised to see that it was his uncle Henry's car. He decided to call him Henry in future.

Seeing the car, his expectation was of noise and movement and caused him to hurry forward. He stopped. He was walking towards a silence so enclosed that he could feel himself leaning into its barrier.

He stood quite still for a time to let the noise of his earlier approach rub into smoothness and fade away into the restrained, subdued rustling which held in the cottage. Then he moved forward, soundlessly.

He reached the tree which went up to his bedroom. It would be too noisy to climb that. He walked round to the side of the house. Now, all his action was in slow motion. He quietened every step by forcing it to follow the careful guard of his mind.

Above him was his parents' bedroom. There was a trestle-stool at the foot of the wall directly beneath it, and beside that was the broken low roof of what had been the washhouse. By climbing carefully on to the stool – silent with rot and weeds – and from there on to a solid part of the roof, he could raise himself up to the window and, if it were open, slip in.

He moved slowly from one position to another, testing each new step by pressing his foot, at first lightly and then firmly, against what was to bear his full weight. He laboured over each decision, considering, re-confirming, pausing, double-checking, and then, finally, bringing himself slowly into a new point. He carried an enormous responsibility of silence. He could now hear the sound of voices coming from within the cottage. He was compelled to discover what was happening there.

When, finally, he was on the roof, bent almost double to avoid the bottom of the window, he made out the voices more clearly. He went completely dry with amazement.

He reached up towards the window and looked in. Both of them had their backs to him. Both of them were naked. They were arguing – but he did not hear the words.

His uncle Henry was squatting on the floor beside the mattress. His neck was bronzed and ruddy; his back and arms, white. He was smoking. His clothes were heaped to one side of him. In the same heap were the woman's clothes.

She was lying flat on the mattress, her face buried into it at the end furthest from Tom. Her hair came right down her back. She was naked. Her legs were spread; occasionally she would flick up her foot in a gesture of relaxed irresponsibility.

They continued to talk and Tom continued to stare. He felt completely emptied of anything which he could recognise as his own. He was unconscious of everything except the most minute details of what was occurring in front of him.

Henry reached over for his jacket and fumbled in one of the pockets before bringing out a packet of cigarettes. He placed one in his mouth and lit it from the cigarette he had just been smoking. He then held it out.

Tom's mother turned to take hold of it. She sat up and looked into Henry's face. Then her eyes flicked over to the window and she saw her son. She screamed.

Tom jumped down from the roof and ran.

288

CHAPTER TWENTY-TWO

He drove until he was out of petrol. By that time he was in Lanca-shire. He had turned off the main road and he found himself in a village called Yealing. There was a pub there – the 'Red Fox'. He went into it and bought some sandwiches and beer.

After closing time, he pushed his bike along the road until he came to a park which went into a wood. He followed it and found a den where he slept for the night.

His mind had been made up while he slept. He would go back to Thornton, collect his things and leave home. He could get a job to see him through the summer. After that, he would go to university – or not, depending on how everything worked out. But he would leave home.

He found a garage and set off. He drove very steadily. He was fresh from his night in the open.

The nearer he came to Thornton, the slower he went. He felt the complexity of what now faced him closing around him like a suffocating heat. Above all, he was tormented with the shame of what he had seen.

He drove into the town by the Sands. Everyone would know everything about him. All he wanted to do was to leave.

His mother was waiting for him. He was helpless in front of her. She told him to sit down, and he did.

'I'm glad you know,' she began. 'I suppose that I would've told you some time – or Henry would. He always wanted to.'

'That's it, then,' said Tom.

'Yes. Henry is your father. Only he didn't want to admit it at the time. He didn't want anything to do with it. That's why I married Edward.'

'But Norman Dalton.'

'I went with him for a few months – on and off. Edward thought it was him the same time as you did.'

Anne was completely calm. She spoke almost offhandedly, as if Tom deserved some sort of an explanation – even though, to her, it was not very important.

'Norman thought that as well,' she said. 'He wasn't sure.' She laughed. It was like a splinter of burning wood jumping out of the fire. 'He still isn't.'

'But you are.'

'Pretty well. Yes.'

She paused. Tom just shook his head. He could feel the tears waiting to well up into his eyes. But they seemed far away.

'Well,' said Anne. 'What do you think of it all?'

Tom wanted to say nothing. But he had to begin re-establishing himself immediately. If he allowed her to dominate him now – he would always be afraid of her. And everything built would be founded on weakness.

'You could have told me,' he said. 'It was a dirty trick not to tell me.'

'I should have done,' replied Anne. 'You're right. But there you are. I didn't.'

Tom went on.

'What does – Henry – what does he make of it now?'

'Oh – worried. Scared it'll all come out. He wants to talk to you.'

'He can want.'

Anne laughed. She was relaxed, almost careless, but her eyes never left Tom's face for a second.

'What are you going to do now?' she asked.

'Leave here. Get a job somewhere before I go—' He waved a hand to fill out his meaning.

290

'Are you sure about that?'

Tom nodded. He wanted to ask more questions. He wanted to have everything clear before he left.

'Have you and Henry been – all the time – ever since you were married?'

'Not all the time. It hasn't been that sort of big thing.' She spoke emphatically. She, too, saw that this was to be their last real talk. 'We couldn't let go but we couldn't keep on – if you know what I mean.' She impressed her argument by jabbing the air with one hand.

'You were always going out on your own, though.'

'Yes,' she replied. And Tom knew that there had been – and were – others.

'One thing's always worried me,' he said, quickly. 'Why did Henry suddenly give Edward that money?'

'He wanted me to stay. No. That's not true. I wanted to stay. I made him.'

'I see.'

'Besides – he owed it to Edward in a way. Edward never got a penny out of that business, you know, and the money in it all belonged to his mother. Old Falcon, Henry's father, only married Mrs Graham, as she was then, for her money. And all that was left of that was in the business.'

'Why wasn't I told anything?'

'I don't know.'

'But why not?' Tom was shouting. 'Why did you keep me out of everything? Why didn't you tell me?'

'It wouldn't have helped.'

'At least you could have said something. A lie would've been better than nothing.'

'I suppose so. I didn't think it would at the time.'

'You didn't think of anything at any time as far as I can see.'

'There's no need to be like that.'

Tom paused. His force had been in his voice alone. He felt no fury.

'I'm sorry.'

'That's all right.' Then. 'I'm the one who should be sorry.'

There was nothing else to say – but, for a time, they sat without moving.

Then Tom went upstairs to pack. He took a long time over it. He had to force himself into the slightest move. He was on the edge of giving in, of lying on his bed and going to sleep, of standing forever in front of that Longfellow quotation: 'Lives of great men all remind us . . .'

He decided that he would take no books, none of his notes, none of his sports' outfits, nor any of the objects he had packed up. These could always be sent on when he was settled down. He packed as for a holiday. His clothes, a towel, his shoes, toothbrush, comb, handkerchiefs. He felt so lonely that it was only the fear of cracking up totally if he stayed in Thornton that kept him going.

Finally, he was ready. He carried his suitcase bumpily down the narrow stairs. The kitchen was empty. His mother had gone out. He went outside and tied the case on to the back of his bike. Mrs Blacklock asked him if he was going away 'on a trip'. He told her that he was.

He went into the house for the last time – and made himself some coffee. He tasted it – but found it impossible to swallow.

His mother came back.

'I've been to see Henry,' she said. 'He wanted to come here but I told him he couldn't. You don't want to see him?'

'No.'

Anne nodded. She had been right. She held out a bundle of notes.

'This is to see that you don't get stuck.'

Tom shook his head. Anne came up to him and pushed them in his top pocket.

'He can afford it and I know you haven't got anything.'

They looked at each other, awkwardly.

'Are you sure you've packed everything you need?'

'Yes.'

'Your books?'

292

'I can send for them.'

'Just let me know where you are and I'll post them. I'll even deliver them myself!'

She brushed at some specks on his shoulder.

'You'll let us know where you are?'

'Yes.'

'And you'll come back as soon as you want to? Whenever you want to?'

'Yes.'

Anne took a step back and looked at him, critically.

'It's better that you go away for a bit,' she said. 'You'll be able to make your own mind up about things then.'

Tom pushed himself forward, almost colliding with her on the way to the door. One more thing.

'What about Edward?' he asked.

'I'll tell him.'

'What does he think?'

'Edward? He knew me when he married me. I never said you were his.'

'About this?'

'He doesn't know.'

'Will you tell him?'

'No. I'll tell him – you wanted to go away.'

Tom went to the door.

'Tell him I'll write to him,' he said. His voice was barely audible. 'And tell him – thank him very much.'

He left his mother standing in the middle of the kitchen.

He drove very slowly out of Thornton. It was noon and the town was almost empty. The day had turned cool and there was grey cloud everywhere. He went up one of the hills which led out of the town. He had held out against her.

Two mornings later he woke up unable to move. Inside of himself, he was covered in a black sweat which had broken again and again through the night. All that he could hear was the endless drone of his own suppressed cries. All that he could see was his home and his mother. He was dry with a wasting panic.

He had found a bed sitting-room. The walls which guarded the bare stairs leading up to it were painted cream above waist-level, brown below it. This decoration continued into his room. There was one picture – a framed Union Jack, one table, one wardrobe, one mat, one bed, one sofa and two chairs. Outside the window was a building site. He was in London.

It had not been so bad the previous morning. Now, he could not move. His arms and legs were soft. He could neither think nor move. He was shackled to the feeling, the presence, the memory of his mother.

The pit had opened. He fell down and down in darkness. Always falling. No one to hear his shouts. Nothing to break his fall. Ever. He would fall forever. He had no past to start from. He had to start again.

On and on this droning, this driving, dry terror. To cry out would be to go mad. He had to let it come.

The ceiling was grey and cracked above him. A piece of flex hung down from it, stuck on like the leg of a spider. His bed was completely disrupted. The sheet had come away from under him and he was lying on the bare mattress. The sun came in through the window above his head.

He flinched from the prospect of doing any single thing. The thought of any effort immediately crumbled into lachrymose blackness. He began to think of the simple act of throwing off the blankets as beyond him. He was strapped down as surely as if he had been tied with rope.

Only street noises came through the window. No birds. No trees. Cars went by like so many swings on a roundabout. One after another after another. Occasionally there would be a hollow clattering down the bare stairs. A door banged. No one shouted.

His breakfast was waiting for him beside the gas ring. Bread in a cellophane wrapper. Coffee in a tin. A packet of sugar. Butter.

He could not move. He had left all movement behind him. All

movement, all knowledge, all experience, all ambition. He was emptied, emptied, scoured. There was nothing to break his fall. Down and down through steady blackness. Nothing to pass, nothing to leave, nothing to arrive at.

Anne would be – wherever. He could not let himself imagine her.

Outside, a large motor started up. Loud voices shouted at each other and the noise kept on. The building site was starting up. The shouts were like the shouts of men being sent to exile: he was in a prison, he was in exile. And he could not move. He dare not move.

The sun, which was catching the wall in front of him, became less clear. Something was moving across it. Soon, the shadow filled the room just as the sun itself had done. Something was swinging towards the window. A black bat on the blank wall.

He jerked up his head and saw the end of a crane. He jumped out of bed to get a good looked at it. It was enormous. A great scaffolded tree which swung its long neck like branches in a wind.

He watched it dip and swing for some time. Then he went to make his breakfast.

MELVYN BRAGG

The Soldier's Return

'His masterpiece'
Peter Kemp, *Sunday Times* Books of the Year

'Unsentimental, truthful and wonderful'
Beryl Bainbridge, *Independent* Books of the Year

A Son of War

'Full of a simple poetry that is deeply evocative . . . even
better than *The Soldier's Return*'
Carol Birch, *Independent*

'Deeply humane and acutely truthful'
Peter Kemp, *Sunday Times*

Crossing the Lines

'I was bowled over by it . . . an enormously important
piece of literature about post-war Britain'
AC Grayling, *Guardian*

'Enthralling, a joy to read'
Allan Massie, *Scotsman*

SCEPTRE

MELVYN BRAGG

Remember Me . . .

'Daring and brave . . . With great skill and stunning
insight, Bragg doesn't just tell a very tragic tale, he
explores what it really means to love and be loved . . .
eclipses anything Bragg has written before'
Daily Mirror

'A powerful novel that communicates difficult
emotional truths. Yet its dark themes are balanced
by the vivid portrait it paints of 1960s London'
The Times

'Utterly absorbing. Melvyn Bragg is worth a host of
more fashionable writers. He never shows off, but tells
us how it is.' *Scotsman*

'A tribute to the ways in which language and imagination
attempt to reconstruct the past and a moving
acknowledgment of the tormenting power of memory'
Sunday Times

'Disarmingly honest . . . a terrific book'
Daily Mail

'Melvyn Bragg has added another formidable
chapter to one of the most distinguished
literary series of recent times'
Sunday Telegraph

'Searing and unforgettable'
Sunday Express

SCEPTRE